SINGLE ALL THE WAY

PORTIA MACINTOSH

Boldwood

First published in Great Britain in 2022 by Boldwood Books Ltd.

Copyright © Portia MacIntosh, 2022

Cover Design by Leah Jacobs-Gordon

Cover Photography: Shutterstock

Every effort has been made to obtain the necessary permissions with reference to copyright material, both illustrative and quoted. We apologise for any omissions in this respect and will be pleased to make the appropriate acknowledgements in any future edition.

A CIP catalogue record for this book is available from the British Library.

Paperback ISBN 978-1-80048-797-0

Large Print ISBN 978-1-80048-798-7

Hardback ISBN 978-1-80483-847-1

Ebook ISBN 978-1-80048-799-4

Kindle ISBN 978-1-80048-800-7

Audio CD ISBN 978-1-80048-792-5

MP3 CD ISBN 978-1-80048-793-2

Digital audio download ISBN 978-1-80048-795-6

Boldwood Books Ltd
23 Bowerdean Street

London SW6 3TN
www.boldwoodbooks.com

For Joe – This one is definitely for you

1

In the movies, you can see a break-up coming from a mile away, can't you? Some poor woman shouting into her phone about how her signal is fine, only to realise that her significant other doesn't mean that the call is breaking up, *they* are breaking up. Or when a loved-up woman's boyfriend says he needs to talk and she gets all excited, thinking he's going to propose, but this usually happens at the start of the movie, so everyone watching knows she's going to get dumped sooner or later. Probably sooner. That's just how these things work.

I have seen so many movies and TV shows where couples break up – you'd think I would have been better prepared for my own, or at least been able to see it coming. Instead, it hit me like a train.

I'll tell you something else I never forecast – that I would have to keep working for my ex, because *of course* he's my boss too. Life is always horribly complicated that way, isn't it? As if getting dumped isn't torture enough, I have to keep taking orders from him. If it isn't 'Clear all your things out of my apartment, Dani' then it's 'Dani, make me a coffee'. Do you have any idea how demoralising it is, making coffee for the man who broke your heart? Do you know how tempting it is to put real milk in his coffee instead of oat milk?

Don't worry, it wouldn't kill him, he'd just be stuck on the loo for a while. I doubt it would make me feel better anyway and it's far less than he deserves. I think it annoys me more than anything because making him coffees isn't actually part of my job. It's something I always did because I was, y'know, in love with him. Somehow, he's cut me loose in all ways apart from getting me to make his coffees, and I don't know how to say no, not because I'm weak, but because he is my boss and the last thing I need right now is to lose my job too.

Tom and I were together for two years – not that anyone we work with knows that. I'm a writer and he's my editor, although he wasn't when we started dating. I stupidly stepped aside to let him get promoted because I thought we were on the right track. I thought we were making smart choices for our relationship. We had talked about getting married and having kids – at least three. I've always been an only child, and Tom was one of five. He would tell me stories from his childhood, about what he and his siblings would get up to, and while he might not have had some of the same financial advantages as me growing up, I always wish I'd had brothers and sisters.

I didn't mind at all when he became my editor, at the lifestyle magazine we both work for. It's not a problem, when the man you're with is telling you that when you eventually start your family, it will make it easier for you to take time off. A huge problem, however, when he dumps you. I should have been making career moves of my own. I put all my eggs in the Tom basket. Yes, I do feel like a mug, but it's always easier to spot what you tripped over when you're down on the floor.

That's what relationships are like, though: one minute you're all loved up, the next minute your long-term boyfriend is dumping you for the girl he's been cheating on you with. A twenty-two-year-old medical student called Mia who he met at the gym. I didn't think that actually happened in real life. It was six months ago now and I still can't quite believe it.

The day I found out that Tom was cheating on me (by actually walking in on him while he was doing it, which was as excruciating as it sounds) was the same day that *he* left *me*. This is going to sound absolutely pathetic, but when I found out that he had someone else, I didn't get mad at him to begin with. I didn't dump him or hit him or even use so much as a PG-approved swear word. I panicked at the thought of life without him. Our lives felt so intwined, being together, living together, working together – I relied on him for so much that the thought of life without the lying, cheating bastard seemed like a worse prospect than staying with him, knowing full well he was treating my heart like a punching bag.

Looking back now, I realise how lucky I am that he did kick me out, because I might have stayed with him and he would have done this to me again and again. Well, I say lucky, I don't feel that lucky living in my pokey rented flat, working this crappy job, and having to look at his smug face every single day. But I can see now that I was so miserable with Tom, and I know that I wouldn't have ever been happy with him. After the initial panic of being dumped wore off, my feelings naturally progressed from wanting him back to hating his guts – so now he's just like any other boss, I suppose.

Of course, the first thing I did at the time was blame myself. Well, I'm a decade older than her. I don't go to the gym much these days, so I'm a few pounds heavier than I should be by whatever standards we're supposed to obey – meh – but I've been struggling to find the time to go. Tom kept politely reminding me

– at least it seemed like a polite reminder at the time – so I politely thanked him but still didn't have time. I'd drag myself out of bed on a morning, do a full day in the office, and I'm always knackered when I get home but I would still make the dinner and do the dishes – always me, every night, and now I feel like an even bigger mug.

Eventually, I realised that Tom was just a selfish, horrible person who had been making me feel like I wasn't good enough ever since he decided I wasn't. He's the kind of person who would cheat on the woman who did nothing but support him – and then kick her out to move his other woman in! That is *not* the kind of person I want to be with and I'm better off without him... except I'm not without him because I'm still working with him, and these days, I'm working *for* him, which is even worse.

I know what you're thinking, that I should quit my job – believe me, I would love to – but this is real life and people can't just quit their jobs, especially not right before Christmas.

When it all kicked off in the summer – and I was subsequently kicked out – I spent a couple of nights in a cheap hotel before I found myself an even cheaper flat. I say it's cheap but somehow most of my money still goes towards my rent. I am on the lookout for a new job and as soon as I find one that works for me, I'll delight in giving my notice to Tom... but in the meantime, I have bills to pay, and I would be crazy to lose my foot in the door here, even if I have only managed to squash a little toe through it at best.

My only other option would be to move back in with my parents up north in Yorkshire – I'm sure they would have me – but that feels too much like admitting I've failed. Failed to find the right man, failed at making a decent life for myself in London, failed to get my career going, failed to be financially independent... No one wants to admit to themselves that they've failed at all things in life, never mind to other people.

At least I'm going to spend Christmas with them this year, and I'm really looking forward to it, because it's the first Christmas I will have spent in my home town in a long time. I spent the last couple in London, with Tom (mug!). We were trying to establish our own family traditions – his words, not mine. I wonder if he'll be doing that with Mia this year...

They'll still be in that first flush of romance, I'll bet. When everyone is on their best behaviour, still keeping their bad habits and annoying traits under wraps. Just wait until she finds out that he listens to country music at deafeningly loud volumes when he's showering in the early hours of the morning, or the fact that he obsessively rewatches those crappy *Not Dead Yet* action movies, but insists on keeping the DVDs hidden, so no one knows he's into something that he considers to be lowbrow. Living with Tom was not a walk in the park, that's for sure. For someone so obsessed with the place being spotless, and everything being in its place, he was terrible for leaving bits of human debris, for lack of a better term, lying around, like his toenails or his rolled-up bogeys. Honestly, given how hard he was to live with (and obviously the fact that he cheated on me), it's almost impossible to miss him, or to feel all that sad about our break-up. If there's anything to mourn, it's just the time and the effort that I threw into our relationship. I always throw my everything into anything I do. It feels like such a waste, to see that it was all for nothing.

Enough about Tom. The important thing is that I'm going to spend Christmas with my family, I'm job hunting, I'm saving up. I'm going to turn things around.

I twirl around on my desk chair. I've done my job search for the day. I've doodled in my notepad until my hand hurts, sketching ideas for festive cakes and biscuits that I could bake with my mum in her massive kitchen. I'm all for looking forwards and putting the past behind me, so I'm focusing on what a wonderful Christmas I'm going to have with my family, all the fun we're going to have, and all the amazing things I'm going to eat. Speaking of which...

I hop up from my chair, a little uneasy on my feet from the twirling, and head into the kitchen to pop the kettle on. It's definitely time for my mid-morning break. A cup of tea and a blueberry muffin is exactly what I need right now.

By the time I get back to my desk, my phone is ringing so I quickly grab it to answer.

'Good morning,' I chirp brightly.

'Hello, Dani,' Tom replies in a similarly cheery tone.

I didn't look at the phone before I answered it. If I'd known it was Tom calling from his office, there's no way I would have been so friendly.

'Good morning, Mr Jones,' I reply.

'Come on, Dan, you know you don't have to call me that,' he replies, dropping his usual professional tone for a moment.

I used to love it when he called me Dan. What is it about when a man gives you a personalised nickname? Why does it make you feel so special? These days, I hate to hear it. I hate to hear his voice generally, never mind my name on his lips.

'What can I do for you?' I ask, keeping things professional, despite his instructions.

As far as I'm concerned, it's Mr Jones all the way from now on – the only other names I'd like to call him are much, much worse. Not the kind of things you would say to your boss, even if he is a colossal wanker.

'Can you come into my office for a moment please?' he asks.

'Okay,' I reply as my brain goes into overdrive. There's something about his voice that makes this seem unusual...

I walk into his room and stand in front of his desk like a terrified child, waiting to be ticked off by the head teacher.

'I wanted to talk about us. Please, take a seat,' Tom instructs me, his eyes fixed firmly on his screen. He never seems uncomfortable at my presence, not like I am in his. I suppose that's because he feels like he has the upper hand. I suppose he does.

I reluctantly sit down opposite him at his desk. The last thing I want to talk about is us – there is no us any more. It's funny, since we broke up, I don't even find him all that attractive now. It's like something inside me has been switched off. I hate his slicked-back hair – I can recall the smell and the feel of it, even though I keep my distance from him these days, and while it didn't bother me at the time, it seriously gives me the ick now.

Just before we broke up, he started going to the gym and dyeing the grey hairs he had on the sides of his head – both of which should have been major red flags that he was cheating on me, I suppose. The only thing is that he's clearly stopped going to the gym, because the smaller, super-expensive shirts that he bought are starting to pull on his stomach, and he hasn't quite colour-matched his hair right, giving the sides a strange sort of red tint. I never cared what he looked like – I care that he never tried this hard for me, though.

'I know we said we'd keep things professional in the office, but a lot went on and we can't keep on pretending it didn't,' he starts.

Funny, he's done an excellent job so far. People in the office didn't even know we were together, never mind that we broke up.

I nod my head. The way he's talking feels awfully formal, like I'm someone he's interviewing for a feature. It feels so strange to be on such weird terms with the man I spent two years of my life with. He knows everything about me (the good stuff, the bad stuff and the just plain ugly stuff), he probably knows my naked body even better than I do, and now he talks to me as he would a potential magazine sponsor. Actually, he would be much nicer to them, they give him money, all I give him is dirty looks and coffee I sometimes stir with a discarded spoon from the sink.

I may be over Tom, and as bleak as my situation is, there's no way I'd ever want to get back with him, but one thing about our break-up that really bothered me – and it still annoys me to this day – is the fact that he never actually apologised for what he did. Tom hasn't shown a hint of remorse over the way he treated me (which is probably why I'm finding it so easy to despise him now) despite the fact we spent two happy (ish) years together. Perhaps an apology is what he's building up to now? He's finally going to apologise! I can feel myself softening towards him already, it's a big deal that he's going to do it, even if it has taken him months to get around to it.

'You need to look for a new job,' he tells me bluntly.

'Well, that's very... wait, what?'

That doesn't sound like an apology, it sounds like I'm going to be adding losing my job to the list of crappy things that have happened to me this year.

'You're sacking me?' I squeak.

Oh, God, I can't be sacked. I need this job – I need the money. I wouldn't be in this room, with this tosser, if I weren't desperate. Can he even sack me for no reason?

'No, of course not,' he replies. I breathe a very slight sigh of relief. 'Anyway, I'm not sure our strained relationship is a sackable offence.'

It probably isn't, but it definitely sounds like he googled it to see if it was.

'Your position is more like that of an intern, someone with less experience,' he explains – I'm not sure that's true, but I let him continue. 'So, we need to vacate your role for the internship programme, which means perhaps we might need to reshuffle you, until we find something better, but having just hired a string of new writers, I don't know how likely it is we'll find you something suitable. We do have something else lined up for you, though, in the meantime, which you'll be doing when we return after Christmas.'

I wonder if this is supposed to be purposefully confusing. I feel like something is happening, something more than his tone suggests, but I can't quite work out what he's saying. Am I getting promoted finally?

'Okay,' I reply weakly. 'So, what will my new role be?'

'You'll be taking on the role of office administrator,' he replies. 'Making copies, setting up meeting rooms, coffees and so on.'

'You mean an office junior,' I correct him with a frown, thoroughly unimpressed by what is now so very clearly a demotion.

'Well, Dani, I don't think anyone calls it that any more,' he insists. 'Office administrator is the preferred title, it makes clear that you don't have to be young to take on the role.'

I widen my eyes. I'm in my early thirties and he's giving me a euphemised job title, not only to make it sound like a bigger deal than it is, but also because he no longer considers me to be in the junior age bracket. He's dating someone who is barely out of her teens and suddenly *I'm* an old lady.

'The pay will be slightly less, unfortunately,' he adds.

So, it's not enough that he kicks me out of our home, cheats on me, and dumps me, now he's docking my wages and demoting me to making cups of coffee and photocopying. What a piece of work!

'Someone new will be taking on your role in the new year. I'm going to need you to train him up, show him the ropes for a few days, then you can start your new role without any worries, okay?'

I nod. I don't know what to say.

'This is good, isn't it?' Tom claps his hands together. 'Perhaps if we're working around each other less intensely, we can maybe see about being friends?'

I nod my head, again, without saying a word. Well, what can I say? I'll just have to put up with my new position until I find another job. I wasn't planning on staying here any longer than I had to anyway. What I'd like to do is pick up that cold cup of coffee that's sitting on his desk and pour it over his head before telling him I quit, and that he should go fuck himself, before walking out with my head held high. That's what the old Dani would have done, but this Dani can't afford it.

2

If you could have any superpower, what would it be?

I've never understood that question. Mostly because I just don't get those people who answer saying they'd like to be invisible, because what's so great about being invisible? Take it from someone who has felt invisible for a while now, it's not all it's cracked up to be.

I've been working at *Livin' It London* lifestyle magazine for three years now. I thought I'd finally made it, when I landed a job as a writer at a big, proper magazine, with huge swanky offices, a fantastic team of creatives, endless opportunities... That's not exactly how things have worked out, though.

To say I've been working as a journalist would be a huge stretch. Yes, I work in the newsroom, and I do technically write articles, but I write the paid-for advertorials, which are exactly what they sound like, just adverts masquerading as real stories, except due to rules and regulations, adverts have to be clearly marked as adverts, so no one even reads them, and even if they do, it's not like they're credited to me. I don't get my name in lights, not like the real journalists here. And now I'm not even going to be doing that any more. I can't even keep a crap job.

The undoubted star of the show at *Livin' It London* is Rex Buckley. Rex is the dreamy all-American hunk all the female employees (and some of the men, to be honest) go crazy for. He's tall, muscular, with messy dark hair and brown eyes – a regular jock, straight out of a high-school movie. Well, they're always played by people in their twenties, right? Rex turned thirty last week and I know because there was a party I absolutely wasn't invited to – this is what I mean about being invisible, it sucks.

Beth and Elle in Fashion hang off his every word. Roxie in Theatre is always laughing at his jokes. Mike, Sam and Rocky in Sports are basically his posse of dudes. Even Tom seems to be head over heels in love with him, which is surprising given that he isn't a twenty-something woman, but there you go. Rex can do no wrong – he knows it, though, which means the *Livin' It London* office is his playground. Sometimes it feels like I'm the only one who isn't a sucker for his charms.

Rex is head of Showbiz, but you would be forgiven for thinking he was a celebrity himself. He's got photos on his desk of him with various celebrities, from Harry Styles to Barack Obama (but I'm nursing a theory he had the boys in digital Photoshop that one for him) but he also gets his own cheesy photo above his articles, along with his name, in big golden lettering.

Showbiz is what I want to be writing about. Not just because I spend all my time watching TV and listening to music, but because the Showbiz writers get the best jobs. But that would require getting on Rex's team – a team Tom always actively discouraged me from joining, saying it wasn't the lifestyle for someone hoping to start a family – and Rex doesn't even know I'm alive, even if he did have a spot open up, so he'd never choose me. I'm not exaggerating. My cubicle is right outside his office and I don't think he's ever actually looked at me. He almost walked through me, when he passed me in the corridor the other day, to the point where I genuinely considered if I might have died on my lunch break and just not realised I was a ghost yet.

So, Rex won't be recruiting me for his team of cool kids anytime soon, and I certainly won't be catching his attention. I wouldn't know how to, unless I flirted with him, but first of all, that wouldn't work because I am terrible at flirting, and second of all, he is not my type at all.

Sure, Rex is good-looking, I'm not saying he isn't, but James in IT is more my type. Kind of shy and quirky with curly brown hair that sits messily on the top of his head – I find it so cute when he has to brush it from his eyes just so he can see his screen. He has all these nerdy toys on his desk, which I think shows personality, even if I don't know what they all are, and a framed photo of his mum, which is always a good sign, right? James doesn't really know I exist either, to be honest, and, with him being shy, and me being invisible, it's not seeming like we're about to get our happily ever after anytime soon anyway.

I know, I shouldn't be entertaining the idea of another work-place romance (even if it has been six months since Tom and I broke up), not even in my fantasies, but with my social life being pretty much non-existent, how else am I going to meet anyone?

I suppose, somewhere along the line, I hid myself. Perhaps I was so focused on Tom that I didn't make enough of an effort with everyone else, or maybe it already felt like everyone was firmly in their friendship groups when I arrived. Working in a team of one doesn't help me make friends, that's for sure, and my confidence has taken a bit of a knock since Tom and I broke up. Whatever the reason is, it's a mess I haven't managed to get myself out of yet.

'Everyone, listen up,' Tom announces to the newsroom. 'Just a quick announcement to say that *Livin' It Leeds* is looking to shake up their editorial team, they've let a few people go and they're hoping to hire from right here in our London offices.'

I'm sitting in my cubicle, at my desk, which isn't too far from where Tom is standing, so I slump down into my seat a little. Right now, being invisible might come in useful. Just hearing the words 'let a few people go' fills me with fear. I feel like if Tom could fire me, he would, and soon enough, he's going to work out how to do that.

There are various groans around the room.

'I know,' Tom says, echoing the general sentiment of the office with a theatrical roll of his eyes. 'Who would want to move to the dreary north? But if anyone does fancy a change of scenery, Rex, our very own head of Showbiz, is the man you want to talk to, he's going to be setting up a Showbiz department up there but, don't worry, ladies, he's coming back after.'

Almost everyone laughs. Ergh.

'Okay, back to work.'

The fact that Tom knows I'm from Yorkshire, and still hasn't put me forward for the job, speaks volumes. He never valued me, or my skills. He doesn't think I'm up for a role in the Showbiz department.

I shift in my seat as the cogs turn in my brain. Being *Livin' It*'s resident northerner – and an unhappy resident at that – I'm starting to wonder whether a move back home might be just what I need. Well, I'm miserable here, I didn't make friends like I had hoped I would when I moved here, it would be the understatement of the century to say I'm pretty jazzed about the idea of never seeing Tom again, and I'm definitely not happy with the work I'm going to be doing here in the new year. No one could blame me for wanting to retreat back to the north.

The only problem is that Tom said they were looking to shake things up in Leeds, and set up a new Showbiz section, and they're not exactly going to do that by hiring the girl who just got demoted from writing the adverts to making the coffee, are they? Especially not if Rex is picking the team. I suppose I could try to come up with something, a way to prove myself, to show Rex that I absolutely can do this job if he gives me a chance... but would he give a chance to a girl he doesn't even realise he's met?

I'll just have to think of something else – find a new job, maybe start looking closer to home again and move back to Yorkshire. Perhaps not to the coast, where I grew up, but Leeds or York must have some writing jobs going. I'm not sure what I'll do yet, but if I can just get the right people to notice me, that would be a start. I wonder if I could rely on Tom for a good reference. I doubt it.

Perhaps setting my sights on working in other, smaller cities is the way to go. I'm not sure what London has left to offer me now unfortunately.

3

_____

I grew up on Hope Island, a tidal island just off the coast of Marram Bay, a cute coastal town in Yorkshire, which means that twice a day it's cut off from the rest of the country by the sea. When I think about it, it's so cool, a real wonder, but when you're a teenager rushing to the mainland to catch a bus, to get a train, to trek to the nearest Primark, it's just an annoyance. It's a shame but, when you grow up seeing the same things every day, they don't seem like they're anything special, they're just the things in your home town.

The more I think about it, the more I feel like the new job going in Leeds really would be perfect for me. I would be so close for visiting my parents, but I would still have all the perks of a city on my doorstep, and... ugh, my imagination is running away with me. There's no way Rex is going to just pick me out of the blue.

I guess I would miss a lot of the wonderful things about living in London if I moved back up north. I love this city, the buildings, all the tourist attractions.

One of the main things I would miss about living in London is the variety of shops, even if they aren't all as close together as they are in other cities. Today I'm shopping for a Christmas present for my mum and dad during my lunch hour – well, my lunch forty minutes. You can't get far, or much done, in forty minutes. It's not like you can just browse the high street here. So, with not much time to choose something for my mum and dad, I am putting my faith in the hands of a very helpful John Lewis employee who reckons he knows just the thing.

'It's a Simple Simon,' he tells me.

'If I don't know what that is then my mum and dad definitely aren't going to know what it is,' I point out with a playful laugh.

It's funny, but it's true, I've seen my dad try to change the channel with his phone, shouting, 'Okay goo-goo,' at it.

'It's a smart speaker,' he explains. 'Like an Alexa or a Google Home.'

'I tried them with a Smarty, but they couldn't get on with it,' I reply. 'I made the mistake of connecting it to their lights and wound up with a panicked phone call from my dad because the house was pitch-black.'

The man allows himself a slight chuckle. My dad is old school – especially when it comes to lights. An automated timer for all his Christmas lights is the extent of it (lord knows he needs it, with his city-centre-worthy Christmas lights display), but to someone as technophobic as my dad is, doing something like that is on a par with defusing a bomb. The only thing I've ever been able to get them on board with is Facebook. My mum took to that with a disturbing ease. Honestly, the day I showed her how easy it was to see everyone's *everything*, I saw a light turn on in her eyes, and a smile spread across her face like nothing I've ever seen before.

My parents, Arnold and Mary, own holiday homes all around Marram Bay, but these days they employ people to run the business for them, so they're pretty much retired. I really think they would benefit from having something like a Simple Simon around the house.

'Don't worry, Simple Simon was designed with older users in mind,' he reassures me. 'My parents couldn't get on with smart speakers either, until I got them one of these, and it's got a money-back guarantee, if they don't like it, so it's worth a try. My parents can't believe how much easier their life is, now that they have a smart speaker they can work.'

It sounds like this Simple Simon will be a great way to sneak a bit of hardware into their lives without baffling them. It must be so hard for their generation, not growing up with all the technology that I did, but managing to master Facebook easily enough gives me faith – even if Mum does sometimes accidentally post the most hilariously inappropriate GIFs in the comments on people's statuses.

I pay for my Simple Simon before dashing back in the direction of the office. Not long to go until Christmas break now. I'm so pleased I saved up my holiday days (even if it wasn't entirely intentional, more just a by-product of working too much) because I really need this break. I feel like I'm always rushing, or working, or rushing to work. It's been non-stop lately, I feel like I've hardly spoken to my mum and dad. We've never been the type to have long weekly phone conversations, preferring to swap instant messages on Facebook, always via my mum, of course. They keep in touch with everyone on there, they get their news on there (whether it is true or not is besides the point), and there's even a Marram Bay Facebook group for residents where they all talk about local events, swap gossip and offload old furniture on to each other.

I make a mental note to call my mum and dad, to make a proper plan for Christmas. We've talked about it, but only in the sense that they've told me I'm always welcome, in the same way they always do. My parents pretty much do the same thing every Christmas, and something about that sounds especially inviting to me right now. It's usually just the two of them. Both sets of my grandparents have passed away and both my parents grew up without siblings, which is probably why my parents stopped at the one kid too. They'll get up and go for a walk, cross the causeway to Marram Bay, have a drink in their favourite pub, before going home for Christmas dinner. It is a simple but perfect Christmas, and I can't wait to be a part of it.

There's a slight elephant in the room, though. When I have spoken to my mum about maybe coming home for Christmas, I have neglected to mention that if I did, I would be coming without Tom. To be honest, I haven't told them about our break-up yet. I know, it's been six months, but I feel strangely embarrassed about it, in a way that I shouldn't because none of this is my fault, but the longer I've left it, the harder I'm finding it to say.

I suppose I've also been worried that, if they found out I was living alone, they might try to convince me to move back home, and it's not that I wouldn't want to, I just hate the idea of being such a failure that I have to go back to basics, start again, move back into my childhood bedroom, in my parents' house, like the past decade meant nothing. It can't all have been for nothing, can it? I can't go back to square one.

Perhaps the best solution to this problem is to surprise them, by turning up on their doorstep, as a living, breathing Christmas present. They'll be over the moon, and I won't have to make any difficult phone calls about turning up alone. By the time I'm there, clearly alone, I can mention it briefly while showing them that I am clearly fine, and that way it won't be a thing. I quite like the idea of surprising them. Mum loves big gestures.

The more I think about Christmas with my parents, the more excited I get, and I'm pretty pleased with my purchase, I think they're going to love it, even if I will have to teach them how to use it first. My post-shopping high doesn't last long, though, because I am heading back to work now. I'm no sooner rushing back towards reception when a tall, fair-haired man goes to walk through the door at the same time. He's an Alexander Skarsgård type, but with the kind eyes of Ryan Gosling. There's no one at the reception desk currently. I pause, to see if he knows where he's going. He clearly doesn't.

'Hello,' I blurt a little awkwardly. It's not every day someone so handsome walks into this office. Well, it's that, or maybe I've just finally started looking at strangers again. Maybe I am finally moving on from Tom.

He's wearing an absolutely pristine navy suit with a matching overcoat and he doesn't have a hair out of place. He doesn't look like he's just got off the Tube in a sweaty hurry, like I usually do when I arrive here (even in freezing winter weather), that's for sure.

'Hello,' he says. 'I'm here to see Tom Jones.'

Yes, my ex really is called Tom Jones. His parents didn't even call him Thomas, so he can't even use that to make it seem a bit less funny, his actual name is Tom. Tom Jones.

'Okay, I'll see if he's free,' I reply.

'Tom Jones,' the man says out loud. 'Is it dorky that I find that so funny? Do people usually laugh?'

'It's not unusual,' I reply, deadpan, and no, I *never* get tired of making that joke.

The man laughs again.

'Can I take your name, please?' I ask him.

'Yes, it's Barry Manilow,' he replies.

I stare at him.

'Just kidding,' he says with a laugh. 'I'm Russell Redford, I'm starting work here in the new year, writing the paid-for content.'

Oh, wow, this is who is replacing me? This gorgeous, stylish man who oozes charm? I mean, he seems like a dream... but something about being replaced by a man (especially a younger one) rubs me up the wrong way. Then again, Tom replaced me as his girlfriend with a younger woman, so at least this is slightly different.

I buzz Tom, who comes rushing out to give Russell a big old manly handshake. Russell gives as good as he gets. I'm tempted to ask if I should pass them a ruler – what is it with men, thinking they need to have the strongest handshake to show how powerful and important they are?

'So, Danielle can help you fill in your paperwork, so you're all set in the new year,' Tom tells him, talking about me, but not to me. Can I? 'She'll get you a coffee too. I'll leave you in her very capable hands. Great to have you on the team.'

'Danielle,' Russell repeats my name back to me when we're finally alone.

'Call me Dani,' I insist.

'Only if you call me Russ,' he replies with a friendly smile.

'Okay, sure,' I say. 'I suppose I should show you the ropes. I guess I'll start by showing you around the office.'

I lead Russ into the kitchen, where we find Amelia using the microwave to make her lunch. She's working alone on reception while Donna is off on maternity leave. That explains why there was no one on reception then.

'Oh, hello,' she says brightly, Russ catching her eye. 'Who is this?'

'This is Russ,' I tell her. 'He's going to be writing the advertorials.'

'Isn't that your job?' she says. 'Are you leaving?'

Russ looks at me.

'Erm, no, I'm going to be office administrator moving forwards.'

Amelia pulls a face at my blatant demotion. It's a mixture of pity and disgust, which is pretty much all you ever get from Amelia.

'Eek,' she says. 'Well, so lovely to have you with us, Russ. It's nice to get some new blood in the office, and I know good people, and you look like you're good people.'

Ergh, how subtle. A handsome man walks into the office and she's all over him.

'Aren't you a sight for sore eyes,' Alan Marsh, the editor-in-chief, says to Amelia as he walks into the room. This is pretty much all you get from Alan too. A level of sleaze you hoped had died off decades ago, but he's still very much the big man of the office, he still smokes at his desk, and all the women are 'little lady' this and 'pretty young thing' that and are all here to be crept on – it's practically part of the job. Then he notices Russ. 'Who is this?'

'This is Russ, he's taking over from Dani,' Amelia tells him.

'Are you leaving?' he asks me, looking at me as though it's for the first time, even though I've been here for three years.

I sigh, before repeating myself.

'Amelia, I love that dress,' Alan says. 'We should think about making it the office uniform. You're much thinner than Donna, though...'

'Well, Donna *is* pregnant,' I remind him, quickly holding my tongue so I don't say something that will definitely get me sacked.

Alan simply pulls a thoughtful face before wandering off towards his office.

'Wow,' Russ says quietly. 'He seems old school.'

'You don't know the half it,' I tell him, leading him out of the kitchen, towards my desk – well, his desk now. 'Alan is our resident sleazebag. It's a miracle no one has taken legal action against him.'

'Wow,' Russ blurts.

I do wonder if I should be telling him this, but I'm in a bad mood, and he'll find out sooner or later anyway.

'Otherwise, he's quite boring. He has a lot of war stories – he'll tell them to anyone who will listen, even back when he used to interview people for features, he would always try and make it all about him. Tom used to do this thing where he would say "fire away" and make a gun shape with his hands. He soon cut that out after a few hours' worth of Alan's war material, and a lecture on how firing a gun wasn't a casual reference to be made. I wouldn't mind, but I don't think he ever left Liverpool or wherever it was he was based when he was in the army.'

Russ laughs.

Okay, I'm sure I shouldn't be telling him this stuff, but I want to make him laugh, I want him to like me. I don't know why, there's just something about him. I can tell just by looking at him, just by hearing him talk, that he's a cool guy (okay, not quite Rex levels of ultra-cool), and who doesn't want to be liked by the cool guys?

'It sounds like this place has some stories,' he says. 'And you know them all.'

'Oh, you wouldn't believe half of them if I told you,' I reply with a cheeky grin. 'I could ruin everyone here.'

I laugh, to make sure he knows I'm joking about that last part, because that's an exaggeration and, even if I could, I would never do anything like that, not even to Tom.

'Want to go for a drink after work and tell me all about it?' Russ asks me.

I am taken aback. I'm almost tempted to look behind me, to see who he's really talking to, because it can't be me, can it? Do *I* want to go for a drink with him? I mean, yes, of course I do, I just can't quite believe he's asking! Normally, the only person who asks me to have a drink with him is the drunk who sits outside the off-licence that I live above. I usually just tell him I'm washing my hair but, with Russ, I want to say yes.

'Yeah, sure,' I reply, as casually as I can.

'Great,' he says. 'I get that it's hard to talk in here, but I want to learn all about everyone. Who is who, what they're like, who is single...'

I pinch myself. Is he flirting with me? I can't get ahead of myself.

'Yeah, sure,' I say again, still casual as I can. 'I'll tell you everything.'

'Looking forward to it,' he replies with a grin.

As I continue to show Russ the office ropes, I can't seem to wipe the smile from my face. I am going for an actual drink, with a handsome man, and *he* asked *me*.

4

———

Madeline Perry is the latest addition to the team here at *Livin' It London*.

Being brought in to head up the Style section, Madeline unsurprisingly looks fresh off the catwalk, 24/7. My own long blonde hair always looks kind of dull, and dry as hell at the ends, but Madeline's longer, blonder hair looks so bright and sleek – so perfect that the lengths can't be real, but if they're extensions I can't tell, because it looks that good. She's also slim and impossibly stylish and her handbag looks like it costs more than my rent.

I would say that Madeline is everything I wish I were, except I don't think I've ever seen her say or do a nice thing to or for anyone since she started working here last week.

I am not surprised (although I am disappointed) to report that her 'treat 'em mean, keep 'em keen' approach works equally well on both men and women. The ruder Madeline is, the more people seem to fall all over themselves to please her. The girls want to be best friends with her. The guys want to be with her. I was no different, at the start of last week, when I introduced myself to her and offered to make her a coffee. Madeline just laughed wildly, closing her eyes and throwing her head back, at the way I said the word 'coffee' in the Yorkshire accent I've had all my life – one I'm ashamed to admit I've been self-consciously trying to phase out ever since.

I pretty much gave up interacting with Madeline after that, but I'm certainly seeing a lot of her still, because every time she passes Rex's office, the two of them chat outside his door, just feet away from me. You can tell he's into her, but he hasn't let on yet. This is how Rex works, he pretends he's too cool to care, flirts in a way that he thinks is subtle, and then asks a girl out when he is certain she'll say yes. I've seen girls who didn't even know they were interested until Rex flicked the charm on and off, and then suddenly they were crazy for him, doing anything to try to get his attention. Annoyingly, I've never actually seen anyone turn him down and, with each woman that falls for his charm, it's almost as though he grows stronger and more confident.

It isn't much more than an annoying part of my day, having to endure watching him flirt, seeing him bounce from woman to woman. The only good thing about sitting here, watching Rex in action, seeing all his plays, is that it reminds me why I would never go for a guy like him, and that I'll certainly never let myself get used by him.

'So, you're settling in here nicely, huh?' Rex asks her.

'Just about,' Madeline replies kind of coolly.

God, don't give him an inch. Sometimes I feel like he lines up questions just to get the responses he needs to turn everything into a come-on. Like, oh, you're not settling in, perhaps I can help settle you in? Well, not exactly like that, because that's rubbish, but you know what I mean. I'm not a serial flirt, *he* is.

'Good to know you're getting a feel for things,' Rex replies.

See! Just like *that*.

'Do you need someone to show you the sights?' he asks her.

'I think I'm doing okay,' she says through a slight smile. 'Although, I swear, there are no good restaurants around here.'

I snort. To myself, ever so quietly. There are no good restaurants around here? What? Around London? Is she crazy? Even if she's talking about here in the office specifically, we're in the West End, for crying out loud. There's everything you could ever hope to eat and more. Why does Rex always go for these sorts of women? Snooty, entitled, generally unfriendly women who can't be at all pleasant to be around for long.

'What do you like to eat?' Rex asks. There's a look in his eye, as though he's hoping she's going to reply with: 'Egotistical American men'. I want to throw my keyboard at him.

'Japanese food,' she replies.

Right, I can think of at least three great ones not too far from here, so this is clearly some kind of flirting tactic. Oh. Right. Silly me. Of course it is – this is all a ploy, to get him to invite her out for Japanese food, so that he can show her where is best to get it. And I'll bet Rex knows exactly where Madeline can get *it*.

'Huh, that's a coincidence,' Rex tells Madeline as he casually leans against his door frame, giving it his usual cool-guy level of aloofness, which really pisses me off, because it just seems so manipulative.

'Japanese food is my favourite too,' he tells her.

I've heard him say that line many times, to many girls, about many different cuisines. And you'll never guess what line comes next.

'Oh, really?' Madeline replies, her eyebrows raised. I think she knows where this is going too.

'If you wanted to grab a bite some time—'

Madeline raises her hand, cutting Rex off mid-sentence. I've never seen that before.

'Let me stop you there,' she tells him. 'I know what you're doing and it's not going to work.'

'What do you mean?' he asks with a faux innocence.

'Oh, don't give me that,' she scoffs. 'You've been flirting with me for a week, trying to play your little mind games with me, well, I've heard all about your office antics and it's not going to work on me.'

'I'm not flirting with you,' Rex insists with an overly theatrical laugh. Wow, I've never seen him this close to losing his cool. 'You've got me all wrong.'

With things taking an unusual turn for Rex, I can't help but enjoy spectating now. Seeing Rex getting shot down is a rare sight, like Halley's Comet, and as such, it is absolutely not to be missed.

I'm currently peering nosily over the side of my cubicle, loving my front row seat, right on the edge of the action, until I catch Rex's attention. For a second, we hold eye contact. There's a glimmer of something in his eye. I'm so embarrassed to be caught watching the two of them that I take back all those times I complained about no one noticing me. Shit. I forget I'm not actually invisible.

To style it out, I grab some papers to take to the copy machine. Perhaps it will just seem like I was looking for the right time to stand up, so as not to interrupt them, rather than just being a nosy parker.

'I have a girlfriend,' Rex tells Madeline after turning his attention back to her. 'I was going to say you could go for dinner with both of us. You're new in town, right? I was just trying to be nice.'

Madeline rolls her eyes.

'Oh, don't give me that,' she insists. 'Do you honestly think I believe that?'

It's hard to explain but it's almost as though she takes as much joy from turning people down as Rex does from wooing them. She's clearly having the time of her life, which seems odd. I am rooting for absolutely no one in this scenario.

'It's true,' Rex insists.

'Even if you did have a girlfriend,' Madeline says, humouring him, 'you were still flirting with me. You were still asking me out. How do I know you weren't doing it all behind her back?'

'Well, because she's over there, obviously,' Rex says, gesturing across the office.

I'm standing in my cubicle, clutching the papers I'm going to photocopy, for absolutely no reason, but I can't help but follow his hand, to see who he's pointing at. I realise he's pointing at me a split second before Madeline turns around to look at me.

'*Her?*' she says in a way that sounds like she can't quite believe it.

I furrow my brow at her. I think I might have to take offence at that.

'Yeah,' Rex says as he walks over to me. 'Do you really think I'd flirt with you while my girlfriend watched?'

He walks over to me and slinks an arm around my waist. I feel my body go stiff, my mouth go dry, and my legs turn to jelly.

Madeline's jaw is on the floor.

'I just... I...' She pauses for a second. '*Really?*'

Rex takes my chin in his hands and pulls my face to his. He gives me a lingering, sensual peck on the cheek. Then he lets me go, smiles at me, and turns back to Madeline smugly.

'Anyway, don't let us distract you from your work, we'll see you around,' he tells her. 'But let us know if you fancy that dinner.'

Madeline looks a little embarrassed as she skulks off.

'Thanks, babe,' Rex tells me with a cheeky smile, still mindful that a few eyes are on us.

'Oh, you're welcome, *babe*,' I reply sarcastically.

Rex gives me a wink before heading back into his office, closing the door behind him. I drop down into my chair, stunned into a state of shock, as I try to make sense of what just happened. Obviously, the one time Rex does notice me, it's just to use me as a prop. I can't help but touch my cheek, feeling where he kissed me, as though that can confirm or deny whether I imagined it all or not. My cheek feels warm. I'm flushed – probably with embarrassment, not because I enjoyed it, why would I enjoy being kissed by Rex, of all people?

I just need to forget about it and get on with my work. Plus, I'm meeting Russ later, so at least I have that to look forward to. Today has certainly been my most interesting day in the office, that's for sure. A date and a kiss – with two different people, no less. It's a shame that, in the new year, working here is going to be unbearable. On days like today, I could actually imagine myself starting to enjoy my job.

5

After squeezing myself into a black dress (after first squashing myself into a pair of tight black stomach-holding-in knickers) and spending ages carefully curling my mid-length blonde hair, I am out. Out-out, for the first time in ages.

I'm at Obar, with Russ, chatting away, drinking cocktails. I've wanted to visit Obar for a while now, but I've never actually had anyone to go with. Cocktails are two for one some nights, which is great, but the only thing sadder than me sitting in here alone with a drink would be me sitting here alone with two drinks. I'm delighted to have an actual human to come here with, never mind the fact that it's an actual male human. Not only are we here together but we're getting on really well. I feel like I'm having an out-of-body experience. It's almost as though I'm watching a TV show about myself – and a highly implausible one at that. I know, it sounds tragic, that I'm so shook by something so small, but it's been one hell of a year, so cut me some slack. Tonight is about more than just a night out. Tonight is the night that marks the end of my pity party. I'm the first to admit that I've let myself become a bit of a sad sack. I really made myself at home in Tom's shadow to the point where I let the light become something that scared me. Well, I'm stepping back out into the spotlight now, I am my own person, and I'm finally on something that at least resembles a date.

The bar is in full festive mode, with decorations everywhere, which I like. We're surrounded by work Christmas gatherings, though. You can spot a work party a mile away, because it's always such a mismatched crew, people of all ages, all with different styles and personalities, who for some reason just don't quite look like they usually hang out. Work parties are always so much louder, though. I suppose that goes hand in hand with everyone finally letting their hair down and getting excited for Christmas. Most of the clusters of people in the bar are a blur of tinsel and novelty headbands. Occasionally you see a serious conversation between colleagues who have clearly brought the office to the office party, but that's just what happens with colleagues, isn't it? Even Russ and I are talking about work.

'Finally,' Russ calls out to someone over my shoulder. 'We were beginning to think you had stood us up.'

'Sorry, we don't usually come here, so we thought we'd best arrive together,' a familiar female voice replies.

I already know it's Amelia by her tone and I can tell you what the look on her face will be like without even turning around. Annoyed, disgusted to be out of her trendy bubble, but smiling in a way that is intended to neutralise how she feels, but in no way masks it, not even an inch.

I do eventually turn around and see Amelia and a handful of people from the office. Bumping into my work colleagues on a night out is something that I would actively avoid generally, but it doesn't sound like we've bumped into them at all, it sounds like Russ has invited them, meaning I haven't just caught the wrong end of the stick, I've accidentally glued my hands to it, and now I feel stupid. Russ invited the whole team for drinks, not just me, so this isn't anything even close to romantic, and we're probably not getting on as well as I thought. He's just been making small talk with me, until the rest of the work crew arrived. Mortifying.

'You two look so funny, like you're on a date or something,' Amelia tells me, squeezing my shoulder, as she laughs.

I'm not even sure she means anything by it. I genuinely think she simply finds the idea of me on a date hilarious. I do too now, I suppose.

Russ laughs. Ouch.

'Anyway, we'll go grab our drinks,' she replies.

Russ gets our conversation right back on track.

'So, you were saying how long it took Tom to land his current role, and where he might go from there?' Russ prompts me.

'Right,' I reply, mentally shaking myself, trying to get back to our conversation. 'Well, first he...'

Shit. It's just hit me. The reason why I'm here. Russ is mining me for intel. He's been doing it all night. Asking me questions about work, about the dynamics, how best to deal with different people, and now he's grilling me on Tom – he wants his job, eventually, I suppose.

'I, erm, I'm just going to grab another drink,' I tell him.

'You've not finished that one,' he points out.

I pick up my glass. It's a cosmopolitan with about a third left in it. I knock it back. Russ's eyebrows shoot up.

'I'm finished now,' I tell him.

I head to the bar. I can see the door for the exit just to the side of it and I am so, so temped to just leave. Would anyone even notice if I did? I hover on the spot for a second, while I decide what to do, but Amelia collars me before I get the chance.

She hooks her arm in mine and pulls me closer, dragging me

past a few people, to the front of the bar queue with her. A few people groan but she either doesn't notice or doesn't care.

It's starting to get quite busy now, and it's packed around the bar, so she has to raise her voice so that I can hear her.

'I don't often see you on work nights out,' she points out. 'I'll buy you a drink.'

'Oh, that's okay,' I insist but, once again, she either doesn't hear or doesn't care. I suppose it's nice of her. I shouldn't throw her kindness in her face. I need all the friends I can get in that office.

'Two Cherryberry Bombs, please,' she shouts to the barman.

Oh, right, I remember now. It's buy one get one free. So she's not actually buying me a drink but, still, it's good of her to give me her freebie.

'So, what's the deal with Russ?' she asks me. 'Is he single? Can you find out for me? Put in a good word for me?'

Wonderful. She's using me too.

Amelia cackles for a second.

'You know, I actually heard someone in the office earlier, saying that you and Rex were an item.' She clearly finds this hilarious and entirely unbelievable. 'Imagine that. I set them right, don't worry.'

I sigh as Amelia thrusts the drink into my hand. She's the last person I want to socialise with. The same goes for anyone from work, really. It's our work Christmas party tomorrow night and I'm strongly considering bailing on it. Let's face it, I have no work friends to hang out with there, and the fact that partners are invited is a double whammy of crap for me, because not only do I not have a partner, but it also means that my ex-partner will be there with the girl he replaced me with. Absolute torture, no thank you.

'You can be my wing woman tonight,' she tells me. 'Operation: Rusmelia. He's so going home with me tonight.'

So I do stand a chance of pulling Russ after all, it just turns out it's going to be for Amelia instead. Fantastic.

6

I stumble through the doors of the twenty-four-hour off-licence
that I live above. I lose my footing a little and crash into a display
of Pringles. Luckily, it's sturdier than I am so it doesn't budge but
it still makes a noise. So do I, as I bang my elbow.

'Motherfu—'

'Don't you think you've had enough?' a forty-something man
buying a four-pack of lager asks me. I think it's intended as more
of a statement than a question. Either way, it's none of his
business.

'Erm, I live here,' I tell him, but that probably doesn't make
much sense to him. Then again, maybe it does, because I've had a
fair bit to drink tonight.

I head through to the back room and up the stairs to my sad
little flat, carefully weaving my way through piles of stock as I go.
Even looking at bottles of booze is making me feel sick. Whose
idea was two-for-one cocktails anyway? It makes it too easy to
have too many.

You know when you drink so much you embarrass yourself?
Yeah, well, I've done things the other way around tonight. I was so

mortified that I'd misunderstood Russ inviting me out that I drank a whole bunch of cheap cocktails to try to forget about it.

It shouldn't have been a shock, really, when it turned out that Russ hadn't been flirting with me at all. Or maybe he had been, just a bit, but only to get the low-down on the office from me so that he can try to climb the ladder the second he starts his new job. It also soon clicked that when he asked me to give him the low-down on who was single, he didn't care if I was single, he was trying to work out if Amelia was single. And she is. Well, she might not be now, depending on how it's going, because I left around the time the two of them started grinding on each other on the dance floor. They're probably at third base by now, at least.

I feel like such a bloody mug. Like moving on from having your heart broken is ever as simple as some handsome, charming man turning up at your work and sweeping you off your feet. Russ is there for my job, not for me. It was more of a car crash than a meet cute, and while I don't care about not getting together with some bloke I only just met (because of course I don't, I barely knew the guy, and the more I saw the less I liked), it's more the fact that I am hardcore embarrassed that I let my mind run away with me like that. When will I ever learn?

Now, more than ever, I want to get out of here. It's everything. It's Tom, it's Russ, and let's throw the weirdness I'm sure to feel around Rex into the mix too. I'm nearly finished for the holidays, and there's no way in hell I'm going to the work Christmas party, so I'm thinking about heading home for Christmas a little earlier than I planned.

It's a week or so until Christmas Day, and I know normally people drop home for a few days over the holidays, but my parents are never going to send me packing, are they? Anyway, once I finish work, it's not like I'll have much else going on, so I might see if I can book some extra last-minute days of holiday. In fact, I'll log in and put the request in now, there's no way Tom will refuse, given that he's actively told me to wind down doing my job anyway.

I really do quite like the idea of surprising my parents, even if they have already assumed I'll be turning up at some point. It will still be a lovely surprise for them, when I turn up early.

I'm sure my mum will want to change my bed sheets and make my favourite thing for dinner, like she always does when I visit, so I could perhaps give her a few hours' notice, but, then again, I always feel so guilty when she launches into hardcore cleaning mode before my arrival. Like I'm going to care if she hasn't vacuumed the stairs, or if she doesn't have at least ten different kinds of nuts to snack on over the holidays. I just want to see them and for us to have a nice, relaxing time together.

I probably haven't visited home as much as I should have. It's just been so hard with work and money, but none of that matters, what matters is that I'm going home for Christmas, and I'm going to forget about all the bullshit for a couple of weeks. Forget Tom, forget Russ, forget that I hate my job and I don't know what I'm doing with my life. I'll have a good Christmas, put this year to bed and I'll start afresh next year. Surely things can't get any worse now. The only way is up.

Yuck. The aftertaste of a mismatched selection of different cocktails is nowhere near as nice as the cocktails tasted individually. Well, the ones I vividly remember drinking, at least.

Once I'm safely upstairs in my flat, I fill a glass of water for future Dani to drink in the morning – or in the middle of the night, depending on how deeply I sleep. I don't drink often but when I do, drunk Dani is constantly thinking about future Dani. That's why I left the impromptu work party, rather than sticking around and making a fool of myself. Well, even more of a fool of myself.

I brush my teeth and while it feels amazing to clean the night off them, going too near my back teeth causes me to gag. It will be a miracle if I don't throw up sometime during the night, or in the morning. Now I feel even more sorry for myself.

I plug my charger into my phone and treat myself to an antacid while I put in my holiday request. No one told me that my thirties were going to be so stressful that my stomach was going to try to dissolve itself. What fun!

I can feel my eyes getting heavy, so I shuffle back down into my bed and mess with my wire, but I can't get my phone to charge. Fantastic. It must have a loose wire. Nothing I can do about it tonight. At least I don't need it for anything before I go to sleep anyway, what am I going to do, drunk-dial someone? Tom? Ha! No, no. I'll just sleep this off, get up, drink a bunch of coffee, make sure I am completely sobered up for work in the morning. The sooner I'm done there, the sooner I can sign off for the holidays. Now I really can't wait.

7

I woke up with the hangover to end all hangovers and it sucks. And I wasn't just hung-over when I woke up, I was running late for work, because my phone died and my stupid alarm didn't go off. If I hadn't woken up gasping for water, I might have slept through the whole morning.

I imagine I would have been in a bad mood anyway today but the pounding in my head is definitely making me feel worse. I'm at work now, scowling at my screen, annoyed at the sight of the last advertorial I'll write. Sure, I hate them, they're paid-for articles that require absolutely zero creativity, it's just a case of assembling the words you are told to say, but my God, it's a damn sight closer to being a journalist than making coffee is.

The saddest thing of all is that I was almost an hour late today and no one even noticed. It's back to being invisible, I suppose.

I feel a pair of hands on my shoulders and my body turns to stone. Tensing up makes my headache feel a million times worse. I'm also completely alarmed at the idea of anyone who works here touching me, especially when I was just starting to feel like I was off the radar again. As demoralising as it sounds to have no one really notice you exist, there is a bizarre and confusing sense of self-confidence that comes with it. If no one is looking at you, there's so much you don't need to worry about, from how fast you're working to how crap your hair looks that day. And my hair really must look awful today, because the best I could do in a hurry was unload a quarter of a can of dry shampoo all over it, in the hope that it did *something*. Dry shampoo is good, but it can't work miracles. I suppose if I had woken up earlier, I could have avoided re-wearing the same skirt today as I did yesterday, but my white shirt is clean at least, even if it could have done with an iron. There isn't exactly a need for me to dress to impress here, is there? I chose the extra minutes in bed over smartening up for the benefit of no one.

'Hey, baby,' I hear an American man's accent say. *Rex!* 'How's it going today?'

I'm genuinely speechless. Suspended in time. Not moving, not speaking – for a second or two, I actually hold my breath.

'You wanna step into my office, talk in private?' he asks me as he leans into my ear, giving my shoulders one big squeeze that sends a shock wave through my body.

I just about manage to force a nod.

Rex steps to one side to let me in before closing the glass door behind us. His entire office is made of glass so, with the blinds open, everyone can see us. I glance, to see if anyone is looking, but I don't spot anyone at the moment. It's funny, I've always sat outside this office, and I can almost always see everything inside it, but I've never crossed the threshold until today.

'Erm, what is going on?' I eventually blurt out. My voice wobbles slightly.

'I didn't realise my *bird* was a northerner,' he says with a cheeky smile. 'I'm Rex, nice to meet you. And you are?'

I'm baffled. My confidence starts creeping back as I begin to feel annoyed by whatever game he's playing. I'm really not interested in being used by anyone else in this bloody office.

'*Obviously* I know your name,' I tell him, starting to get a little angry, but still being painfully polite, as per my very English upbringing. 'And you know mine, you were introduced to me when I started.'

'Right,' he says as he sits down behind his desk, leaning back in his chair, putting his feet up. 'Catherine.'

'*Dani*,' I correct him.

He clearly had no idea.

'You only miss the shots you don't take,' he tells me through a cheeky smile.

'Speaking of the shots you take, erm, what the hell was that?' I ask him.

'What?' he asks innocently.

'You, touching me,' I point out. 'And you kissed me yesterday. I'm pretty sure I could report you for that.'

'Oh, yeah, right, well, you were watching, you saw what was happening with the new girl, she was on to me, I had to do something.'

He says this like it is a perfectly reasonable explanation.

'Oh, well, in that case I'm happy to have helped,' I reply sarcastically.

I really don't need this sort of drama in my life. I head for the door. If this is being noticed, then I definitely preferred things the way they were before. It turns out there really is a lot to be said for invisibility.

'Thanks,' he says. 'It's a blessing in disguise, really. If she thinks we're together, she'll know I'm not shallow, and it will make her want me all the more, if she knows I'm taken. So long as you keep up the act.'

I stop in my tracks and slowly turn around.

'Erm, you what?' I blurt.

'*You what?*' he says back to me, mocking my accent again. 'That's seriously adorable. You really should talk more.'

I ignore what might be a compliment to focus on what is definitely an insult.

'Let me get this straight, you want me to pretend to be your girlfriend so you can pull a different girl?' I say, just checking I have all of the seriously dumb details right.

'Yeah,' he replies, once again like it is a perfectly reasonable thing that normal people do all the time. 'Just think of what it will do for your street cred, huh?'

'I don't care about street cred,' I tell him, which is mostly true. At least, not the kind that comes with being one of Rex's conquests. It doesn't seem like it's a very exclusive club, to be honest with you. Take it from the girl who sits outside his office all day.

'Come on, Dani, there must be something you want from me.'

Rex says this with a wiggle of his eyebrows but, by the time I've finished shuddering, I realise that he may be right. There *is* something I want from him.

'Well, now that you mention it...' I start, mustering up my last scraps of confidence, to try to pull this off. 'I want the Leeds job.'

You have to understand, I never do anything like this. I've never asked for anything in my life. But I do deserve the chance to get out of here, and I do really, *really* want to move closer to home. I feel like a new beginning is exactly what I need but I can't just quit my job and move home, that's not a real plan, that's not going to work out well for me. I need a job to move for, a new direction to take my life in, and some security when I get there. This really could be the answer to all my problems.

'What?' he says, his eyebrows shooting up towards his perfect hair. He seems serious for a split second, but then his face softens again. He seems almost amused. 'Do you even write?'

'*Yes*,' I inform him. Honestly, it's embarrassing how little he knows about me. 'But they've only been giving me the crap. But if you were to choose me as part of your Leeds team...'

'Well, that's not going to happen,' he says with a snort.

'Well, then, guess who is about to be dumped for having an STD in front of the whole office,' I say, my game face firmly on.

I can't stress this enough: I'm not usually like this. None of this is me at all. Not being pushy at work, making deals with co-workers to get ahead, and definitely not the kind of shenanigans where you pretend to be someone's girlfriend. But if I want to move back up north *and* manage to keep the magazine job that I worked so hard to get, then perhaps this is the kind of person I need to be from now on.

Rex smiles at me. I actually think he might be impressed.

'Where have you been hiding, huh?' he asks through a smile.

'Literally right in front of your face,' I point out plainly, gesturing towards my desk that has been outside his *glass* office for as long as he's been working here.

'Okay, fine,' he gives in. 'I can try to help. I'll give you some of my junk to write up, giving you a chance to show me that you can do it. I'll give you some advice on how to be cool too – it's a huge part of the job.'

'I'm sure it is,' I reply with a roll of my eyes. 'Perhaps I'll give you some advice on how to get girls.'

'I definitely don't need that,' he says confidently. 'Have you ever seen me struggle to get the girl?'

'Yesterday,' I remind him.

He frowns.

'Game on,' Rex insists. 'But you have to go to the work

Christmas party with me tonight. Just to really make Madeline mad with jealousy.'

'Deal,' I tell him. I wasn't going to go to that but okay. 'If you give me some of your work to do today. I'm on holiday from tomorrow.'

It's my turn to feel a little confident. If all I have to do is turn up at some Christmas party with him, then it's got to be a sure thing? Rex really does seem like my best shot for getting out of here. All of a sudden, it seems within reach.

'We'll have to spend a little time together anyway, won't we?' he points out. 'If we want people to think we're dating. And, you know, so we can coordinate outfits for the party.'

I raise an eyebrow. I'm sure he's kidding.

'So long as you give me some work to do, to prove myself, and then give me a job in Leeds, then I'll wear whatever you want,' I reply. 'I'll be at my desk when you're ready to send some over.'

'I'll drop by soon,' he tells me as I open his door.

'Okay, thanks,' I reply.

'See you later, babe,' he calls after me overenthusiastically.

I've never actually heard Rex call a girl 'babe' before. I think he thinks this is what people in relationships do. The word sounds so awkward when it leaves his lips. Usually he's so cool.

I give him a sickly-sweet (kind of sarcastic) smile. I hate being called babe at the best of times, but from Rex it rubs me up the wrong way even more than it usually would.

I just need to stick it out for a couple of days and hope that Rex follows up on his end of the deal when I get him the girl.

I'll just have to work on my sweet smile in the meantime.

8

Rex did drop some work by my desk, as promised, but with it was an invitation to eat lunch with him in the chill-out room – not the most romantic location for a lunch date, but Rex is counting on us being seen together, so he isn't going to take me to a real place and pay for my food, is he?

So here we are, sitting at one of the tables eating our lunch together. It's strange, because I don't really know what to say to Rex, and I don't think he knows how to talk to me either. I can't imagine we have all that much in common.

'You don't eat your crusts,' Rex points out, nodding towards my plate.

'I don't,' I confirm, glancing down at the discarded edge of my cheese sandwich. What else can I say?

'I cut off my crusts too,' he says, possibly a little too excitedly given that we're talking about bread, but I think he's just relieved to have thought of something to say to me, and to have found some common ground between us.

'Oh, wow, it's amazing we haven't got together sooner,' I say with an almost aggressive level of sarcasm.

Rex laughs.

'English girls are so mean,' he says. 'That's your thing, isn't it? Treat them mean.'

'Erm, isn't that a bit like me saying all American guys do is pretend they don't like you, so that you want them more?' I reply.

'Well, it does work,' he says with a laugh.

'It's not working on me,' I remind him. 'I'm definitely immune to your so-called charm.'

'Right, okay,' he replies. 'Well, I won't point out the fact that you're on a lunch date with me.'

I scowl.

'Look, you need to lighten up, Dani,' he says as he pops a crisp into his mouth. I don't know why, but there's something sexy about the way he eats – and I hate myself for saying it, because I do not want to find Rex attractive in any way, shape or form, but I love the way he somehow simultaneously looks like he enjoys everything, but also like he doesn't need to eat, he's so casual with the way he throws things back, lightly sucking the salt from his fingers.

I pinch my own thigh under the table. Stop even contemplating Rex in that sort of way, Dani!

'You need to opposite of lighten up,' I reply, growing slightly more hostile now that I'm annoyed at myself for acknowledging the fact that Rex is sexy in some ways. 'Surely someone who takes everything so seriously would be a shoo-in for a new job?'

Let's get this conversation back on track.

'Showbiz is fun, though,' he says. 'Are you fun?'

'Of course I'm fun, everyone is fun,' I point out. 'Fun is subjective. We don't all share the same idea of what is fun – for example, not everyone thinks it's fun to shag their way through the office.'

'Ooh, shots fired,' he replies with a laugh. 'I definitely haven't

done that. And anyway, you seem like you're going to be an especially hard nut to crack.'

He's joking, but he's not wrong. I would *never* sleep with
someone like Rex.

'Anyway, I can't imagine you going in for an office romance,'
he adds.

It's something about the way he sounds so certain that he
knows me. It just rubs me up the wrong way. The words leave my
lips before I can consider them.

'Well, that's where you're wrong,' I correct him. 'The only
difference is I never broadcast the fact. Discretion is the key – you
would do well to be a bit more discreet.'

'BS! No way!' he blurts. But then he must notice the look on
my face. 'Who?'

And this is why I should have kept my mouth shut.

'I'm not going to say,' I reply, before taking a sad little bite of
my sandwich.

'You have to say now,' he insists. 'I'm never going to believe
that without evidence.'

'I'd never rise to a comment like that,' I say with a snort.

'You know who is good at gossiping?' he starts. 'Showbiz writers. It's a part of the job, in fact.'

I narrow my eyes at him. He's got me there.

'They're also good at keeping sources a secret too, right?' I
reply with a sigh.

'Oh, of course,' he says. 'And if you can't trust your boyfriend,
who can you trust?'

I suppose I am currently keeping a secret of his, so it seems
very unlikely he would blab and risk me outing him in retalia-
tion. Oh, God, please don't let this be a mistake.

'Come on, I'm on the edge of my seat, who is it? Is it Ruben,
who does all the weird countryside stuff?'

'Absolutely not,' I insist. 'You know he supports fox hunting still?'

'I've seen him wear socks under his sandals too,' Rex adds. 'Shocking.'

He thinks for a moment.

'Cian, who does the accounts?'

'I'm pretty sure Cian is gay,' I reply.

'Then why are you dating him?' Rex asks through a cheeky smile. 'Sorry, I just can't picture you with anyone here.'

I take a deep breath before I let the cat out of the bag.

'Tom,' I say simply.

'Where?' Rex asks, looking back over his shoulder.

'No!' I can't help but laugh. 'It was Tom.'

'Bullshit,' Rex says. 'You and Tom were dating and no one knew?'

'We never told anyone,' I reply with a shrug. 'It didn't seem relevant at the start and then, when he got his promotion, we didn't want anyone to think I was going to get special treatment.'

'You write the ads, right?' Rex reminds me. 'No one is going to think that's special treatment. And anyway, I've been for dinner with Tom and his latest girlfriend three times now. He doesn't seem like the kind of guy who wants to keep things under wraps.'

I can't help but wonder if one of those times was while he and I were still together. It's probably for the best that I don't know.

'Then I guess it was just me he wasn't proud of,' I point out pathetically. 'And I'm not even going to be writing the adverts any more soon enough. Tom has pretty much demoted me. That's why I'm so desperate for a new job – and even more so to move back up north, so I can be closer to my family.'

I do feel like a total loser, spelling all this out to Rex, although Tom must look much worse than I do. It's one of those things where, at first, hiding our relationship felt like a smart decision we were both making, in both of our best interests. Well, hindsight really is 20/20 vision, because it's pretty obvious to see now that Tom was the one pushing to keep things under wraps. Once you can look back like this, things really do seem so clear, and so many questions pop up. For example, all those work nights out I couldn't go on – was he really just out seeing another woman? Probably. It's not worth thinking about it now, though, is it?

'Dani, I'm so sorry, that's rough,' Rex says. He pushes his brownie towards me. 'Here, have this.'

'Thanks, but I don't want a brownie, I want a job,' I reply, although I absolutely do want the brownie too. Why did I say I didn't want it?

'Jokes aside, I only have the budget for one more hire,' he points out. 'You would have to be right for the job.'

'Just say you'll think about it,' I reply. 'That's all I ask.'

I do think Rex feels genuinely sorry for me. I can see it in his eyes. He's right to question my experience, though, perhaps I don't have enough, maybe I'm not right for the job. I would do my best, though – there's too much riding on it. I need to make it work.

'Hi,' Madeline says brightly, taking a seat at the end of our table.

'Oh, hello,' Rex replies. 'How's it going?'

'Yeah, good,' she says with a smile. I notice her look back and forth between us. It's almost as though she can't quite believe the two of us are an item. Well, obviously, because we're not well matched at all, Rex is the most popular person in the office, and I'm the one people actually forget works here.

There's a bar a couple of doors away from our office where most people go for drinks after work – it's where our Christmas party is being held, in fact – and I once went up to say hi to one of the girls I recognised from the art team, and she thought I was a waitress and asked me for an espresso martini. So, yeah, I get why Madeline is baffled, but it still stings, just a little.

'Rex, can I pop into your office after hours?' she asks.

I watch Rex's face. Madeline says this in an almost flirtatious tone. His eyebrows begin to shoot up, but he stops them in their tracks. He's too cool for that.

'Oh?' he replies simply.

'Yeah.' She turns to me. 'Don't worry, it's a professional matter, I just want to pick this one's brain before the party later.'

Could she be any more obvious right now? I know that Rex isn't really my boyfriend, but clearly the fact that she thinks he is means something to her. It's like she wants him more for thinking she can't have him, like the thrill of the chase, the act of stealing someone's man, is what she enjoys the most. It's so gross. These two are probably perfect for each other.

'Shoot, sorry, I'm all for helping others at work, but I promised Dani I'd take her shopping after work, get her a new dress for the party tonight,' he replies as he takes my hand over the table, squeezing it lovingly. 'She told me she would wear whatever I wanted.'

He winks at me. That's true, though, I did say that. I was kidding, of course.

The only thing I enjoy more than seeing the smirk rapidly plummet from Madeline's face is the fact that I feel a little something from Rex's touch. It's nothing – just my mind playing tricks on me. It's like when you're at school, and you've got the coolest guy in your year, and he's kind of cute and funny but he's also horrible to you. Yet you still fancy him, because you're attracted to the idea of him, not him specifically. I'd say thankfully I'm an adult who doesn't have to worry about things like that but, I have to admit, I am feeling some sort of pathetic validation from sitting here with Rex. He reaches out and places his hand on mine. This is so bizarre.

'Erm, hi,' a voice says.

We all look up and see Tom Jones himself standing by our table, holding his lunch on a tray in front of him. He looks frozen in time. His body is still facing in the direction he was walking in, but he's got an owl-like thing going on with his neck, twisting it in our direction. Eventually, the rest of his body follows suit. Then I realise it's because Rex has my hand in his on top of the table, squeezing it, stroking it lightly. Tom looks like he's been hit by a bus.

'Oh, hey, Tom,' Rex replies. 'What are you having?'

Rex nods towards his lunch tray.

'It's, erm, it's... it's quiche,' he eventually blurts. 'You?'

'Just my girl,' Rex replies, taking my hand, raising it to his lips and kissing it gently.

My eyes dart back and forth between them, like I'm watching an especially gripping tennis match.

Honestly, you would think it was sour grapes Tom was having, judging by how tight his jaw muscles look, and the way his eyes are darting back and forth between us. It never ceases to amaze me how jealous men can be. He clearly doesn't want me, and yet the idea of me moving on visibly upsets him.

'Anyway, see you at the party later, yeah?' Rex says, in a friendly way, although it's clearly designed to move Tom along. 'You too, Madeline.'

'Erm, yeah, see you,' she says.

Tom skulks off. As Madeline pulls herself to her feet, she gives me the filthiest look. She's clearly gutted that a plain Jane like me (at least I'll bet that's how she views me anyway) could be standing in the way of her getting with Rex. I'll bet she's fancied him since the moment she laid eyes on him but, in an attempt to keep the upper hand, she rejected him in front of everyone. Well, ha, how is that working out for her?

'You're so good at that,' I blurt out when it's just the two of us again.

'At what?' he replies. 'Kissing hands? Because, let me tell you, if you think that's what I'm best at...'

Everything is a joke to him, and it's as annoying as it is charming.

'At manipulating people,' I correct him.

He winces playfully.

'I don't manipulate people,' he insists. 'I just know how to work them. But, come on, tell me you didn't feel any satisfaction from watching how jealous Tom was seeing the two of us together.'

'Okay, it did feel good, seeing him so bothered, especially considering it was him who dumped me,' I reply.

Rex raises an eyebrow.

'He dumped you?' he replies.

'Yeah, when I caught him cheating on me, that absolute prat,' I tell him. No point skimping on the details now.

'Huh,' he replies plainly. 'I would have thought it would have been you who dumped him.'

'How do you figure that?' I ask, practically cackling at the concept.

'Don't get me wrong, Tom's a good guy, he's a decent editor, never had any problems with the dude, he's just a bit...' Rex pauses for a second, while he considers his words. His eyes dart around before he lands on something that helps him articulate his thoughts. 'Okay, see those potato chips you're eating? What kind are they?'

'Salt and vinegar,' I reply. 'Well, technically they're sea salt and cider vinegar.'

At £2 for a small bag, I may as well give them their full title.

'Tom is just plain potato chips,' Rex says, finally to the point. 'He's bland. He's boring. He isn't exactly flying off the shelves.'

He's got a point about Tom. He is very vanilla. I couldn't tell you much about him, despite being with him for so long, because he's just not that into anything. He doesn't really have a favourite food. He's easy-going to the point where he is verging on the bland, it's true. I don't know what that says about me, though.

'What flavour would you be?' I ask.

'I'm your fancy flavour,' he replies with a smile. 'I'm sea salt and cider vinegar. Better. Cooler. More upmarket – definitely more exclusive.'

I snort. Not just because of his playful crisp analogy but because it doesn't sound like he's all that exclusive.

'Dare I ask what flavour I would be?' I ask curiously.

'Oh, that's easy,' he replies confidentially. 'It's a flavour you only have here in the UK: smoky blackmail.'

I chose the wrong time to take a sip of my orange juice. It almost comes out of my nose. I'm amused, sort of, but I feel sort of bad now.

'Listen, I know it might have sounded like I was blackmailing you because, well, I guess I did kind of blackmail you, just a bit... but that's not what's going on here,' I insist. 'I'm happy to help you. No strings attached.'

No strings attached but please, please still give me the job. Please!

'I'm just joshing with you,' he says with a smile. 'But I was serious when I said I need to go shopping. I've gotta hit up a clothes store where I can buy something expensive enough to impress someone in the style section. Wanna come with? I could use a second opinion.'

'From me?' I reply.

'No, from my other fake girlfriend sitting behind you,' he jokes. 'Yes, you. It will get you out of work early.'

'Will it?'

'Yeah, I'll tell Tom I'm following a lead and that I'm taking someone with me,' he replies. 'If anyone notices you missing, then I'll just explain everyone else was busy, so I took you.'

As if anyone is going to notice me missing – even Tom.

'I don't know how good my high-end fashion advice is,' I admit. 'But I'd jump at the chance to get a tooth filled, if it got me out of here early.'

'Don't worry, I'm not going to give you a filling,' he replies.

We both laugh.

'Right, I'd better get back to work, but I'll come find you when it's time to go, yeah?'

'Okay, sure,' I say, trying to keep a lid on my excitement.

'Where's your desk?' he asks me with a completely straight face as he pulls himself to his feet.

He's got to be kidding...

'Psych,' he eventually blurts through a smile. 'Wow, you should have seen your face.'

'Oh, hilarious,' I call after him. 'You'd better be nicer to me, or I won't come with you.'

Now it's my turn to joke because, honestly, no matter how I feel about Rex, an afternoon off sounds great. Even if I probably can't afford to shop wherever he's going.

9

The idea of me spending my afternoon shopping in a bougie department store like Oliver Strand, when I really should be working, is something I never expected. There's something more unexpected, though. Rex and I are getting on really well.

It turns out that he's actually about more than just his job and his quest to pull women at work. I hate to admit it, but there's something quite enthralling about being around him. It's different at work, watching him charm people, but, even though it pains me to say it, it's hard not to feel special when it's you who is the object of his attention.

The saleswoman is clearly feeling it too. She's an attractive twenty-something who gleefully hangs off his every word. I wouldn't expect any less from a salesperson, obviously she wants him to buy as much as he can afford (and maybe then some), but it's more than that. She's got the googly eyes, the ones all women get for Rex, the ones I cannot under any circumstances allow myself to develop. I need to keep my eyes sharp and on the prize. That prize is my ticket out of here. Back to my old life without going completely back to square one in the process.

'I'll be back with a selection of ties in just a moment,' the salesperson says.

Rex, who is currently behind a fitting room door, waits a few seconds until he's sure we're alone.

'Do you think a tie is a bit too much?' he asks me. 'Tonight isn't exactly a formal affair.'

'Maybe,' I reply, but I *definitely* think that a tie is too much. I'm just nervous about having too much of an opinion.

A surprising but pleasant by-product of me being nice to Rex, so that he'll give me a job, is that it's actually forced me to give him a chance as a person, to talk to him like I don't resent him. And I'm really enjoying his company. I'm finding out all kinds of things about him and he's even asking questions about me. If this scenario hadn't come from something so twisted, bizarre, and ultimately manipulative, I might have felt like we could genuinely be friends. Not that I've ever seen Rex with any female friends. Dates, sure. Groupies, absolutely. Even the odd stalker. Never real, true female friends, though.

'I get why you would want to leave London,' Rex says. 'Growing up by the ocean is a lot different to living in London, isn't it? The shoes, the ties, trying to catch a wave on the Thames.'

He laughs at his own joke. It's kind of cute.

'Right, I'm not having that,' I insist. 'You can't lump us in together, saying we both grew up by the ocean. I grew up in a Yorkshire village on the edge of the North Sea. You grew up in Malibu!'

'The coast is the coast,' Rex replies. 'It's a different lifestyle to city living.'

'Okay, tell me the name of the street you grew up on,' I reply. 'Let's see.'

'Paradise Avenue,' he says.

I snort.

'That's not real,' I call back.

'It is, look it up.'

I punch 'Paradise Avenue, Malibu' into Google Maps. It zooms in on an area that is categorically nothing like the tidal island I grew up on.

'All I'm seeing is a bunch of houses with pools and tennis courts. I grew up down a cul-de-sac in the middle of our island. The closest thing we had to a pool was occasional flooding in the back garden when it rained too heavily – and, believe me, it rains heavily there all the time. Your ocean looks amazing, even on Maps. So blue. You want to look up where I'm from. The sea looks like it's a dark, murky colour.'

My rant amuses Rex. I've been making him laugh all afternoon, actually. It feels good to have someone find me so entertaining.

'A tidal island sounds awesome,' he eventually says. 'I'd love to see it. How far is it from Leeds?'

'It's not too far if you have a car,' I reply. 'There are people in our office with worse commutes. But as far as public transport goes, it's a whole thing. Walks, trains, buses, taxis. It was like a budget *Lord of the Rings*, when my friends and I used to trek to Primark to get our hands on cheap leggings and shoes.'

'Well, I'm heading up to Leeds tomorrow, to get things started before the holidays,' he tells me. 'If you're home for the holidays too, perhaps I could swing by.'

I laugh. He's obviously joking.

'Okay, well, just remember that if the causeway isn't safe to cross, it can add another, like, seven hours to your journey,' I tell him, playing along. 'I'm heading home myself as soon as possible, probably in the morning, seeing as though I'm staying for the party now. I thought it might be fun to surprise my parents, although it won't be much of a surprise when I call my dad to come and pick me up from the nearest train station, but I can still surprise my mum right up until the last minute, maybe.'

'Ties,' the salesperson announces.

She reaches over the top of the door, handing them to Rex.

'I would go for the blue,' she tells him.

'Thanks,' he replies, before getting back to our conversation. 'That's pretty cute, surprising your folks like that. I'm sad, not seeing mine this year, but it's a long way home, and the workload never ends.'

'I bet,' I reply. 'I'd still love a job, though.'

I say this with a jokey optimism. It can't hurt to keep mentioning it, can it?

'So, what do you think?' Rex asks as he steps out of the fitting room.

He's absolutely dripping in Gucci.

I pull a face and wobble my head with uncertainty.

Of course, at the exact same moment, the salesperson tells him how incredible he looks.

Rex laughs at our completely opposite reactions.

'Can you give us a minute, please?' he asks the salesperson.

She gives me a look – furious that I dared to disagree with her, and absolutely questioning my credentials with her eyes – before reluctantly doing as she is asked.

'Go on, what's wrong with it?' he asks me. 'Be honest.'

'It's just... it's all wrong,' I say. I'm unsure how much to say. I know what I'm thinking but I need to keep in Rex's good books. 'I don't think the salesperson has done what you asked her to do.'

'To be fair to her, I told her I wanted to impress a style writer, and to dress me in something fashionable,' he says, looking at himself in the mirror. 'You can't beat Gucci, everyone knows it's fashionable.'

'That's just the problem,' I tell him. 'It's too try-hard. If you're trying to impress someone who knows fashion, then turning yourself into a walking billboard for a designer brand isn't the way to do it. It's so blatant.'

Rex turns to me, cocking his head thoughtfully.

'Go on,' he insists.

'Being genuinely stylish isn't about layering up in designer gear,' I continue. 'Anyone with a credit card can do that. It's about wearing things that generally look good on you, that you're comfortable in. The people who can easily afford this stuff often go for the items without the heavy branding. Take those Valentino shirts, on the mannequins over there. I clocked that white shirt, not a logo in sight, but it costs almost a thousand pounds. Your average eye will never see the value in it, but Madeline will know. So if you're going to spend as much as you are on an outfit, trust me, you don't need to go so hard.'

I exhale quickly before immediately holding my breath, only for a second or two, while I wait to see what Rex has to say.

'That's a really good point,' he says. 'What would you recommend?'

'I'm not an expert,' I insist quickly. Should this backfire, I don't want to seem like I ever made myself out to be the authority on looking cool, because lord knows no one in the office finds me cool in any way. 'But I saw some cool-looking stuff in the Brioni section. Smart, no logo – you'd look great in the black shirt. And not at all like you were trying.'

'Okay, I'm taking this billboard off, and heading over there,' he says as he disappears back into the fitting room.

'Okay,' I reply. 'I'm going to pop upstairs and have a look. There was a Vivienne Westwood display in the window, I'm going to go pretend I can afford it.'

Rex laughs.

'Okay, see you soon,' he calls back.

I make my way through the different departments before sauntering through the women's clothing floor. It's funny, the deeper I head into the department, the more expensive the clothes around me get, and the more out of place I feel. I'm wearing black jeans and a grey jumper that I poked thumb holes into myself. Not exactly haute couture, is it?

Still, Vivienne Westwood is calling my name, but once I arrive at the right section, my leisurely stroll turns into a meaningful strut. I've just spotted the dress of my dreams and it's sucking me closer like a tractor beam.

It's a tartan minidress – absolutely perfect for a Christmas party. It's short, with long sleeves, and is nipped in at the waist by a long skinny belt that hangs down at the front. It feels like a wonderfully soft mixture of wool and cotton. Yes, I am just being dramatic when I say this, but I've never been quite so sad to be skint. I can't really afford to heat my flat but, if I could, you'd best believe I would swap that heat for this dress. Okay, look, I'm not exactly freezing, I do put my heat on when it's cold, but there is no way in hell I can afford to buy a dress if I want to keep it that way. I glance at the price. £615. Even if it was £61.50, it wouldn't be coming home with me.

A sales assistant approaches me. She says hello brightly before her smile falters, just a little. I imagine shops like these are the only places where the staff can actually measure your worth by what you're wearing. She's clearly taken one look at me and decided I'm only here to window-shop and that there's no way in hell I'd buy anything. She's right, obviously, but I resent the fact that she's judging me. Well, it's not like she's bloody Vivienne Westwood herself, she's a person working a retail gig like so many other people in the country do, without judging the customers by such extremely high standards. Just for that, I kind of want to waste her time. So this is what it feels like, to be *Pretty Woman*'d.

Sort of. Vivian from *Pretty Woman* could actually afford to shop there.

'I'd like to try this on, please,' I announce proudly, with a confidence that suggests maybe, just maybe, I can afford to buy it.

'Right this way,' she replies dutifully.

I enter the fitting room with extremely low hopes. It's a beautiful dress, sure, but I'll bet it looks like crap on me. Never mind the fact I had to grab the biggest size they had, just to stand a chance of fitting into it.

I kick off my boots, wrestle off my jeans and pull my jumper over my head without damaging it any further. It's only a matter of time before my makeshift thumb holes turn it into a vest. I slip the dress on and, oh my God, it's a real Cinderella-type situation. I'm not joking, it's like this dress was made for my body. It fits me to perfection. Wow, it looks so good. I've seen better days, sure. My blonde balayage needs taking up a little higher, my skin is so pale it's practically giving away my secrets, and if a concealer exists that can hide these bags, well, I definitely can't afford it. But none of it even matters in this dress, it's carrying me, distracting from all my style don'ts with one big do. £615, though... do you think they take kidneys?

'Dani?' I hear Rex call out.

Shit.

'Just a minute,' I reply. 'Just changing back.'

I need to get out of this dress now – ideally without ripping it, though, because the last thing I need is to have to buy it damaged. I can't quite seem to undo it, though – because *of course* I can't.

'Can I see, before you do?' he asks. 'I took your advice, bought what you suggested, so I need to see if we match.'

His cute little joke makes me even more determined. I'll just tell him it didn't fit – no, wait, that makes me sound like something is wrong with me, I'll just tell him I didn't like it.

'You can go in and see, if you like, if that's your girlfriend,' I hear the salesperson say.

How is she flirting with Rex using those words? I can hear it in her voice. Baffling.

'Oh, great,' he tells her. 'You hear that, Dani? Can I come in?'

I sigh.

'Yep,' I reply, a little too loudly, with an almost sarcastic level of enthusiasm.

I feel all hot and flustered from trying to undo the dress. At least Rex can help me out of it safely. That will be marginally less embarrassing than me Hulking out of it. It's definitely the cheaper option. Unless fatally wounding my street cred hurts my chances of bagging the Leeds job. He did say that personality was a big part of the gig.

Rex walks in and just stares at me for a second or two.

'Okay, I know, I look ridiculous,' I reply. 'I only let you in to unfasten it for me.'

I turn around so Rex can get to the back, to help me out. Instead, he stands close behind me, his hands on my sides, his chin on my shoulder as he looks at me in the mirror. He looks the dress up and down a few times before his reflection makes eye contact with mine.

'Dani, you look awesome,' he tells me.

'Shut up,' I say with a goofy snort.

'I'm serious, you look amazing, you have to wear this tonight,' he insists.

He seems like he's being serious. I've seen him work his magic on many a woman, though. Compliments from Rex give a person life. You can get drunk off them. I can't fall for it.

'Nah,' I say simply.

'What are you wearing tonight?' he asks.

'Erm, probably the Primark leggings I mentioned to you

earlier. There's no way I can afford this dress, or anything new really,' I admit, in hushed tones, hoping that will be an end to that. 'I love it but it's like six hundred quid.'

Obviously I'm joking about the Primark leggings from my teens, but I'll definitely be wearing something I already own.

'It really suits you,' he says simply. 'And it's exactly the kind of thing a date of mine would wear.'

'Well, unlucky for you, you've got a skint girl on your arm tonight,' I tell him with a smile. 'Now, quick, undo me – I mean *it*. Undo *it*.'

Rex does as he's told before leaving me alone.

I look at myself in the mirror one last time, sigh, and then change back into my scruff. My normal clothes will never feel quite right again.

The salesperson is nowhere to be seen so I head back out on to the shop floor, to put the dress back where I found it, and myself back in my place.

Rex catches up to me on my travels, his shopping bags in hand. He passes one to me.

'An empty bag,' I point out. 'How symbolic.'

'It's for the dress,' he says.

I stop in my tracks.

'How do you mean?'

'It's for *that* dress,' he clarifies. 'I just bought it.'

'Well, Madeline is definitely going to think you're trying too hard if you wear that,' I tell him. 'And it's definitely not your size.'

Rex takes the bag back from me, and the dress, which he meaningfully places inside the bag before handing it back to me.

'To be clear: this dress is for you,' he says, slowly, as though he were talking to an idiot. 'The sales assistant scanned through one off the rack, it's all paid for.'

'What? No!' I hand him the bag back. 'You're not buying me a dress. That's so weird.'

'It's not weird at all,' he insists, handing me the bag once again. 'I owe you something, for helping me.'

'Okay, but all I want is a job,' I reply. I try to place the bag back in his hand, but he refuses to take it.

'Consider this dress an apology,' he says. 'It's not for doing me the favour, it's because I shouldn't have kissed you. Not like I did. It was cocky and arrogant, and I didn't stop to think about whether you had a boyfriend or anything like that. You could have me fired so, yeah, take the dress, we'll call it quits.'

I can't help but detect a thinly veiled note of sympathy in Rex's voice.

'You don't have to do this,' I insist. 'It was only a peck on the cheek and I'm not going to say anything. I'm complicit now anyway. Plus I am actually quite enjoying seeing Tom look so uncomfortable.'

'Well, imagine how devastated he's going to be seeing you in this dress,' he says with a smile. 'And I told the lady who rang it up to throw the receipt in the trash, so we're stuck with it now.'

I smile.

'Thank you, Rex,' I tell him. 'You really, really shouldn't have. You've got to let me repay you just, you know, really slowly.'

He smiles that devastatingly charming smile of it.

'You could buy me a Five Guys and we'll call it even?' he suggests. 'The food will be crappy tonight. So, if you want to grab a bite now?'

'Yes, absolutely,' I say, perhaps a little too keenly.

Geez, a man buys me a dress, and suddenly I'm down for whatever. I really can't believe he's done this. It's so, so generous of him. It's obvious that he's quite well off, both from his job now, and from his upbringing, given the aerial view I saw of his street, but that's not the point. Just because he can easily afford something doesn't take away from his kindness and his generosity. Although I suppose ultimately it boils down to the fact that he really, really wants to shag Madeline and I'm his ticket to do so. When I think about it that way, accepting the dress doesn't seem so hard, it's a prop. He's probably only doing it so I don't show him up with my own clothes.

Still, it's a stunning dress, I'll happily trade it for a burger. And it won't be so awful, spending a little more time with Rex, I am having fun with him. I just need to try to charm him right back, show him that I am absolutely the right person for the Leeds job. It all hinges on tonight. Let's hope I'm up to it.

10

While this year's work Christmas party may come with a slight difference, I must admit, attending one of these things whilst in a sham relationship is not exactly uncharted waters for me.

When Tom and I were a thing – a thing that, for some reason, we couldn't tell anyone about – we would all but ignore each other at the Christmas parties. We would interact just enough that our marked avoidance of one another didn't raise any suspicions. I'm hesitant to make myself seem even more tragic than I'm sure I already do but, at the time, it was almost sexy, hiding our relationship from everyone else. The sneaking around, the stolen kiss outside the toilets (it was more romantic than it sounds, honestly). It's only now, looking back, that I can see how unhealthy it was, being in a relationship that was kept under wraps for no good reason. Oh, and it's worth noting that he's here with Mia tonight, which is a real slap in the face. She obviously makes the cut.

That's why I'm delighted that (speaking of unhealthy) I'm here tonight with Rex. Another sham relationship, but one that I feel like I'm getting so much more from. I was in a real relationship with Tom, and he treated me like crap. With Rex, our cards are on the table, we know exactly where we stand, what we're both getting out of the situation, and so on. Hilarious really, making it sound like such a formal, serious affair, when in reality, I'm doing it because there's a chance it might land me a job and Rex is doing it to shag the new girl in the office. And they say romance is dead.

Tonight we're at Martini's, a bar not too far from the office where staff often go for after-work drinks – something I have heard of, but something that I am not invited to. When the Christmas party comes around, I always have this feeling, one that I can never quite shake, that at any given moment someone is going to ask me to leave.

When you were a teenager, and you went into a shop alone, or with a friend, did you ever get that feeling that the security guard was watching you, sometimes even following you, and you would work overtime to try to look relaxed, like a normal shopper, picking things up and putting them down to prove you were not a shoplifter? But when you would go in that same shop with your mum or dad, no one would bat an eyelid at you. Well, that's what Rex is giving me tonight, he's my parent, hand-holding me so that I blend in. He's quite literally hand-holding me, actually, taking mine in his the second before we stepped through the door, and he hasn't let go of it since. I know none of this is real, but it's still sort of nice. It's almost as though it's a preview of what it would be like to have a cool, attentive, loving boyfriend. Even if it is fake, it still feels good.

Martini's is all ours tonight. It's so beautifully decorated, with lights and blue and silver Christmas decorations. It has a chilly, winter wonderland vibe, although it's boiling hot in here.

I feel like I look, okay, not quite hot, but pretty warm-ish maybe, in my new dress. More than the tepid I felt last year, in whatever I wore, it was so underwhelming I honestly can't remember. I've even had a few compliments from co-workers, which is new. I can't tell if they're finally seeing me because of the dress, because I'm here with Rex, or both. Whatever the reason, I hate to admit it, but I love the way it feels.

Rex looks incredible, as he always does, but he looks even better in his new outfit. I would never flex any kind of fashion credentials to anyone, but I'm really happy with the advice I gave him. Tonight Rex doesn't look flashy, he looks effortless. I guessed this would do the trick with Madeline and I'm starting to think I was right. She can't take her eyes off him. I think I even saw her wink at him, not too long ago, and she keeps walking over to where we are, trying to insert herself in the conversations we're having with other people, getting as physically close to Rex as she possibly can. Of course, as soon as she does this, Rex makes some excuse for us to move on, circulating us around the room, talking to everyone – everyone wants to talk to Rex. Clearly, the more she wants him, the more he acts like he's not interested in her, which only makes her want him more. It would be brilliant, if it weren't so gross and demoralising.

It's a scary time to be single. How the hell are people supposed to contend with this? How do we know what's real and what's fake? Even the things that feel real aren't necessarily that – it's so confusing.

Rex held my hand for a while, before he let it go when food was served, and I swear, I missed it the second it was gone. As his palm left mine, and the cool air hit my sweaty skin, it was that cold sensation that exaggerated the impact of Rex holding me. When he took away his hand, he took away the warmth and left me feeling exposed. Now I almost feel like I'm being clingy with him but – surprise, surprise – I don't usually do things like this. I'm scared of being left alone.

'Let's hit up the buffet for round three,' Rex suggests, leading me over there.

When all is said and done this evening, one fact will remain: the food is amazing. Who doesn't love a buffet? There is a graze table set up that is nothing short of stunning. It has Parma ham, cheeses, figs, a selection of colourful crudités, pretzels scattered everywhere. It's an Instagrammable dream. But, when it comes to buffets, we all know where the best stuff is at. A beautiful, colourful spread is nice and all, but the best bits on the buffet table is all the beige stuff. Sandwiches, sausage rolls, various other pastry parcels with all sorts of things inside, mozzarella sticks, pizza rolls, chicken bites. I'm shunning the celery sticks, the tomatoes can take a hike. As far as I'm concerned, the beiger the better, and Rex seems to be in agreement.

'I'm driving to Leeds tomorrow,' he tells me. 'It's not going to be a fun road trip if I eat and drink too much tonight.'

'At least you can stop a car,' I point out. 'I'll be getting the train most of the way home. It's not nice being stuck on a train with a hangover – especially not a busy one, which it usually is. I'm really not looking forward to the journey.'

'That's true,' he replies. 'You know, I never really ate sausage rolls before I came to England,' he tells me, eating what must be his twentieth mini sausage roll. 'I would eat the occasional corn dog at a baseball game, but they're a whole different thing. But now I'm obsessed. You know what it is, it's Greggs. I didn't know about Greggs and now it's going to be on my death certificate. Pasties are a big part of my life now. We really need to get Greggs in the US – we gave you McDonald's, it only seems fair we get Greggs in return.'

'If you could only have food from either Maccies or Greggs for the rest of your life, which one would you keep?' I ask him.

This conversation reminds me that there are mini cheese-burgers, so I grab one – well, *another* one, I had two earlier.

'That's such a difficult question because I've been eating McDonald's all my life,' he explains. 'With Greggs, it's definitely love, but it's that first flush of love. What?'

Oh, God, I must have made a face.

'No, it's nothing,' I say quickly. 'You just don't seem like the kind of person who would know what love is. Romantic love, at least.'

'Ouch,' he says through a laugh. 'Well, I'm definitely qualified to talk about food love, you can't argue with that, and your question is a pretty tough call. Perhaps it is just lust, with Greggs.'

I move in closer to Rex and lean in, placing my lips just inches from his ear.

'What about a Big Mac burger, except instead of beef, the patty is made out of Greggs sausage roll meat?' I suggest, in a faux sexy voice.

Rex turns to me and playfully rolls his eyes into the back of his head, as though the idea drives him wild.

'Now you're just talking dirty to me,' he replies.

Someone clears their throat.

'Tom, buddy, how are you?' Rex asks, realising we have an audience.

'I just wondered if I could borrow Dani for a moment,' he replies awkwardly.

I'd never really figured Tom for a bumbling Hugh Grant kind of character, but next to Rex he seems so uncomfortably English. You know the extreme caricature of a young, posh English man, almost embarrassed to be alive, mumbling, clumsy body language. 'Oh gosh' this and 'bugger' that. I wasn't sure people like that existed outside of romcoms but, when I view Tom along-side Rex, that's the kind of person I see. What I definitely don't see is whatever I saw in him to begin with. It's easy, looking back, to see everything that was wrong with a person, but I've always gone into relationships with a hopeful optimism. More fool me.

I stare at Tom blankly. He wants to talk to me, here, now? I need to be cool.

'What's up?' I ask him. 'It's okay, we can talk work in front of Rex, he is my boyfriend, after all. You're not going to demote me again, are you?'

I throw my head back and laugh. This isn't me, this is me drawing confidence from Rex, from our sham relationship. I feel like I can say anything, do anything, I'm untouchable.

'It's a, erm, it's a... it's a personal matter,' Tom eventually says.

'Well, that's all right,' Rex tells him before kissing me on the cheek. 'You can look after her while I go to the bathroom.'

I take what cool confidence I can from his kiss, but I feel it fading fast with every step Rex takes away from us.

Once we're alone, Tom unbuttons the jacket of his black suit and exhales deeply, as though he's finally safe to stop holding his stomach in. Amazing really, that he would do that for Rex's benefit, but not mine.

'Mia looks beautiful tonight,' I tell him.

Steady now, Dani. That was almost passive-aggressive. It's frustrating, though, seeing him here with the girl he cheated on me with, as his date, when he wouldn't even tell people we were together.

Tom looks tired. His suit isn't fitting him quite right at the moment, not like it normally does. I do occasionally torture myself by looking at Mia's Instagram and from there I can see that the two of them are going out all the time, always in some restaurant or B & B. Mia is young – and posts countless photos of herself in yoga positions that seem too provocative to be real – but Tom is getting older, he's gaining weight, developing bags under his eyes. If he's clearly living his best life, then why has he got a face on him right now?

'You and Rex,' he says, cutting to the chase. I'm not sure if it's a question or a statement.

'Me and Rex,' I reply with a smile.

'You can't be serious,' Tom replies. 'What do you even talk about?'

I would wonder who he thought was out of whose league if I didn't think the answer would offend me. I need to remind myself that Tom cheated on me. He hurt me. If letting him think I'm with Rex annoys him, and gives me the slightest hint of satisfaction, then why not go with it?

'We talk about all sorts,' I insist. 'Movies, our childhoods, work... Although, to be honest, we don't do all that much talking at the moment.'

I watch my words wind him up. It's not as satisfying as I thought it would be, to be honest. I don't really care what he thinks. I certainly don't want to be here talking to him.

'He's not right for you,' Tom points out, seriously, like he's a worried dad and I'm a rebellious teen.

Oh, for God's sake.

'Go back to your girlfriend,' I tell him before turning around and walking away.

I don't know where I'm going but I'm only doing it to kill some time. Time until my security blanket gets back from the loo.

'That was fast,' Rex says when he finds me.

'Yeah, well, that's just Tom's style,' I joke.

Rex laughs.

'Are you okay?' he asks me.

His words make it sound like he knows I'm not. I didn't realise I wasn't, but...

'Ah, I'm fine,' I reply. 'When someone breaks your heart, the damage is done before you realise that breaking up was for the best. I only have a small scar left and that man's existence just picks at it now and then. I just want to get the hell away from him but everywhere I look he's there. And her. Here. It's just—'

'It's okay, I get it,' Rex replies. 'Forget them, let's play a game.'

'What sort of game? I ask curiously, welcoming the distraction.

'Watch this,' Rex says before slowly walking over to a table of people.

Frances from HR and Curt from accounts are sitting next to each other, but talking to people on their other sides, meaning they're facing away from each other. Rex walks up behind them, undetected. He picks up a mini pork pie from Frances's plate and puts it down on Curt's plate. Then he walks back over to me.

'I can't believe you just did that,' I blurt through a snort.

'Your turn,' he replies. 'Do something small. Move something, swap something – but don't get caught. The idea is that no one knows you've done anything. I do it all the time in the office, when I'm bored, or if someone annoys me.'

'My God, you don't mess with me, do you?' I ask, although of course he doesn't, he didn't know I was alive until the day he kissed me on the cheek.

'I've never messed with you,' he reassures me. 'You always look so busy, so serious – not someone to be messed with. By the way, no one knows about this, so you can't tell anyone.'

I get a little pang of something, from knowing that Rex has noticed me, but it's short-lived because it sounds like all he's ever noticed is that I'm boring, and I do sit right outside his office, so *obviously* he's spotted me before, it would be crazy if he hadn't.

I glance around the room. Rex is clearly an expert at this game. I can't think where to begin.

Frances still hasn't noticed that Curt has her pork pie. I

wonder if... I've got it. Curt's jacket is over the back of his chair, so I start small by wandering over, carefully removing it, and placing it on the back of Frances's chair instead. It's such a small thing but standing there, behind their chairs, knowing either of them could turn around any second fills me with excitement. At one point, Frances runs a hand through her red bobbed hair, only to tuck it behind her ear, and I flinch because it seems like she's going to catch me, but she doesn't. When the deed is done, I hurry back to Rex.

'Good job,' he says, wrapping an arm around me, squeezing me with pride. 'A worthy adversary. Okay, what's next...'

Rex and I take it in turns to perform small, harmless pranks on the other people at the party. Highlights involve removing the helium balloons from their weights and putting Tom down for the karaoke, multiple times, to sing 'It's Not Unusual', 'Delilah' and 'What's New Pussycat?' Tiny, harmless pranks that are probably only humorous to the two of us. I'm having an absolute whale of a time.

I take a break, to pop to the toilets. As I'm washing my hands, I smile at myself in the mirror. I'm actually having such a great time, and it's all thanks to Rex. If we hadn't come together, well, I wouldn't have come at all, but if I had, I wouldn't have swapped more than a few words with a few people all night.

I finally head back out to find Rex, a wad of toilet paper in my hand, ready for our next prank. He's where I left him, but he isn't alone. Madeline is chatting with him. She must have waited until I was out of the way to make her move. She has one hand on his arm. As she leans in to whisper in his ear, she runs her other hand up his body in an undeniably flirtatious way. She says whatever she was going to say but continues to linger next to him, her face inches from his. I hang back for a moment. This was what it was all for, I suppose, I've just been having such a good time with him. This is definitely the most fun I've ever had at one of these parties. It may be sad to say, but it might be the most fun I've had since I moved to London.

Rex's lips move. I can't tell what he's saying but Madeline quickly pulls away. Her face falls. She opens her mouth, as if she's about to say something, but then she stops. There's a look on her face that I can't quite read. She makes this face for a second before walking away. With the coast clear, I join Rex again.

'You know, there is such a thing as overcooking it,' I point out.

'What do you mean?' he asks curiously. Then he notices what's in my hand. 'Ah, great, you got the toilet paper. Need me to flank you on this one?'

'I mean, with Madeline,' I say. 'You're so very clearly in there. Go, get your woman, before she finds new prey. You did it.'

I sing those last three words like I'm pleased about them. I'm not, though. Now that I'm getting to know the real Rex, and enjoying spending time with him, I don't want to give it up, even if our relationship is entirely for show.

I'm letting myself get swept away. I'm drunk on the party atmosphere (not just the drinks Rex and I have been enjoying together). Christmas really is the most wonderful time of the year. Everyone is happy, everything is sparkling. But all that glitters isn't gold. This is nothing but a showmance, I need to remind myself of that fact – *again*.

'Yeah, you know, I'm starting to think she's not my type,' he says casually. 'I'm not really all that interested any more. Plus, I'm having a blast with you. I'd rather keep playing. Oh, and I don't want to stay up too late, if I'm driving tomorrow. I had a thought, though. I'm heading north. You're heading north. Why don't you travel in my car with me? I'll take you right to your door. I don't mind if it's a little further, I'm curious to see this magical island, plus it will be nice to spend some time with you. We can figure out if there's a way we can sort this Leeds job for you because, I totally get it, you don't want to be around Tom any more. Let me see what I can do, okay?'

Rex gives me a smile that, coupled with everything he just said, finally melts me. I finally get it. I see it, that thing that everyone sees in him, that makes him so impossibly attractive. I don't know what to say so, instead, I go with my gut. I close my eyes, I pucker up, and I lean in to kiss him.

I feel Rex take my hand. No, wait, he's taking the toilet roll from me. I open my eyes.

'Let me try do this one,' he says. 'I think I can get away with it.'

I hand the toilet roll over to him.

Oh God. Ohhhh God. There's no way he didn't notice that I was trying to kiss him. No way at all. And this is the man who kissed me when he didn't even know me, just to try to get another girl he didn't know. He's not exactly fussy when it comes to who to kiss. How absolutely, totally, completely embarrassing. And now he can't even look at me.

And I just agreed to spend hours in a car with him tomorrow. *Fantastic.*

11

You know, I didn't think there could be anything more awkward than me trying to kiss Rex and him trying to pretend he didn't notice. It turns out there is. It's me, trapped in a car with him, working overtime to make out like I didn't actually try to kiss him in the first place or – if I did – I didn't mean it.

We've been on the road for hours now. We're both pretty knackered after our late-night partying, but there's also this polite uncomfortableness between us. We're listening to the radio and chatting, to make the journey go faster, but there's an undercurrent of 'I know that you know that I know', etc.

If I can just show Rex that I don't really care about him like that, make him think it was all part of the act, or just me being a cool, fun gal who just goes about kissing people – perhaps if I say the right things then he'll think I was doing it just to make Tom jealous? If I'm being honest, though, and I really hate to say it, but last night, in the moment, I did sort of care about Rex in that way. I was totally smoothed over by him. Charmed by him, attracted to him, totally intoxicated on everything that comes with having his full attention. And that's the only thing I was intoxicated on, unfortunately, or I could have blamed the alcohol for me trying to put the moves on him.

God, I'm such a moron. More than this being completely embarrassing (which, trust me, it really, really is) is the fact that I've briefly taken my eyes off the prize. The goal here wasn't to kiss Rex, it was to get him to give me a job, and now I'm worried that I've ruined it by trying to kiss him. He's not going to give a job to someone who fancies him and makes hasty moves on him, is he? I'll bet he's really regretting offering to drive me all the way home now. Thank goodness we're almost there. But that also means I don't have much time left to undo the damage I caused last night.

'Thanks again for helping me make Tom so jealous last night,' I tell him. 'I'm definitely over him – and baffled why I was ever under him – but it is funny, seeing him so uncomfortable.'

'You're welcome,' Rex replies. He keeps his eyes on the road, but he smiles.

I'm not really a car person so I can't tell you much beyond the fact that Rex drives a sporty little BMW, but it's exactly the sort of car I expected him to drive.

'It's good to be so sure that I'm over him,' I continue. 'Because I've been messaging with my ex-boyfriend, Ben, who lived on the same street as me growing up, and things have been getting quite flirty. We're going on a date, actually, while I'm home for Christmas.'

Pretty much the only thing that is true about that statement is that I grew up on a street. I did have a huge crush on a boy called Ben, but he wasn't ever my boyfriend. But if Rex thinks that I'm on the verge of getting involved with someone, and chatting about it so casually, then he'll know that I'm not obsessed with him, and therefore there's no reason not to give me the Leeds job. It's a pretty foolproof plan.

'That's great,' he replies. 'It sounds like you're going to have an awesome Christmas.'

'How are you spending the holidays?' I ask him.

'I have a friend,' he replies. He pauses, slightly awkwardly, before he continues. 'They said I could spend the holidays with them. They'll be alone too, so it's kinda perfect for us both.'

They. There's something about when men use the word 'they' so clumsily, when they're telling you about someone, that tips you off to the fact that they are talking about a woman, but don't want you to know that they are. So Rex is spending Christmas with a woman. That's that, then. Thank God I just told that porky about Ben.

'Well, you're right, even in the dark I can tell it's nothing like Malibu here,' Rex says as we drive through Marram Bay. 'But it does look beautiful. Really cute and quaint.'

'Yeah, it's really nice,' I reply. 'When you grow up somewhere, I don't think you always realise just how beautiful it is, until you spend a little time away, and then come back.'

I look out of my window as we drive across the open causeway. It's dark, so you can't exactly see much, but I've always found something so comforting about looking out into the dark horizon beyond the sea. I'm not sure what it is. Perhaps it's the comfort of feeling like the rest of the world is nowhere to be seen, like I'm safe in my own little bubble, the *Truman Show*-style existence you have from living on the island. I've been really craving it of late.

My relationship with the causeway that connects Marram Bay and Hope Island has always been a rocky one. I mean, come on, a tidal island is a natural wonder, absolutely fascinating, a real spectacle to behold, even if you've seen it a bunch of times... that is, until you have somewhere you need to be and it's the only thing standing in your way. If you don't get your watch and/or calendar right, if your timing is off by even a matter of minutes, you're going to find yourself stuck at home – or, sometimes even worse, stuck away from it. Marram Bay is a tourist town, full of holiday homes and B & Bs, so if you do find yourself missing your last chance to get home before the causeway closes (and by closes, I mean completely disappears under the sea) then at least there is a choice of places to stay for the night on either side of the water. It closes two hours before high tide and for three hours after, and this happens twice a day, always at different times, so it can be quite tricky trying to time your life around it.

Locals know how much leeway they have with the closing times of the causeway, but you always get some tourist who thinks it's just like a big puddle they can drive through. At high tide, the road can be covered by up to four metres of water. Just imagine, one minute it's a road, then suddenly it's at the bottom of the sea. It's a dangerous game, trying to cross when the tide is in, so much so that they taught us all about it at school. They wanted to drill the message into us so powerfully that they even taught us a song, to remember the key facts and rules of the road, and to be fair, as annoying as it was, it's stayed with me my entire life so far. People often need to be rescued, either by the coast-guard, or in even more extreme conditions from the air, and it costs thousands. It's never worth risking it.

'It says we're here,' Rex announces as he pulls up at the side of the road. He glances around the junction. 'Where do you live?'

'Oh, not far from here, but it's not accessible by car,' I insist.

Another lie.

'Shall I walk you to your door?' he suggests. 'There's something seriously unchivalrous about dropping off a lady on a dark street and driving off.'

'No, no, no, honestly, I'm fine,' I insist.

'Is there somewhere I can grab a coffee around here?' he asks.

Is that a hint? Does he want to come into my house? To my

parents' house? I mean, obviously no, for so many reasons. I don't want him meeting my parents, that's too much of a thing, and I only asked him to drop me here so that he doesn't see the street I grew up on.

'Yes, if you drive back down this road, and turn left instead of heading back the way we came, you'll eventually find the street where a handful of shops and restaurants are. There's a few places there that are open on an evening.'

I keep things to the point. If he can ignore my advances, then I can ignore his hints.

'Okay, great,' he replies. 'Well, I'll get settled in Leeds, and then we'll see about calling you in for a meeting or something.'

'Great,' I reply.

Rex gets out of the car to remove my case for me.

'So, erm, yeah, we'll talk soon, and I guess, have a good time, in the meantime,' he says kind of awkwardly.

'Yeah, you too,' I reply.

Rex goes to open his arms, as though he's going to hug me, but then retreats. He quickly lifts them up again.

'We can hug,' he says through a laugh. 'We were a couple yesterday. Let's end this relationship amicably.'

'Something I've never been good at,' I joke. I have to admit, he gives good hugs. That or it's been a long time since anyone hugged me. Wow, actually, I think it really is the latter. That's tragic. 'Anyway, see you later.'

'Yeah, see you, Dani,' he replies.

I watch Rex get back in his car and drive away before I make a move. Once he's gone, I walk down the road a little, dragging my suitcase behind me, and turn on to the cul-de-sac where I grew up. The intense glow from all the Christmas lights almost knocks me off my feet.

The one good thing about Rex giving me a lift is that it means

I can well and truly surprise my mum and dad. I'll bet they've thought, because they haven't heard from me, that I'm not coming. When I walk through the door, they're going to be over the moon. This couldn't have worked out better.

I finally rock up outside their house, but it's in total darkness. No lights inside, no Christmas lights on outside. There are only a handful of houses on the cute little street I grew up on, but with everyone else's house literally lit up like a Christmas tree (everyone takes Christmas lights so seriously here, honestly, it's like walking on a film set or something) it makes my family home look like an uninviting black hole. My dad usually goes all out with the best of them (in fact, his display is usually quite literally the best of them) so it's unusual to see that his lights aren't on. Don't tell me he's finally put his friendly neighbourhood rivalry behind him.

So far, things haven't felt all that festive. It's been around me in bars and there were the obligatory decorations up at work, but I haven't really been feeling it, I've kind of just been ignoring it, not allowing myself to feel it until the time was right. I knew all that would change when I walked down the street here, and I saw my parents' house all decked out for the holidays, waiting to invite me in with open arms, a Christmassy barrage on the senses. How typical that, for the first time ever, Dad's lights are off when they would usually be on. Ah, well.

Okay, see, this is why I needed to call and tell them that I was on my way, they've obviously gone out for the evening. Never mind, though, I know where the spare key is, underneath the garden ornament on the doorstep (which is swapped out for a festive ornament at this time of year), so I can let myself in.

'Hello,' I call out, just in case one of them is here, because I don't want to spook anyone. There's no reply.

I carry my bags up to my room, admiring the festive garland

lovingly wrapped around the banister on the way upstairs. My parents live in a gorgeous detached house with an old curved staircase that is just begging to be covered in Christmas decorations.

My mum is very house-proud. The place has always been absolutely spotless – a trait I unfortunately haven't inherited from her.

There isn't a thing out of place in the house and almost every inch of it is beautifully decorated with fancy festive things. It's so extra, but so worth it. Exactly what I hoped for, coming home for a family Christmas.

I dump my case down in my room and let out a big, theatrical yawn. I rifle through my bag to find my pyjamas. Well, it's practically a festive tradition, especially in your family home, to spent as much of the holidays as possible in your PJs, isn't it? I was going to wait up for my mum and dad, but who knows what time they'll be home? Thankfully, Mum always keeps the bed made up, so at least I don't have that to worry about that. To be honest, I'm that tired, I'd probably climb into it unmade. It's not even 9 p.m. yet and I'm absolutely shattered.

I plug my phone into the charger and climb into my bed, safe in the knowledge that when they do arrive home, they will see my coat and shoes in the hallway and know that I'm here.

I can feel my eyes getting heavy, I'm pretty shattered from the late night and the long drive. The only thing keeping me awake is fantasising about what my mum will be making me for breakfast in the morning. Your mum making you breakfast has to be the best thing about going home. Reverting back to being a child. Perhaps it's because I haven't had any dinner, but I can't stop thinking about a boiled egg with soldiers. My mum would often make them for me when I was a kid, and no one can make them like my mum can, believe me, I've tried to hit the spot myself (it's not that hard to boil an egg, is it?) but it just isn't the same.

I really can't wait for tomorrow. I'll have breakfast, then I'll probably help my mum with the last bits of shopping, I'll watch a movie with my dad – it's going to be the best Christmas I've had in years. I feel like a kid on Christmas Eve, but we're not quite there yet. That's okay with me, though, because I don't want Christmas to be over too quickly. I've no idea what is waiting for me on the other side of it.

12

I would love to say that I just woke up from the best sleep I've had in months, but it's not true. It might have been true, were it not for the fact that I am so used to sleeping in a double bed that sleeping in my old childhood single was just awful. It's as though I've forgotten how to keep away from the sides. I kept feeling like I was going to roll out of it in my sleep and wake up with a painful start, only to find myself on the floor. It's nothing shy of a Christmas miracle that I didn't fall out of bed.

The house feels cold. I haven't slept here in a long time, but I don't remember it feeling so chilly on a morning. My parents fight for the thermostat like the best of them, but my mum has always won the battle when it comes to the temperature on a morning. I grab my phone from my bedside table and rifle through my old wardrobe for a dressing gown. Sure enough, hanging up exactly where I left it the last time I was here for Christmas, I find the silly (but oh-so comfortable) reindeer dressing gown my mum bought me. I can't remember how old I was when she got me it, I was definitely a teenager, though. A few of my friends and I got them from our mums, who had all bought them from the annual Christmas festival we have by the beach here. It's a gorgeous, silky brown material but the hood had antlers and a red nose on it – and I thought I was far too cool to wear it. Well, I'm far too cold to *not* wear it now, and fully accepting of that fact that I'm not that cool now that I've matured. It's just a dressing gown, nothing to be embarrassed about.

I love how quiet it is here. It doesn't matter where I lived in London, when you're in an apartment, with the city outside, it's rarely silent. My parents don't exactly make much noise, but I just love how peaceful it is here. This morning, honestly, you could hear a pin drop. Oh, and if that's not idyllic enough, I've just looked out of the window and there's a fluffy blanket of snow covering the garden. Thank God I made it here before the blizzard hit. I had started to catastrophise about what would happen if the snow hit sooner, and Rex's silly little car couldn't handle it. I worried about winding up trapped God knows where with him, having to check into some weird hotel together, for who knows how long, trying to avoid the elephant in the room. It would've been like my own personalised version of *The Shining*. I'm even more grateful to be here with all that in mind.

It's after 10 a.m. now so my parents will be up. I practically gallop downstairs, giddy to announce my surprise arrival, excited to tell them that I'm here for Christmas, and fill them in on everything that has been going on with me that I'm yet to tell them about. I need to tell them about Tom too, although I'm sure they'll realise when they notice he isn't here with me. It would be nice if it was implied that I was single, rather than me having to chat it out with them.

I bounce into the kitchen, ready to give it the big ta-da, expecting to find my parents having breakfast, my mum eagerly hovering by the eggs, ready to make her baby girl her favourite thing, but neither of them are here.

My mum and dad are usually such painfully early risers. Were they out so late last night that they're still in bed asleep? Those party animals! I know what I'll do, I'll march into their bedroom, giving them a playful lecture about how they should be up already – they'll get a real kick out of this, because this is exactly what they used to do with me when I was younger and would stay out late before sleeping in the next morning.

I get to their room, calling their names while I knock on the door, but no one calls back. I wait a few seconds before trying again. Eventually I walk in but there's no one there. Their enormous super-king bed looks so inviting. Inviting, and unslept in.

This is weird. This is *so* weird. They must have stayed somewhere overnight, I suppose, but that's not like them.

I head back downstairs and put the kettle on. I guess I'll make myself a cup of tea and fix my own breakfast today – I can always have my boiled egg tomorrow.

I grab my favourite festive mug from the cupboard and place a teabag inside while I wait for the kettle to boil. I tap my nails on the worktop. Where the hell are my parents? I don't want to freak out unnecessarily but... you know... they're not here. So, where are they?

I'm debating whether or not to call them, giving the game away, when I spot a man peering in through the kitchen window out of the corner of my eye. I immediately drop to the floor, hiding between the worktop and the island where I can't be seen from any of the windows. Who the hell was that?

Perhaps this is just my imagination running away with me, but it isn't easy to slow it down, all things considered. My parents are missing and there's a creepy man looking in through the window. It's like something out of a crappy Christmas action movie except, y'know, it's real life.

The kettle finishes boiling and the room falls silent. I can't hear anything apart from my own heartbeat in my ears, which only makes me more anxious. Well, there's nothing like being reminded that you're alive to make you worry that you might soon be dead.

I open one of the lower drawers, one of the only ones within my reach, and root around for a weapon but the best I can come up with is a palette knife, so I just sit on the floor with it, brandishing it with intent.

A knock on the front door makes me jump out of my skin. The good news is that if this is some kind of psychopath, then he's not going to knock on the door, is he? Unless that's what he wants me to think...

I stand up and cautiously make my way towards the front door. Behind the glass, I can make out the silhouette of two men. A tall one and a short, round one.

'Hello?' I call out.

'Hello, it's the police,' the man replies.

Is it, though?

'Really?' I reply weakly.

The second the word leaves my lips, I realise how much it must sound like I've seen too many movies.

'Erm... yes, really,' the man replies. He sounds bemused by my caution. I suppose there isn't much crime in Marram Bay – especially not over here on Hope Island. Well, you can't exactly make a quick and reliable getaway with the causeway in the mix, can you?

I open the door to reveal a tall, dark-haired man in a leather jacket. He's so ruggedly handsome, I'm tempted to get myself arrested for something just so that he manhandles me. Next to him is the short, round man, who I now recognise as my parents' neighbour, Dennis. He's your classic nosy neighbour, always has been. It's nice to see he's still keeping a keen eye on the place, at least – I'm sure he can tell me where my parents are.

'Hi,' I say simply.

'Oh, Dani, it's only you,' Dennis says with a sigh.

'Yep, only me,' I reply. 'Is everything okay?'

I turn to the handsome policeman.

'Hello.'

'Hello,' he replies. 'I'm DC Dean Gardner.'

'A detective,' I squeak. Now I really am worried.

'It's nothing to worry about,' he reassures me, reading my mind. 'A call came through on the radio about an intruder and I live locally so I said I'd swing by.'

'Well, with your parents being on holiday,' Dennis explains, 'I was worried when I saw people hanging around in the house.'

'On holiday?' I repeat back to him.

'Yeah, they're in France for Christmas,' he replies. 'It's just like your dad, to upstage us all, with a last-minute surprise for your mum.'

Oh... my... God. I never considered in a million years that my parents wouldn't actually be home for Christmas – they always spend Christmas at home! Oh, God, I'm so embarrassed. See, this is why you should never try to surprise people, because it will almost always backfire on you.

'Oh, no, didn't they tell you?' Dennis says. 'Are you here alone? Do you want to come over and have Christmas dinner with us? There's me, Mother, Carole, her new husband and young Paul – he's twenty-three now, and he's thinking about courting.'

I look over at DC Gardner, who is stifling a giggle. He reminds me a little bit of Jeffrey Dean Morgan, he's a dead ringer for him. He has the same cheeky look in his eye when he's amused too.

Wow, hmm, let me think, do I want to spend Christmas with fifty-something Dennis, his elderly mum, his ex-wife and her new husband, and his odd son who it sounds like he's trying to set me up with? I remember Paul well. When I was a teenager, he used to terrorise me, he was such an oddball. He'd sit on his doorstep holding his pet frogs, dressed all in black, rocking his 'kid from *The Omen*' haircut. And despite Dennis being super nosy, he spent so much time looking out of his windows that he didn't realise what was going on in his own home – Carole was having an affair. I guess it's nice that they can all get together for Christmas, but I absolutely do not want to be a part of it.

'*Of course* I know they're on holiday,' I say with a laugh, trying not to lay it on too thick. 'It would be pretty weird if I didn't. They said, because they're away, that I can use their house for a Christmas party.'

'Oh, right, well, that's okay. I'm relieved it's only you. I was worried it was your dad's Christmas rivalry gone too far,' Dennis replies.

'Well, if everything is okay here, I'll leave you two to it. Nice dressing gown,' Dean says with an amused grin. This whole scene must be hilarious for an impartial spectator. It's less fun for me.

After we say goodbye to Dean, I am quick to get back to our conversation, keen to defend my dad, even if he did go on holiday without telling me.

'It's only a friendly rivalry,' I remind Dennis.

'It doesn't seem all that friendly to me,' he replies. 'I don't know, all this drama over a bunch of Christmas lights. It's supposed to be for charity.'

I can't help but laugh.

My dad does have a friendly Christmas rivalry with Gerry, his neighbour, a little further down the road. I've known Gerry all my life – I went to school with his kids – and he's not a bad person. He's a bit of a boaster and a bit loud perhaps, but that's about it. The thing is, over the years, my dad and Gerry have been competing with their outdoor Christmas displays. Every year, they both go bigger and brighter – I was surprised when I arrived here last night to see that my dad hadn't left his lights switched on, to be honest. He usually has a timer that makes them switch on and off at the right times. In recent years, not only do my dad and Gerry try to one-up each other with their Christmas lights, but they've started taking playful swipes at each other, and even playing small pranks. I once asked my dad when he was going to start taking it easier with the lights – well, he's not getting any younger and I know my mum is terrified when he goes up the ladder – and not only did he say that he would never back down, but he also said that I, as his sole heir, was responsible for continuing his work after he dies. I'm hoping he was just joking and doesn't really expect me to keep sabotaging his neighbours' Christmas display after he's gone.

It is all for a good cause, though. Both locals and tourists travel to our little street to check out the Christmas displays. In fact, so many people drive by that my dad and Gerry installed a secure collection box, to raise funds for the local hospice. All the houses get involved now, but it's always my dad and Gerry who go the hardest.

'Well, my dad is away, so no drama this year,' I point out.

'I wouldn't be so sure about that,' Dennis tells me. 'The two of them made a truce, I saw them from my garden.'

I bet he did.

'They said they wouldn't compete this year, with your dad being away, but the day after he left, let's just say I saw someone in your garden and ever since, the lights haven't worked. It was a man in a hoodie, it looked like he was messing with the lights.'

I'm annoyed for my dad. Classic Gerry, calling a truce and then sabotaging Dad's lights while he's away. I'll bet he's removed a bulb from each set, so that none of them work – that's one of the tricks my dad taught me. I might not be interested in inheriting my dad's rivalry, but the least I can do is tighten the bulbs that Gerry loosened, so that the house lights up as usual tonight. If I really were having a Christmas party, I'd want the Christmas lights to be on, right?

'I'll sort it, Dennis, thank you.'

'Good,' he says firmly. 'I'm not having it. I have to live between you both and it's like being between the Montagues and the Capulets. Sneaky and illegal behaviour invites more sneaky and illegal behaviour and if I see any more, I won't hesitate to call the police. I'm not having my home turning into a crime hotspot.'

'I see that,' I reply, keen to end the conversation ASAP.

Wow, Dennis really needs to chill out. Gerry unscrewing a few of my dad's light bulbs is hardly going to turn into a shoot-out across the road, Gerry building a meth lab in his cellar, and Janice in number eight putting a red light in her window, is it?

'Good,' he says before his angry expression turns into something softer. 'Are you sure you won't join us for Christmas dinner, Dani?'

'Sorry, I have plans,' I say again. 'Thank you, though.'

'Well, you know where we are if you change your mind,' he says as he heads back towards his house. 'By the way, your doorbell is broken.'

'Thanks,' I call after him.

I don't need to worry too much with Dennis around, I'm sure he'll keep a very close eye on me.

I grab my boots from next to the front door and pop them on before tightening my dressing gown belt. I just *had* to be dressed like a reindeer for this.

The snow has really come down overnight, there's a thick covering everywhere – it could be a perfect white Christmas, if I wasn't going to be home alone. I should be able to make it to the

shops on foot okay, grab myself some food for the next few days. I
might as well stay here now, I have nothing to go back to London
for, and I don't know how I'd get anywhere in this snow anyway. I
doubt I'm going to be able to get to Leeds, but I'll worry about
that later. At least I'll be more comfortable here than I would be
in my tiny flat. I can eat, watch Christmas movies – sure, I'd rather
not be alone for Christmas, but I'm playing the hand I've been
dealt. Better to be alone in a warm, comfortable house with
superfast broadband and Sky TV than in a freezing-cold flat
above an off-licence.

With no dignity left to lose, I go to inspect the Christmas
lights. It turns out that Gerry hasn't just loosened a bulb from
each set, he's stolen one. And anything he couldn't disrupt by
removing a bulb, he's unplugged. I puff air from my cheeks. Oh,
boy. For some reason, being the only one here, I feel like I owe it
to my dad to plug everything back in and replace the bulbs so
that I can get the lights back on for him, even if he doesn't know
that they're off.

I remove another bulb from each set, to take with me, to make
sure I buy the right ones, and carry them inside with me.

My dad has always had this thing – like a lot of folk here –
about shopping local, so I'll bet he bought his Christmas lights
from Marram Bay's open-all-year Christmas shop, Christmas
Every Day – because of course we have a Christmas shop that's
open all year round, why wouldn't we? It was my friends' mum
who owned it back in the day, so I used to go there quite a bit to
see them. I'll try and get replacement bulbs there – plus it will be
nice to go back there for old times' sake.

I boil the kettle again but when I go to the fridge to get some
milk, there isn't any. There isn't much of anything. I suppose, if
they knew they were going on holiday for Christmas, they won't

have bought any food, will they? I was planning on shopping for food anyway, so I guess I need to buy the basics too.

I remove my phone from my dressing gown pocket and tap a message to my mum, just saying hello and asking how she is. I know that she would be mortified if she knew I had come home for Christmas and they weren't here. She'd feel so guilty when really it's all my fault for not telling her I was coming. She mustn't find out I'm here.

By the time I am dressed and ready to head out, I notice a reply has come through from my mum. She says that Dad decided to surprise her with a trip to France for Christmas. He'd booked a last-minute B & B, so they packed their bags and set off. I can't stress how unlike my parents this is, but I'm so happy for them. My mum says she's going to call me when she gets settled but I can't stand the idea of lying to her over the phone, pretending I'm not in her house, so I send her a message saying that I'm away for Christmas too (which isn't technically untrue) and that she should concentrate on having a good time, and I'll message her later.

Right, now I've got that out of the way, I need to go out and buy Christmas light bulbs. Oh, and food, otherwise I'm not just going to be home alone, I'm going to starve too.

13

The strange thing about Marram Bay is that, while a lot seems to have changed, things never really seem any different. It's a place that does move with the times, only the movement is so subtle, it's almost undetectable.

I noticed a few new businesses as I passed Main Street. There was Fruitopia – a jam shop with what has to be the greatest name in history – and the Apple Blossom Deli, which is new to me too, but everything that pops up here has to be so Marram Bay-appropriate that it looks like it's been here forever. There's an entire team of locals who are dedicated to making sure the Marram Bay aesthetic is preserved, and God help anyone who gets in their way.

One thing that does look very different to how I remember it (but still looks just right in the village landscape) is Christmas Every Day, the festive shop that's open all year round. The last time I was here, it was an old stone cottage that had been converted into a shop with a flat above it, sitting on the edge of a field, all alone, in the middle of nowhere. I knew this place like the back of my hand because it was my friends, twins Holly and

Ivy, whose mum ran the place. That little village Christmas shop is well and truly gone now. Standing in its place is a gorgeous, modern arrangement of different buildings. At a glance, it's made up of holiday homes, shops, a café... I can hardly believe it! It looks amazing, and busy, and most importantly, a new and improved Christmas shop sits right in the heart of it.

I'm freezing by the time I get inside. Marram Bay is thankfully quite a small place but walking across the open causeway has chilled me through to the bone. As I step inside the shop, and I'm greeted by a combination of warm air and the sweet smell of the confectionary, it's like getting a hug from Tom Hardy.

'Ho, ho, ho!' a man dressed as Santa Claus greets me.

'Oh, hello,' I reply, a little taken aback.

Santa Claus, despite having the well-padded red suit and the stick-on beard, doesn't look like any Santa I've ever seen before, you can tell by his eyes and his muscular figure that he's a young, buff dude.

'Have you been naughty or nice this year?' he asks me. It's hard to tell, because of the white fringe that sits just over his eyes, but I'm pretty certain he winked at me as he asked.

I sort of smile, to be polite, before continuing into the shop. I definitely don't answer his question. The past year has been too boring for me to have been either.

This is obviously the Christmas shop, but it's nothing like the one I remember from when I was a kid. It's much bigger and fancier, but it has somehow managed to hang on to the charm of the original. The miniature steam train from the old shop is still here – or one just like it, at least – running around the shop on a track that weaves in and out of displays and perfectly decorated Christmas trees.

There is a whole selection of lights on display. Under each set is a little drawer, filled with single bulbs. This is exactly what I need, I just don't know which ones are which, they all look the same to me.

I make my way through the shoppers to the front desk where two women are working. It takes me a few seconds before I realise that one of them is my friend Ivy, all grown-up.

'Oh, my gosh, Ivy?' I ask, double-checking. I mean, I'm sure it's her, it looks just like her, and she's still a good six or seven inches shorter than me, so that's a dead giveaway.

'Hello...' she starts slowly as she looks me up and down. Then the penny drops for her. 'Oh, wow, Dani?'

'Yes!'

'Oh, my God!'

Ivy rushes around the counter to give me a big squeeze.

'What are you doing here? Are you home for Christmas?' she asks.

'Yes!'

'Your mum and dad must be made up,' she says, finally releasing me.

'Yes, well, no, they're away for Christmas this year,' I tell her.

'What?'

We're interrupted by the Santa who greeted me on my way in.

'Oh, so you two know each other then?' he asks nosily.

'We're old friends, we went to school together,' Ivy tells him. 'Dani, this is Gaz, our resident Santa Claus,' she tells me. 'Gaz, this is Dani.'

'We've already met,' Gaz tells her. 'She wouldn't tell me if she was naughty or nice, though.'

Ivy rolls her eyes.

'He used to be worse than this, if you can even believe that?' she says. 'I'm the not-so-proud wrangler of Marram Bay's horniest Santa Claus. But wait, back to you, your mum and dad are on holiday, didn't you know? Are you here alone?'

It enters my mind, for a split second, that perhaps I should tell Ivy the truth about me coming here to surprise my parents, only to learn that they went on holiday without telling me, but it just sounds oh-so tragic, I can't bring myself to say it, not in front of Gaz, even though I've only just met him. The last thing I need is 'Marram Bay's horniest Santa Claus' inviting me to the North Pole to sit on his lap for the holidays – especially if it's only out of pity.

'Oh, no, of course I knew they were going on holiday, obviously, I'm not like Kevin McCallister from *Home Alone* or anything,' I babble, throwing in an awkward joke at the end, that's a little too close to my home (in which I am definitely alone). 'I'm using their house to throw a big Christmas party while they're away.'

'I hope we're invited,' Gaz says. 'I can even bring my Santa suit if you like...'

Okay, that was definitely an eyebrow wiggle I just spotted going on underneath his hat.

'Go away, Gaz,' Ivy says with a laugh. 'Go find some kids to annoy, they're more on your wavelength.'

'Fine, fine,' he says. 'See you around.'

'That really is a pretty randy Santa,' I point out through a chuckle. 'He seems like a handful.'

'You definitely can't use words to describe him like "handful" when he's listening. Mrs Claus would not be happy with his behaviour,' she replies with a sigh. 'He's amazing, though. As you can see, this place has changed a lot. Gaz has been with me every step of the way, he helps me run this place.'

'Oh, wow, you're running it now?' I reply.

'Yeah, since my mum passed away.'

'Oh, Ivy, I'm so sorry,' I tell her sincerely. Her mum was such a lovely woman. Christmas was her life. It's such a lovely tribute that Ivy has kept her shop thriving in her honour.

Ivy bats it off with her hand, but you can tell it hurts her every time she says it.

'Does Holly work here too?' I ask, glancing around to see if Ivy's twin sister is lurking somewhere.

'Nah, not really her scene,' she replies. 'She's got enough going on – she's got four kids. *Four!* But I've got things covered here.'

'Wow. I always thought you were going to be a baker,' I tell her. 'I remember, it was your dream when you were younger.'

'Yeah, well, this place got in the way of that,' she replies. 'But that's life, right? Are you a big-time journalist? Last time I spoke to your mum, she said you were working in London. She's so proud of you.'

Awkward.

'Erm, I'm not exactly a big-time journalist, something got in my way too. I do work at a magazine, though, and I'm angling for a promotion at the moment. I do still love baking, when I get time,' I reply.

Ivy and I were always partners in food tech. We bonded over our shared love of baking and were both always top of the class. Everyone – kids and teachers – always devoured everything we made.

'Are you still upsetting the world with those fake mince pies you used to make?' she asks with a chuckle.

'Oh, you know it,' I reply.

'We're looking for someone for here,' she tells me. 'Someone to bake for the café next door, and for the things we sell in the shop, since we expanded. More floor space, food, Gaz harassing the mums – it must seem like everything has changed since the last time you were here.'

I notice Ivy is saying 'we' a fair bit, which makes me wonder...

'Gaz isn't your boyfriend, is he?' I check. I mean, I figured as much when he flirted with me in front of her, but now I feel like I need to make sure.

'Oh, lord, no,' she says with a laugh. 'Just a great friend.'

I wonder, if Ivy is single too, perhaps I could tell her about my predicament. I'm sure she's spending Christmas with her family, but she might take pity on me and hang out with me for a bit? It could be quite fun, being a double act again.

'I do have a husband, though,' she says. 'Seb. He's the guy who built this place.'

I smile. It wouldn't be right of me to tell her I'm on my own, she's such a sweetheart, I know that she would invite me to join them for Christmas and that wouldn't be fair, I can't drop myself on her like that.

'He sounds like a dream,' I reply with a smile. 'Anyway, I am here because I need some new bulbs for Dad's Christmas lights. It turns out his and Gerry's rivalry is still going strong, even while Dad's on holiday.'

'Ah, say no more,' she says, leading me over to the bulbs.

I show Ivy each of the bulbs I've brought with me and she promptly hands me the right bulbs to replace the missing one with.

'Thank you so much,' I say as Ivy carefully wraps them up for me, so that I can get them home without smashing them. 'I know my dad is away, but apparently they called some kind of truce, so it weirdly and annoyingly feels like my job to put it right in his absence. It will be nice for the party too, to have all the lights on.'

I add that on at the end, to try to make my lie seem more convincing.

'Ha, you'll be joining in before you know it,' she says with a laugh.

'Oh, I'm not so sure about that,' I reply. 'Where is the best place for me to shop for food these days?'

'Ooh, for your party?' she replies. 'Exciting!'

I did mean generally but I'm so deep in with the lie now.

'Yes.'

'You want to swing by the deli on Main Street, oh, and pop to the farm shop – Wilson's farm has this massive farm shop now, it's got all kinds of yummy things. You'll love it.'

'Oh, sounds great, thank you. Maybe we can hang out before I head home?' I suggest.

'I'd love that,' she replies.

We swap numbers before I head out again, back out into the cold. Alone again. I do feel awful, lying to her, but I'm just trying to minimise the carnage. I don't want anyone feeling sorry for me, taking me in, messing up their plans. And I definitely don't want to wind up being taken in by the neighbours, so I just need to keep trying to style it out until it's time to go back to London. But, gosh, I really don't want to go back to London. How have I landed myself in this mess?

There are outdoor speakers dotted around everywhere here. I notice that 'Lonely This Christmas' by Mud is playing.

Of course it is.

14

I took Ivy's recommendation and popped into the Apple Blossom Deli on Main Street and absolutely filled my boots with sweet treats to keep me going over the festive period.

A very lovely, very friendly girl called Channy works there, who recommended all these different Italian and French biscuits and cakes to me. She even let me try a few, which made it even harder to leave without buying loads of different things. I also learned that the shop manager's husband owns a local farm that makes fruity ciders, so I bought a few of those too. Everyone likes a drink at Christmas, don't they?

I didn't buy any actual food-food though, so unless I'm going to spend Christmas alone, drinking cider and chain-eating cannoli, then I need to buy some real food for meals, so I'm at Wilson's Farm Shop now, hurrying inside where it's warm. It's getting dark now and the snow is getting heavier. I just want to go home, slip on my reindeer dressing gown and watch TV while I burn through my new food supplies.

I grab a trolley, although there's only so many bags for life I can carry, so I can't let myself get too carried away. As I start making my way up and down the aisles, one thing becomes embarrassingly clear to me: all of the food is gone. Well, the food-food, the *Christmas* food. You can still buy tins of beans, chicken nuggets, sausage rolls – stuff like that – but obviously Christmas staples like turkey and all the usual vegetables are long gone. I suppose people order their Christmas dinner ingredients these days, don't they? I think I've grown too used to a Christmas Eve M&S dash to see what kind of turkey and veg I can still get my hands on. No M&S here, though, not for miles.

So, basically, I can eat kids' favourite meals, like chicken nuggets and baked beans, or I can make myself up a six-year-old's party plate, with sausage rolls, breadsticks and crisps. I do feel like a helpless little kid, left to her own devices by her neglectful parents, except, y'know, I'm in my thirties and they had no idea I was coming. So perhaps I'll go with a bit of both, mix it up.

'Dani,' I hear a familiar voice call out behind me.

I turn around to see a petite brunette charging towards me. The light bounces off her glossy bob – something I've never been able to get my hair to do – and, while I'd say she was about my age, I'd hazard a guess she's invested in a better moisturiser than I have over the years. She's practically glowing.

As she smiles, she flashes her brilliant white teeth and I realise who it is, it's Eleanor, my childhood frenemy.

Eleanor and I were around each other our whole lives, until I moved away. We were born around the same time, we grew up on the same street, and we were in the same classes all the way through school. Gerry, my dad's rival, is Eleanor's dad, which might be why she naturally decided that we should be rivals too. She's always had this same sickly-sweet smile, except when we were younger, it wasn't a friendly thing, it was more like she was baring her teeth.

Eleanor was the kind of kid who was amazing at everything –

spelling, reading, maths, *everything*. And if that wasn't hard enough to live up to, she was the best at PE too. I remember when they started making us do those godawful bleep tests, you know, where you have to run from one side of the gym to the other, timing your running with the bleeps (which were always played from a cassette in my day, which makes me feel a thousand years old) as the sounds grew increasingly closer together. Eleanor was amazing at the bleep test, everyone else would bow out, only to sit on one of those little wooden benches, and watch Eleanor go on and on and on. And it wouldn't be so bad, if she hadn't known she was better than everyone – or didn't act like it, at least. She knew, though, and she let everyone else know that she knew.

Growing up on the same street, and having mums that were friends, Eleanor and I spent a lot of time together. It was torture. She was always in constant competition with me, whether I wanted her to be or not. Even if I wasn't competing, she would somehow always find a way to win. Fair enough, I had to take part in the bleep test (although I would always try to fake a twisted ankle when I knew it was coming) but at Christmas, she would always work out who had the better presents and at Easter who had the most eggs.

Eleanor obviously learned this from her dad. Her mum wasn't like that at all, and neither was her older brother, Ben. Yep, *the* Ben, the one I had the crush on, the one I lied to Rex about, telling him that he was my ex. I really liked Ben back in those days, he was a couple of years older than us, far more mature than his sister, and definitely more modest. I never let him know that I had a crush on him, obviously, but I was always so nervous around him, struggling to talk to him, carefully crafting my sentences before saying them, which often meant I would miss my chance to speak. I must have seemed like such a loser. I don't have much trouble talking now, though – perhaps Eleanor will have changed for the better too?

'Dani, look at you, you look so old,' she squeaks as she hugs me.

Then again, perhaps not.

'Well, you know, not old-old, like grown-up old,' she clarifies. 'You look *very* grown-up.'

She absolutely could have just said that to begin with. Even her emphasis on the word 'very' in her clarified comment makes it sound like it's designed to wound me too.

'Hi, Eleanor,' I say, as brightly as I can. I was over the moon to see Ivy after all these years, but I easily could've gone another decade, maybe even two, without having a run-in with Eleanor.

'How the bloody hell are you?' she asks. She reaches out, takes me by the shoulder, and shakes me lightly for some strange reason. She's probably building up to a physical assault.

'I'm great, thanks. You?'

I ask to be polite – why am I always so polite to everyone, even if I don't like them? It's infuriating.

'Yeah, I'm really good, can't complain at all – well, I can, but you know.'

I smile. Oh, I know she can complain.

'Why are you here?' she asks accusingly. 'Your mum and dad are on holiday, aren't they? Oh, God, has something awful happened to one of them?'

Wow.

'No, nothing awful has happened to either of them,' I say, otherwise holding my tongue. 'I'm just using their house to throw a Christmas party while they're away – with their permission, of course. I'm just scoping out food, actually.'

'I'm just getting some bits for dinner tonight,' she says.

'Speaking of which, where is that bloody muppet with the salt I sent him off to find?'

Eleanor scans the room as best she can, but she's another one who is much shorter than I am.

'Your partner?' I ask curiously.

God, please don't have a devastatingly handsome husband that you're going to lord over me before asking if I'm still single. I genuinely might have to lie, say I've got some stud waiting for me back in London, who is just too busy being a billionaire dot-com something or other to bother with something as trivial as Christmas. Although perhaps that's too far – and, crucially, too unbelievable. Plus, I cannot mentally juggle so many fake relationships at a time. I'm starting to feel deluded. Any day now, I'm going to worry about wondering whether or not one of my fake boyfriends might bump into one of the others, and why none of them are coming home for dinner. It's a slippery slope. Best I do everything I can to stay off it.

'Oh, God, no,' she replies firmly. 'No, no. Quite the opposite. Oh, there you bloody are, you muppet.'

Wow, she hasn't changed a bit. She's still using insults in the place of terms of endearment. I wonder if I've changed much. It's funny, being back here, standing in front of Eleanor, worrying about what she thinks of me, I don't feel like I've changed an inch.

'All right, calm down, they sell nine different types of salt,' the man replies as he tosses it into the trolly.

'Well, what kind did you get then?' she asks. Her tone is just awful.

'Salt,' he replies. 'Salt-salt. You said you wanted salt. Did you want pink salt or something?'

'Oh, my God, seriously, get off my back,' she whines at him. 'Mum would never cook with pink salt because Dad would refuse to eat it, obviously. Dad hasn't touched a pink food since he swore that beetroot salad made him look like he was wearing lipstick at our Julie's wake.'

Wow, there is so much to unpack there, I don't know where to begin.

The man turns to me. Tall, broad, with a mess of brown hair on the top of his head that is just as wild as the last time I saw him. He has a beard now, though – a proper one, far more impressive than the one he tried to grow when he was a teenager.

'Ben,' I blurt. 'Hello, you.'

'Hey, Dani,' he replies through a big smile. 'What are you doing in town? Aren't your parents on holiday?'

I forget that everyone knows everything about everyone else in a small place like Marram Bay, whether you want them to or not.

'She's using their house for a big party,' Eleanor tells him.

'Remember that house party you had when we were kids?' he asks me with a grin.

My first thought is that we weren't as young as he makes us sound by saying 'kids'. I was sixteen and he was a couple of months off his eighteenth birthday, but I suppose we were still kids really. I felt so grown-up at the time, but these days, when I see sixteen-year-olds, they look like babies. Hooray, yet another sign I'm getting old. I'll be complaining about pop music next.

'I remember it well,' I say, a little embarrassed. That was the night that Ben and I almost kissed. The first and only time there was ever a hint that anything could happen between us. My parents were away for the night and left me alone for the first time, so naturally all my friends talked me into throwing a house party. We were playing spin the bottle when Ben took his turn and the bottle landed on me. I couldn't believe my luck... until Eleanor 'accidentally' knocked her drink all over the carpet. I had to jump into action, soaking up the liquid, trying to make sure her alcopop didn't leave a stain. By the time I had cleaned up, the game was over, and I couldn't exactly chase up my kiss with Ben, could I? He definitely would've realised that I fancied him if I'd done that.

'Nothing quite so wild this time,' I insist. 'Definitely fewer bottles of cheap blueberry Kapops that will stain the carpet. It will be a more mature affair.'

A sly dig. I'm definitely braver now I'm older.

'Not if you're serving up chicken nuggets,' Eleanor points out, clocking the random assortment of foods in my trolley.

'Oh, I'm just picking up some extra bits of party food, it sounds like people might be bringing friends,' I lie. Still, I start filling up my trolley with sausage rolls, scotch eggs, mini pork pies, etc., to try to make it seem like it's true.

I notice a family-sized four-cheese pizza, the last one in the fridge, so I place that in my trolley too. That will be perfect for dinner this evening – not all of it, obviously, but I don't see a smaller one available. I can always eat the leftovers tomorrow – if I don't somehow manage to plough through the whole thing alone over the course of a *Die Hard* movie marathon.

'Ooh, get you,' Eleanor sings, sounding almost annoyed. 'Sounds like it's going to be a big do.'

I look at my wrist, only to realise I didn't put my watch on this morning, so I rifle through my handbag, looking for my phone, so that I can check the time, and make up an excuse to get out of here.

'Oh, look at the time,' I eventually blurt after getting my hands on it. 'I'd better get going, so much to prepare. Lovely to see you both, though.'

'Yeah, you too,' Ben calls after me as I shuffle off. 'Albeit briefly.'

'I'm sure we'll catch up before I head home,' I call back, but I don't mean it.

'We can all catch up,' Eleanor adds, firmly inserting herself in the situation. 'We're staying at Mum and Dad's for the holidays, so we're only up the street.'

God, he's still gorgeous. And she's still... far from ideal.

I pay for my shopping, including all the supposed extra party food, because I can't find a subtle way to bin it all off without being noticed, and hurry back out into the cold. I definitely have a little more than is comfortable to carry, but I'm not far from home now. I don't just have more shopping than I can carry, I've bitten off more than I can chew, with this party story that is growing increasingly out of control. I need to find a way to nip it in the bud, to make it seem like the party has happened, and somehow everyone missed it. Although it's not going to be easy, with a nosy neighbour like Dennis keeping an eye on me – and with Eleanor and Ben just feet away too.

Still, I'm sure I'll think of something. Another lie, probably.

15

One of the things I love about visiting home is that my childhood bedroom is, as always, exactly how I left it the last time I was here, and this is something that dates back to when I was younger, still living here.

It's like a weird time capsule of a room, but one that represents my life while I lived here. There are keepsakes from when I was a kid, random bits from when I was a teen that even I can't quite remember the significance of. Another reminder of my teens is the photographs that are still all over my walls – this will also date me, but I pretty much took a disposable camera everywhere I went, the results of which are adorning the walls. My old corkboard is still up there too, covered in all sorts: awards from school, gig tickets, notes from friends, and other random keepsakes that I didn't only not want to part with, I wanted them on display too.

I could probably live without most of this stuff now, happily, but Mum says you never know when you might want to look at a photo with your old friends, or remind yourself that, at age fourteen, you got a star award for your food tech work. I remember the project I got that particular award for, it was for a festive treat that I came up with – one that I still try to find the time to make every year. I remember at the time, when I first made them, how divisive they were amongst the teachers who were doing the judging. Mr Lodge, our secondary school's answer to Paul Hollywood, branded what I had made 'an abomination', but luckily the other judges loved it and it was my project that won.

See, as much as I love Christmas, and almost all of the smells and flavours that go with it, I absolutely hate mince pies. I don't know what it is about the flavour and all that sticky, lumpy fruit, but it's just too much for me. That's why fourteen-year-old me decided that we needed reform and came up with a recipe for something that looked like a mince pie, and retained all the elements that I did like about them, but without the mince. I filled my pies with chocolate brownie filling instead. Some with sweet caramel sauce and some with a sort of rocky road brownie. I feel like people either love mince pies or they hate them – naturally, the people who hate them absolutely adore my take on the classic (especially big fans of chocolate like me) but the people who are big fans of the OG pie think I'm some kind of Grinch with a bee in her bonnet. It's quite funny, really.

See, my mum is right. If I she hadn't held on to all this junk for me then I never would have thought about my pies much beyond Ivy asking me if I still liked to make them. Memories are stored inside our brains but sometimes, when they're pushed right to the back in favour of other more pressing things, they're as good as lost forever until a random bit of junk like a gig ticket or a stuffed animal brings it back to the forefront. I think my mum's plan is to hang on to everything in this room for me, until I have my own home with enough space to house it all. I think she's worried I'm going to throw it all away and then regret letting go of everything, and the memories that are attached to them.

I'm really missing my mum this evening – my dad too – more so than usual but I suppose it's a by-product of being in their house and them not being here. I'm getting the nostalgia hit I love about being at home, but without my parents being here, it's not quite the same.

My ringing phone distracts me from my thoughts. It's Rex. My God, now, more than ever, I desperately want that job in Leeds. I want to be closer to my parents. I want to see them more often. Rex is my ticket to a new life.

'Hello,' I answer brightly.

'Hey,' he replies. 'How's big family Christmas going so far, is it everything you hoped?'

'Erm, yeah! And more,' I say, before reminding myself to tone it down a little. 'How are you doing? How's Leeds?'

'Yeah, good, got here in the end,' he replies. 'Although I think I might be stuck here for a while. I told you that my car didn't like the snow – it's in the shop for the foreseeable. Not that there's anywhere to go.'

'Shit, are you okay?' I ask him.

'Oh, yeah, totally fine,' he insists. 'The downside to all of this, though, is that it's probably not going to be possible for you to get to Leeds for our meeting.'

'Right, no,' I reply.

Well, of course it isn't. The snow is bad, the trains will be off, Rex's car sounds like it needs some major TLC, and it's not exactly a walkable journey like the shops are here. It's no one's fault, of course it isn't, but my God is it disappointing. I want this job so, so badly, for so many reasons, and this just makes it feel even further away than ever.

'I know it's not what we had planned but perhaps we could have our meetings over Zoom?' Rex suggests. 'That way, we don't have to cancel.'

'Oh, that would be great,' I say, practically biting his hand off. 'Yes, please.'

'Great. It's nothing formal. Just the two of us, trying to work out if you're a good fit for the job. It's probably going to take a few calls to figure things out. Hey, don't sound so worried. Do you have your laptop with you?'

Shit, do I sound worried?

'I don't,' I reply, making an effort to sound like I'm not worried, but going too far and sounding almost indifferent instead. 'Oh, but my dad has a PC, and a webcam, so I can just log in on that.'

'Awesome,' he replies. 'So, what's on the big family Christmas agenda tonight?'

'Party planning,' I lie. 'Just doing some bits to get ready for the bash we're throwing for the neighbours. Then it's looking like pizza and *Die Hard* with my dad. What are you getting up to?'

'Out for dinner this evening,' he replies simply.

I wonder if he's going out with a girl – stop it, Dani!

'Ooh, nice, well, have fun,' I tell him.

'Yeah, you too,' he replies. 'Are you free for our first Zoom in the morning?'

'Yeah, definitely,' I reply. 'Just send me a link whenever.'

'Great, looking forward to it,' he says.

Is it me, or do things feel a little stiff and awkward now?

'Yeah, have fun tonight,' I say again. Yep, definitely awkward.

I know how silly it's going to sound, but I miss pretending to be in a couple with Rex. Yes, it was fake, but it still felt good. Hilariously, I have more fond memories of my fake relationship with Rex than I do my real one with Tom. It's funny, but it really puts things into perspective. If all that comes from this is that it reframes how I look at my relationship with Tom, then it will have all been worth it. But I do still really, really want this job.

Ah, well. Time to try to take down a pizza for four people and watch one of the least festive Christmas movies I can think of. And then, after that, God knows what, just killing time until morning, until my meeting with Rex.

One thing's for sure, I need to be up bright and early, and dressed in my best. At the end of the day, this is still a job interview, of sorts, so I need to pull out all the stops. I need to keep things as formal as possible and do everything I can to make sure Rex forgets that I tried to kiss him – it might be difficult, though, because I know I can't stop thinking about it.

16

'Simon, play my music,' I command.

'All right, playing music by Lewis Capaldi,' the voice-activated smart speaker I bought my parents replies.

'Simon, stop,' I say quickly. I love a bit of Lewis Capaldi as much as the next girl, but his music is not the vibe I need right now, sitting here alone, on the floor with my legs crossed, eating my fifth slice of pizza, playing with the Christmas present that was supposed to be for my mum and dad.

Well, it still is for them, and I'll be giving it to them at some point, but I know that when I do, it will be me who has to set it up for them anyway, so I may as well save myself the work later, even if I re-box it and wrap it back up after. If I don't set it up for them, you can guarantee that they'll just use it as a doorstop or something.

In a strange way, it's nice to have another voice about the house. Someone to talk to, even if they're not really listening to me. It's not unlike my relationship with Tom, really, although Simple Simon is much smarter. It will be nice for me to have a man about the house while I'm here alone, even if it is only an artificially (kind of) intelligent one.

After replacing the bulbs outside the house, and making sure all of the plugs were plugged in and switched on inside, all of the Christmas lights came back on again and... wow. My dad really has gone all out this year. I know I haven't visited home for a few Christmases, but he has always sent me pictures of his light display and I can say with confidence that this year he has upped his game significantly. Every straight line of their large detached house is covered with twinkling fairy lights. So are the bare branches of all the trees in the garden, with strings of lights painstakingly wrapped around each branch. The evergreen trees are decked out like Christmas trees, with lights, baubles and stars on top. Finally, his pièce de résistance is the near life-size Santa sleigh with reindeer, made from white metal frames, all covered with fairy lights. It sits in the centre of the lawn, as though Santa had just touched down. Not only does it look beautiful, but I like to think it serves as a reminder to Gerry that Santa *does* stop here, because we've been good. Gerry's display, although I haven't had time to step outside and properly take it in yet, appears to be far tackier, but just as brightly lit, so the competition is still tough, depending on what you're into.

After fixing the lights outside, I turned my attention to the lights inside. Last year, in an attempt to make my parents' lives easier, I sent them some smart bulbs. Of course, they couldn't get the hang of the app, so I eventually had to send the physical switch to go with them, which took them back to square one, but they do like being able to dim them, so we'll call that a win. Now that I've got them a Simple Simon, he'll be able to control the lights for them if they ask him to, which reminds me...

'Simon, start party lights,' I command.

'Okay,' Simon replies. 'Party lights: on.'

A split second later, all of the light bulbs in the living room – from the ceiling ones to the lamps – are flashing different colours. It looks fantastic, although I doubt my parents ever use them for this. I'm sure my dad would, if he knew how, because it must look awesome from outside. Not only will it add to the display, but it will definitely make it seem like a party is going on to the neighbours, should Dennis next door be curtain-twitching, which he almost always seems to be doing. It's hard to feel unsafe, home alone, with Dennis keeping an eye on things.

'Simon, play Christmas music,' I say.

'Okay,' he replies again – my kind of man. 'Shuffling music by Chris Martin.'

'Oh, God, no,' I reply, not that Simon understands my aversion to Coldplay. 'Simon, play *Christmas* music.'

This time, Simon gets it right.

I smile to myself as 'Rockin' Around the Christmas Tree' by Brenda Lee starts playing. Is it strange that the lights and the noise make me feel a little less alone?

I'm flicking through the booklet that came with Simple Simon when something interesting catches my eye.

'Simon, activate burglar deterrent,' I say excitedly.

'Okay,' he replies.

After answering a few simple questions about what level and type of noise I want, Simon plays the sound of people chatting just a little quieter than he's playing the Christmas music. Okay, now it really does seem like there's a party going on, should Dennis happen to be putting his bins out, or pressing his ear up against the front door, or whatever.

As I sit in the centre of my fake party, snuggled up in my dressing gown, eating chocolate coins (you have to at Christmas time, don't you?), I scroll through Instagram to see what everyone I follow is up to. I think it's fair to say that my feed is mostly made up of people I haven't ever met in real life. People with cute dogs, people who do make-up tutorials – just people who generally seem like they have more going on than I do. Then again, I'm sure that my feed makes it seem like I have way more going on than I do, but that's just the way we use social media, right?

With the fake party in full swing, I decide to make myself another cup of tea. I might even grab the cannoli I bought today too, well, Christmas is for spending time with family and eating nice things, and without the family, the eating bit is all I have...

As I walk from the living room to the kitchen, with my large robin-shaped empty mug, a knock on the door really takes me by surprise. It happens right as I'm walking through the hallway, which means whoever is standing outside the door must have seen me walking through before they knocked. I look over at the door, and through the frosted glass I can see one person standing there. Whoever it is appears to drop to the floor.

'Dani?' a male voice calls through the letter box. 'Don't worry, it's just me, it's Ben. You dropped your work ID card in the shop today, I was going to put it through the letter box, I didn't want to disturb your party but, well, I just spotted you and it felt weird not to knock.'

Oh, crap. Well, what am I supposed to do now? He's seen me. I can't just ignore him, can I?

'Just a second,' I call back to him.

Think, Dani. Think. Without any time to get changed, I quickly wiggle out of my reindeer dressing gown and put on my long coat over the top of my pyjamas. So long as Ben doesn't look down, I'll be fine. Perhaps I'll stand just inside the door and peer out, keeping my legs hidden behind it, then I might get away with it.

'Hello,' I say brightly, sticking my head out around the partially opened door.

'Hi,' he replies. 'Sorry, I didn't mean to disturb you, but you dropped this earlier.'

Ben hands me my work ID card. It must have fallen out of my handbag when I was looking for my phone.

'Oh, thanks so much,' I say, reaching through the doorway to take it from him.

'You're welcome,' he replies. 'I rang the bell a couple of times but either it's not working or it's too loud in there. It sounds like the party is in full swing.'

'Yeah, erm—'

I don't know what to say.

'Is it a pyjama party?' he asks.

'What?'

'Is it a pyjama party?' he asks again. 'When I shouted through the letter box, it looked like you were in your pyjamas.'

'Oh, right, yes, well,' I babble, trying to buy myself some time while I think of something to say that isn't totally insane. 'No, of course I'm not having a pyjama party, that would be ridiculous. No one is here yet.'

'It's nearly ten p.m.,' he replies. 'What time does it start? And... I'm sure I can hear people in there?'

Wow, I am so bad at this.

'Yeah, I mean the party... isn't today,' I continue. God, lying is exhausting, and I really am terrible at it. How on earth do I shut this accidental interrogation down?

Ben cocks his head as he continues to listen to the music and chatter coming from the living room. He has the most bemused expression I think I've ever seen.

'This is just like, you know, the dry run,' I sort of explain. 'I'm just testing the lights and the music.'

'But where is the talking coming from?' he asks curiously. 'I can hear actual people.'

'Simon, stop,' I call into the living room.

Ben's face falls.

'Sorry, if you have company,' he starts as he makes an awkward move to leave.

'No, wait, sorry, Simon is the smart speaker I've bought for my parents, not a real person, I was just using his burglar deterrent to test noise levels, to make sure I wouldn't disturb the neighbours.'

Lies upon lies, wrapped in lies, held up by more lies, with a big, lie-shaped festive bow on the top – and almost none of it remotely believable.

'Erm, okay,' he says with a chuckle. 'So, when is the party? It sounds like it's going to be something special, if you're going to all this trouble.'

'Christmas Eve,' I blurt, just because it sounds right.

'Am I invited?' he asks.

'Of course you're invited,' I reply immediately, my voice going up in pitch slightly. 'I was going to invite you and Eleanor tomorrow. You've saved me a job.'

Why, oh why did I just mention Eleanor? I am such a moron.

'Oh, great,' he replies. 'Well, do you want to come over anyway, have a catch up?'

'Oh, erm, yes, okay then.'

I really would love to catch up with him, and it will be nice to have some company – some real company, other than Simon.

'Okay, well, I'm in all day. We're both staying at Mum and Dad's house for Christmas, you know what they're like about having us all under the same roof. Pop round whenever,' he says casually.

'Okay, sure,' I reply, trying to sound casual but probably not hitting the mark. 'I've got a work meeting on Zoom in the morning, but I could pop over after?'

'Always working so hard,' he points out with a smile. 'Okay, see you then.'

'Yeah, see you tomorrow,' I reply.

After we say goodnight and I close the door behind me, I lean back on to it, unable to hide my smile. Tomorrow I'm not only not going to be alone all day, but I get to hang out with Ben. Sweet, charming, handsome Ben. The Ben I had a crush on all through school – hilariously, the Ben I told Rex I was going to be making a date with.

My smile, unfortunately, doesn't last long, because now I have bigger problems on my plate. It's great that I'm going to have some company tomorrow, but I've gone and got myself company for Christmas Eve too, inviting Ben and Eleanor to a party that isn't actually happening. No idea what I'm going to do about that one...

17

Last night, I slept in my parents' super-comfortable, super-king bed, and it was heaven.

With them being out of the country, I decided that I would be much more comfortable in their bed than I would in my sad little single, and it's not like they were in it, so I slept there and it was glorious. If I could fit a super-king bed in my flat – and if I could afford to buy one, obviously – then I would get one in a heartbeat. It was somehow so soft, yet firm enough, and they have some kind of fancy pillows that seem to be made of the same stuff as their mattress. If I weren't scrimping and saving to afford some-where better to live, I'd definitely buy a bed and pillows like this, but in the meantime, I'll just enjoy sleeping in theirs.

Also, and I know this sounds ridiculous for a thirty-something woman to say, but it felt so wonderfully naughty, to be breaking the rules. I got a real kick out of it. In a similar vein, I also got a kick out of drinking from my mum's favourite mug, sitting in my dad's chair, and listening to his records that no one is allowed to touch. I even allowed myself a cheeky five minutes to touch my mum's collection of crystal ornaments – basically, all the things

I've been discouraged from doing my entire life, that I can only do today because no one is here to tell me off for it. To be honest, I'm sure neither of my parents would care about any of these things now that I'm an adult (allegedly), but just let me have this.

One thing I am doing, that I know my mum would be absolutely horrified with, is not keeping the house neat and tidy. Well, seeing as how I'm home alone, I'm leaving dishes in the sink and my clothes on the floor. I will, of course, be tidying all of this up before my mum and dad get home. I'm a rebel, but a low-key rebel, one who eventually cleans up after herself because she doesn't want to get in any actual trouble. Right now, though, the last thing I want to do is spend my days tidying. I've got a job to secure and a party to plan.

I had a lie-in, got up, made myself some breakfast, watched TV for a while and then eventually, by the time midday snuck up on me, I got dressed, ready for my Zoom meeting with Rex at 12.45, except it's 12.49 and I'm not quite connected yet.

'I'm so sorry about this,' I tell him, my phone wedged between my ear and my shoulder, as I faff around with my dad's prehistoric PC.

Rex laughs.

'That's okay,' he tells me. 'Do you want to do this later?'

'No, no, it's okay, I'll sort it,' I insist.

Bloody hell, I don't know what my dad uses this PC for, but it's absolutely riddled with viruses, spyware, random programs, thousands of documents that don't seem to be much more than accidental screenshots or Word files that are so small they must be empty.

His office is the only room in the house that is entirely his – and therefore totally messy. My mum isn't allowed to tidy in here, lest she ruin his system. It's a proper dad office, with dark wood and loads of books. The computer is an old Windows machine that might actually be the one he was using when I was still living here. I don't suppose he uses it for much, but it definitely needs an intense clear-out – even if it's just for his own safety.

'I'd say you were morally obliged to sort it,' Rex tells me.

I don't know what I click to cause it, but a robotic voice starts singing 'You Are My Sunshine', pumping it out through speakers that are set way too loud – probably because my dad listens to everything at an insanely loud volume.

'That's horrifying,' Rex says, sounding audibly alarmed. 'What is that?'

'I have no idea,' I reply.

I notice a small sunflower on the screen. It's popping out of a pot, with a wiggly body, and it's wearing sunglasses on its face, because of course it has a face. Eventually, it stops singing and says hello. A text box pops up underneath it. Then it asks me what it can do for me. The cursor flashes expectantly.

'It's some kind of desktop buddy,' I tell him. 'I haven't seen one of those since the early noughties. I'm pretty sure they were spyware. Oh, my days, there's no way I can use this machine. Even if I could get it to stop running so slowly, I don't think I'd dare log in to anything. My dad's bank account is probably draining as we speak, just because I successfully booted the thing up.'

'Do you want to just use your phone?' Rex replies through a chuckle.

'I think that might be best,' I say. 'I'll download it and see you on there in a minute.'

I sigh. I really, really wanted this to be as formal and professional as possible, something that isn't going to happen if I'm holding up my iPhone like I'm taking a selfie.

I check through all the settings, to make sure everything is working before I go to click the link. There's some kind of setting you can toggle on and off that makes you look a little less tired, so naturally I turn that on. Silly, really, because I was with Rex a matter of days ago. He's knows what level of dark circles I'm working with. I want to make a good impression, though.

'Here she is,' he says cheerily when I join the Zoom.

'Hello,' I say with a theatrical sigh, waving like a dork. 'I made it.'

'I was worried cybercrime cops had burst into your house and taken you away,' he jokes.

'No such luck,' I reply.

Rex is looking good. He doesn't look like he's long out of the shower, his hair is still wet, and I can see the towel on the bed behind him. He isn't in the office, he's in a bedroom. I can't help but wonder whose.

'So, it's a formal job interview then, is it?' I tease.

'It's no fun, being cooped up all alone in a hotel,' he points out. 'I'm taking a lot of showers.'

I raise my eyebrows.

'Erm, not like that,' he insists.

Rex laughs. He looks so good when he laughs.

'The showers are a nice break from the limited TV channels,' he tells me. 'It's also blumming freezing up north.'

He says the second part of his sentence in your typical American-doing-a-'British'-accent. He couldn't sound more Dick Van Dyke if he tried.

'It really is,' I reply. 'At least you're inland. It's always seriously cold on the island at this time of year. I would have thought you'd be in a nicer hotel. A sleek, city-centre bachelor pad.'

'Oh, no, this place isn't remotely cool,' he replies.

Rex angles his laptop around to the left, then the right, to show me around his room. It's really not a swanky room at all, far from it. It's quite small, plain – but not in a cool, minimalist way – and everything looks quite basic.

'You know what's going on, don't you?' Rex says.

'What?' I reply.

'The request for a room goes to Frances, back at the office, but ultimately it's Tom who signs it off,' Rex explains. 'I think he's told her to book me in somewhere crappy, and now I'm stuck here.'

'No! Tom wouldn't do that... would he?' I reply.

My first thought is that he wouldn't but, then again, he did demote me ultimately because he cheated on me.

'He seemed quite jealous at the party,' Rex points out. 'Perhaps he wants you back.'

'Ha!' is about the only thing I can get out in response to that. 'Unlikely. Perhaps Frances doesn't like you – she doesn't like anyone. The second-best thing about getting the new job would be writing my resignation letter and sending it to her. Except she's such a cow, she'd probably just correct my grammar and send it back to me. Do you know what she did? One time, when I signed someone's leaving card, she pointed out some absolutely minor error in something I'd written, I'd missed a comma or something – I wrote it in a hurry and, also, it was a leaving card for someone I'd never even spoken to. Frances said, in front of everyone in the break room, that "being northern" the only grammar I knew was married to my grandad.'

'Wow, you're right, she is a cow,' he replies.

'All the more reason to give me a job,' I say hopefully. 'Also, I *do* know my grammar from my grandma, even if they do sound quite similar when I say them out loud.'

'Cute,' Rex replies. 'Hey, where are you?'

'I'm in my dad's office,' I say, leaning out of the way, so that Rex can see the overflowing bookshelves behind me.

'Can I get a tour of your house?' he asks curiously. 'Are your folks home?'

'They're out,' I reply, which isn't untrue. 'You want a tour of my house?'

'Yeah,' he replies with a cheeky smile. 'Start with your old room. Have your parents turned it into a gym yet?'

'Not yet,' I say with a laugh as I pull myself to my feet. 'Is that what yours have done? That said, I've seen your street from above, they probably have an actual gym.'

'My old room is like this freaky sort of shrine to me,' Rex says. 'My mom won't let my dad touch it. If I go there on vacation, she makes my bed, I can sleep in there, I'm allowed to interact with my things. If I wanted to take something with me when I left, I'm pretty sure she would let me, but she likes the room to stay pretty much as is. That's kinda messed up, isn't it?'

'Erm, you know what...' I say through an almost manic laugh.

I flip the camera on my phone, so that Rex can see where I'm looking, instead of me. I open my bedroom door and show him inside.

'My mum has a weird sort of me shrine too,' I reply, which makes sense to him, but is the kind of sentence that would make old Frances spontaneously combust.

'Zoom in on that wall, let me see your photos,' he insists excitedly.

I dutifully move my phone up to the wall, panning from side to side, so he can see all my photos.

'I wasn't cool either,' he teases. 'Don't worry.'

'Charming,' I reply. 'I was cool then. Maybe. I was trying to be, at least.'

'I was the same,' he replies.

'Were you a jock?' I ask, only semi-seriously.

'No, far from it,' he replies. 'I was a dork. I didn't have many friends, girls wouldn't talk to me.'

'What?' I squeak.

'Oh, yeah,' he says, with a fascinating confidence, considering what he's saying. 'Everyone used to pick on me, because I was short. My growth spurt came real late. If I'm being honest – and if you can't be honest with your ex-fake girlfriend, then who can you be honest with? – it's really shaped who I am. I have zero time for girls like that.'

'Erm, that's sort of your type,' I point out.

'Okay, I don't have much time for girls like that,' he corrects himself. 'Look at Madeline. The more I saw of her, the less I liked. It did me good, to get rejected by her – or what is it you say here, pied?'

'Only people on *Love Island* say pied,' I correct him quickly, hoping he'll get straight back to what he was saying. It's nice to see a more vulnerable side to him.

'Having that bonus time, to see more of her, more than just the way she looked, showed me the kind of girl she was,' he explains. 'She didn't give a damn that I was with you. I thought maybe we would fake break up and then that would open the door to something happening between me and her, but she was ready for it, at the party, even though you were only across the room.'

'Grim,' I say, pulling a face. 'You need to stop going for the hot girls.'

'Where's the fun in that?' he says with a smile.

'I was bullied at school too,' I confess. 'I wasn't short, though, I was too tall, and a bit fat. Kids are absolutely vile, when I think back, and remember how horrible everyone was. There was one boy who bullied me, he was the worst of them all, and it wasn't just mean words. He would jab me with a compass, spit on my blazer – really awful stuff. My head of year said he was just the class clown and that I needed to toughen up.'

'I wonder what a kid like that is doing with his life now,' Rex muses.

'Time,' I reply. 'Last I heard, he was in prison. But don't get me started about how rubbish some teachers can be.'

'I hear you,' Rex says. 'I always felt sorta invisible at school, as far as the teachers were concerned, because I was quiet and a dork, I just blended into the background.'

'Right? It's like, if you're not a super genius, or incredibly naughty – and certainly if you're quiet – it's almost as though you're not there.'

'That's totally it,' Rex replies. 'Huh, who knew we would have such an awful shared experience?'

'It's character-building,' I insist with a smile. 'We turned out okay.'

'I guess we did,' he agrees. 'Can I see the rest of your house?'

'Really?' I ask in disbelief.

'Yeah, I wanna see where you grew up,' he replies.

'Is this important for the job?' I ask, raising my eyebrow.

'Sure, why not?' he says through a playful grin.

'Okay, fine,' I say as I head downstairs.

To be honest, I don't mind, I'm really enjoying chatting with him. Is it odd that I miss him?

'This is the lounge,' I announce, panning around the room.

'I like that fire,' he says. 'It looks super quaint and cosy.'

'Yeah, it's really nice,' I say. It's good to see things through someone else's eyes sometimes, to remind you of just how great it is. 'This is the kitchen, those are the doors to the garden.'

'Can I see your yard?' he asks curiously. 'Does it look good in the snow?'

'Are you always so nosy?' I ask him.

'How much snow do you think we get in Malibu?' he asks. 'I'm still fascinated by it. Even if it is holding me hostage for the holidays.'

'It does look pretty beautiful,' I say as I show him. 'It's hard to see much, given how much snow there is, but you can see my tree house.'

'I had a tree house *just like that*,' Rex tells me. 'My dad even ran power to it, so I could play PlayStation in mine.'

'Okay, well I'm just like a rubbish version of you in so many ways, because mine wasn't even weather sealed,' I tell him. 'But I did spend so many happy summers in there. I kind of like that it's still here.'

I only let myself get lost in my thoughts for a second before I try to get things back on track.

'So, the job...'

'Right, yes.' Rex claps his hands together. 'I'm just waiting on confirmation of something.'

'Is it good news or bad news?' I ask nervously.

'It could go either way,' he admits. 'I'm seeing if I can sort something out.'

'Oh, okay,' I say. 'Well, I've got plans today anyway, so do you want to drop me a message when you want to talk again?'

'Sure,' he replies. 'What are you getting up to today then?'

'I'm just going up the road to my friend's house, for a catch-up,' I tell him.

'Is this the famous Ben?' he asks me. 'Ex-boyfriend Ben?'

'Yes,' I reply, a little overenthusiastically. I'm going to have to stick with that angle now.

'Okay, I'll let you go,' Rex says. 'I'll go watch some more TV and have another shower. Perhaps I'll download Matcher, see if anyone else is lonely this Christmas.'

He smiles, as though he's joking... maybe. I wish I could tell him the truth, that I'm all alone for Christmas, but I'm so deep in the lies now, and it's not like he can get back here to hang out with me now anyway. What a fun Christmas that would be, though, hanging out with Rex, chatting, playing games...

Nope, I can't think like that, I can't let myself think about him in any capacity other than work. He's talking about dating apps, for crying out loud. Whether he's joking or not, it shows where his head is at.

I just need to stop looking at him. Stop thinking about him. Stop noticing how attractive he is, how much we have in common, how he makes me feel. Blah, I'm doing it again.

I haven't had a proper unrequited crush on someone since, well, since Ben. So that's what I need to focus on, until I hear from Rex again about the job.

Easier said than done, though, right?

18

Standing on Ben's doorstep takes me right back to when I was a kid, knocking to see if Eleanor was there, but secretly hoping that it would be Ben who opened the door. I can feel those same nervous butterflies going crazy inside my stomach today.

It's not quite dark yet, so Gerry's Christmas lights aren't turned on. If he takes his lights as seriously as my dad does, which I'm almost certain he does, then I imagine he'll have his lights on a timer too, ensuring that they always come on as soon as it gets dark – God forbid they miss a second of night-time without their lights shining brightly. Gerry's Christmas lights might not be switched on yet, but the large snowman ornament on their front lawn is impossible to miss. It's just your classic depiction of a snowman, nothing too wild, but it's taller than I am – it's really quite creepy, with its piercing black coal-shaped eyes and its twisted twig mouth. I don't like it. I don't like it *at all*.

Today it is positively freezing outside. No snow has fallen but there's still plenty of it left on the ground, so I'm all wrapped up in my long coat, my Ugg boots, and a scarf so big it might technically be a blanket. I've only just taken my gloves off, to knock on the door at Ben's parents' house, and already I can feel the cold creeping up into my sleeves. I'm definitely more suited to living somewhere warm, like the Caribbean, I'm sure, but I'm still more than happy to move back to the cold north. I really hope Rex can make this work for me.

I place my gloves in my handbag while I wait for someone to answer the door. I wish I'd touched up my lipstick before I knocked, then again, it isn't that long since I put it on, it took me a literal minute to walk here. I don't know why I feel so nervous.

Eventually, Ben answers the door. I can't hide my smile.

'Hello, Dani,' he says. 'Come in, come in.'

'Oh, wow, I love what your mum has done with the decorations,' I tell him.

Just like in my parents' house, Ben's dad handles the decorations outside but inside is all his mum. Not dissimilar to my mum's efforts, their large banister is wrapped in a Christmas garland. Ben's mum, however, has attached Christmas cards to hers, leaving a trail of them all the way up the stairs. My mum would never do this because she has a Christmas-tree-shaped frame, custom-made, for attaching greetings cards to so that they look like a Christmas tree. It's absolutely gorgeous and seriously cool but, unless you live in a village where everyone knows everyone, you might worry about not getting enough cards to make up all the branches. I can safely say that I would maybe just about cover the top of the tree, and that would be it.

'I'll be sure to tell her you said so,' Ben replies. 'She's taken my grandma Christmas shopping today, and Eleanor has taken my dad to get something for my mum – I know, it's all seriously last minute – so it's just us. I am the only one who hasn't left his Christmas shopping until last minute, but I didn't know that you'd be here, so I figured the least I could do would be to pop out this morning and get you something nice to have while we catch up. I went to the Christmas shop and got a few of their hot chocolate sticks, and a bunch of Ivy's home-made cookies. She's really killing it there, especially since the renovations.'

'Aww, Ben, that all sounds delicious,' I reply as he takes my coat. 'And it's so nice to see Ivy doing so well, that shop always meant so much to her. I'm surprised she expanded, to be honest, I would have imagined she felt too emotionally attached to the old place, seeing as though it was her mum's.'

'Well, there's a story there,' Ben says. 'But first, what flavour hot chocolate would you like: peppermint, orange or gingerbread?'

'Oh, orange, definitely. Thank you.'

I absolutely love an orange hot chocolate, but I only really drink them around Christmastime for some reason. I suppose it makes them seem all the more special.

Ben empties bags of various flavours of Christmas cookies onto a plate before showing me into the living room to sit down.

Just like in my parents' house, Ben's parents' décor has stayed frozen in time, encapsulating an era. It doesn't seem old-fashioned, though, just like it doesn't at my parents' house, it just seems warm and homely, and I feel so comforted by it.

Ben opens the door to the log burner and adds a couple more logs before sitting down on the sofa next to me.

'I think Ivy was having money troubles,' Ben starts, telling me the story he hyped about the Christmas shop. 'When they built that new road into the village, people stopped driving past her shop and, well, a Christmas shop that is open all year isn't exactly going to be booming with local trade, is it? Not without the tourists who used to make up most of the custom.'

'That's very true,' I reply. 'So, I guess she didn't have much choice?'

'She was trying her best,' he continues. 'Until her landlord sold the place from under her. It was horrible, she did everything she could to save the business, to raise the money to buy it herself. But in the end, she was offered a unit in the building that replaced it – it was the man who bought the place that set her up with it. She's married to him now. She really does seem so happy, though.'

'Well, that's all that matters, isn't it?' I reply. 'And she's working her dream job. You can't really ask for more than that.'

'Like you, you work for a magazine, right?' Ben says. 'Just like you planned.'

'Huh? How did you know that?' I ask curiously.

'I've been Facebook stalking you for years, even though we're not friends on there,' he says with a straight face, which almost immediately dissolves into laughter. 'I'm kidding, I found your work ID at the farm shop, didn't I? I couldn't help but notice, when I picked it up.'

'Oh, right. Yep, I work for a magazine. It's not exactly the position I want to be in but I'm working on bagging a new position, in a different branch of the company.'

'What position are you in at the moment?' he asks curiously.

I've lied so many times about so much. Perhaps it's time to be a bit more honest.

'I've just been sort of demoted,' I admit. 'My boyfriend and I were always vying for the same roles and now he's at the top and I'm at the bottom, somehow.'

'Your boyfriend?' he repeats back to me.

Oh, God, as if this wasn't embarrassing enough, I've found a way to make it worse. Perhaps I should stick with lying, it's messier but it's easier for sure.

'My *ex*-boyfriend,' I correct myself.

'Oh, I'm sorry,' he says.

'It's fine,' I reply. 'It was a little while ago now.'

'Well, it sounds like you're better off without the guy,' Ben says with a frown as he reaches for another biscuit. He grabs the plate to offer me one.

'I am. And I know I'd be much happier if I didn't have to work with him, but hopefully that won't be a problem for much longer,' I say. 'The new job would be in Leeds, so I'll be much closer to home, I'll be able to see my parents more, I really hope it pans out.'

I really hope I haven't jinxed it by saying that.

'That's great,' Ben replies. 'You could move back here and commute, maybe.'

'That's true, although I don't really feel like I have a life here any more,' I say. 'It seems like everything and everyone has changed so much. If I'm starting from scratch, I suppose I can do that anywhere.'

Of course, I know that my life in London is pretty non-existent now anyway, so that won't be a big deal, and while I do have my parents here, I'm not sure I could go back to living on the island. Near it, but not on it.

'I think a new beginning sounds quite nice,' he says. 'But I suppose it's easy for me to say you should move back here. I've never lived anywhere else.'

It's nice that he's so interested. I'm not exactly used to it – before my interactions with Rex, Tom was probably the last male person I had multiple, proper conversations with. Wow, finally saying that to myself in my head really emphasises how tragic it is.

I consider Ben's words for a moment. Is he just talking about the idea of my moving back here, or is he encouraging it? Teenage Dani is doing an excitable little dance in the back on my mind, in my memories somewhere. To be honest, present-day

Dani kind of likes it too. It just feels good to be thought of, I suppose.

'Tell me about you,' I suggest, changing the subject. Now isn't the time to get lost in my own head, trying to decode every little detail.

'Erm, there's not too much to tell, unfortunately,' he replies. 'I'm a carpenter. Not all that exciting. I do have my own workshop, though, in my garage. I make bespoke furniture. Fancy stuff that I sell mostly online. People like to think of their furniture being lovingly crafted by some local on a cute little island – I suppose it gives a bed more character, if it has a story to go with it. Rather than just being the same mass-produced chunk of flatpack that everyone else has.'

'That sounds amazing,' I reply sincerely.

'I'll show you some of my work while you're here,' he says. 'See if I can convince you to buy a piece for when you move back home.'

He says this with a cheeky wink, as though he's joking, but also not joking.

'It would be an honour to sleep in one of your beds,' I reply. Then I consider my words and laugh awkwardly. 'I mean...'

'It's okay, I know what you mean,' Ben says with a laugh.

'This is why I used to love baking,' I say, getting the conversation back on track. 'I miss making things that make people happy.'

'Well, I maintain that you should do what makes you happy,' he says. 'Or at least do whatever it's going to take to help you get there. I know Ivy is looking for someone at the shop, Eleanor was telling me about it, she said she'd go for it if she could bake. We've got to do what keeps food on the table, though. I'm still hanging doors during the day, doing what I need to do to pay my bills until my furniture company properly takes off.'

'So, you're still living here on the island then?' I ask. 'You haven't been tempted by the convenience of the mainland?'

'Yep, still here,' he says. 'I've got my workshop, and my house was a bit of a fixer-upper when I bought it, so I'm constantly working on that in my free time. By the time I've finished each room, I'll be ready to start work on redecorating the first one again, I reckon. It will all look dated soon enough.'

I laugh. I suddenly can't help but wonder if he lives alone, but I don't want to ask because he'll wonder why I'm asking... why am I asking? It may feel like I still have a crush on him, but that's just lingering old feelings, right? As an adult, I hardly know him. I know that he still spends Christmas with his family, that he has his head screwed on right, that he's working hard doing his dream job, and that he's been so lovely to me since we bumped into each other... God, perhaps I do still have a crush on him.

'I live on my own,' he eventually says without me having to ask. 'It's nice being here for Christmas, though, being around family. Mum still insists we all stay under the same roof for the festive period. It just wouldn't feel right being home alone.'

'I totally get that,' I reply – and, my God, I really do get that. 'I'm single all the way this Christmas.'

Ben laughs.

If he knew I were spending Christmas alone, he'd know just how funny that joke really was.

'Hey, there's nothing wrong with being single,' he replies. 'All the best people hold out for the right person. I've never seen the point in dating for the sake of it. A few of my mates use Matcher and I'll never understand why. They tell me stories about their dates and it all sounds so terrifying. I'd rather be alone and wait for something real. Yes, I know how sad that makes me sound. It's not very manly of me, is it?'

Ben laughs awkwardly. It isn't as though he's ashamed of

saying something that makes him seem vulnerable, more that he's just nervous now he's said it, like he's pulled the pin on a grenade, revealing something true that might not be well-received, or might make him look weird.

I can't help but think about Rex, and all the girls I've seen him flirt with, all the dates I've heard he's been on. I imagine more guys are like Rex than Ben. It's nice to talk to a bloke who doesn't feel like he always has to have a girl on the go to be a manly man, whatever that is.

'I totally agree with you,' I reply, quick to put him at his ease. 'I feel the same way – or at least that's what I tell myself, and anyone else who asks why I'm *still single*.'

I say those words in a silly voice. Ben laughs.

We chat for way over an hour, about the past, the present, the future, and it's so lovely. Ben somehow seems no different, but at the same time, it's like he's grown into this amazing man. I smile so much, my face hurts. Everything is absolutely perfect until Eleanor and Gerry arrive home from doing their Christmas shopping.

'Oh, hello, Dani,' Eleanor says as she places her bags down on the living room floor.

'Hi,' I reply.

'Hello,' Gerry says through huffs and puffs. 'Christ, it's absolutely Baltic out there. You all right, Dani, love?'

'I'm great, thanks, how are you?' I ask politely.

'Yeah, can't complain,' he replies. 'Ay, I see you got your dad's lights back on.'

There's a smirk on Gerry's face that he just can't seem to hide. It's like he knows that I know that he sabotaged the lights, even when there was a truce, and it winds me up way more than I ever would have expected it to.

'I did,' I reply, my poker face firmly in place.

'Not that you'd notice, hey? Not with my lights on. My lights are always much better than your dad's, it has to be said.'

'Hmm,' I reply, still not rising to it.

'He thinks he can compete with my dad, with our snowman, with that pathetic little sleigh,' Eleanor chimes in with a cackle.

God, those two really are so alike.

'All right, guys, they're just Christmas lights,' Ben says, clearly a little uncomfortable with the over-the-top competition too.

'I'm just saying, I wouldn't be surprised if that was the reason he went on holiday, so he didn't have to compete with me, so he didn't have to live with having the lesser display,' Gerry theorises.

'Ooh, maybe,' Eleanor agrees. 'You know what, Dad, I think you might be right. I think Dani thinks it too, ooh, look, she's blushing.'

'Yeah, anyway, I'm going to get going,' I say, jumping up so quickly I actually go a little dizzy.

'You're going?' Ben says, standing up after me.

'Yeah, I've got party planning to do,' I reply as I head into the hallway.

'Oh, Ben told me I'm invited too,' Eleanor calls after us. 'So, I'll see you then. Any dress code, anything you need me to bring?'

What I need is for her to not come – even if there was a party, I wouldn't want her there, but there absolutely isn't a party and I'm not sure what the hell I'm going to do about it. I mean, I could actually throw a party, but who would I invite? I know less than ten people and that's if I include my weird neighbour Dennis, his creepy son, his ex-wife, and her new husband, and that doesn't sound like any party I want to attend.

'Nope, no need to bring anything, just yourselves,' I say as I head for the door.

Ben chases after me, catching me in the doorway.

'Sorry, I'll never understand why they take the lights so seriously,' he says with an awkward laugh. 'Fancy making a dinner date for tomorrow evening?'

Okay, I wasn't expecting him to say that.

'Oh, erm... Yeah, okay. I'd love to.'

'Great,' he says.

He grabs the notepad from next to the telephone and writes his number on it before handing it to me.

'We'll make a plan. And I can always come over early, on Christmas Eve, and help you with party prep,' he offers.

I try not to let my smile fall, because that would be great if there was actually a party going on.

'That's very sweet of you, thank you,' I reply.

'Do you want me to walk you home?' he offers. 'I'll just grab my coat.'

'Ben,' Eleanor calls out from the living room. 'Ben! Come help.'

'Oh, no, you go help your sister,' I tell him. 'I can see myself out.'

'Okay, well, see you tomorrow.'

'Yeah, see you tomorrow,' I tell him.

For a second, it feels like we might hug, but we don't. Perhaps we weren't going to at all, it's probably just wishful thinking on my part.

I step out onto the doorstep, closing the door behind me. It's only a short walk down the street back to my parents' house but it's snowing thick and fast now, and I don't want to get too cold or wet, so I take my black hooded scarf from my bag and put it on.

I stop on the drive and take a moment to look back at Gerry's Christmas lights. There is no way his display is as good as my dad's display. Not a chance. God, and he and Eleanor are *so* smug and sure about it too, and it's *so* annoying.

Gerry's lights are kind of tacky. There are too many different types in play – too many colours, too many shapes, too many flashing patterns. It's like a fairground, full on and dizzying. My dad's display is like a delicate walk through a winter wonderland. Absolutely beautiful. And the more I think about it, the more I begin to care about the competition too. Wow, I actually care about my dad's lights. I want him to have the best display. Worst of all – and most surprisingly – I want to get revenge on Gerry, for not respecting the truce. I'm not usually a revenge-y person, at least I didn't think I was, until I look over at Gerry's garage door and realise he hasn't closed it yet.

I skulk over and peep inside, securing my hood around my face, just in case anyone happens to be peeping. Perhaps they'll just think I'm Eleanor, if they can't see me properly.

Just inside the doorway, I can see a multi-plug, with lots of timer plugs sticking out of it. So, this must be where Gerry's lights are plugged in, and these must be the timers for the lot of them. Each plug has a little dial with numbers on it. I can tell from each timer what time the lights come on and go off. I wonder, if I were to mess with the timers, make them all come on and go off at different times, if that might make up for his bulb-stealing trick? I wonder if I should do it... I mean, it's far easier for Gerry to put this right than it was for me, he only needs to correct his timers. I had to go out and buy bloody bulbs.

I shift my weight between my feet for a few more seconds while I figure out what to do and... I'm going to do it. I'm doing it! I leave one timer as it is, and mess up the others in varying directions, to make sure that there are never too many sets of lights on at the same time. If Gerry suspects foul play, he'll know it was me, and he'll probably think that I've removed bulbs, just like he did, but at least I'll have him chasing his tail for a bit before he figures out what has happened.

Pretty satisfied with myself, I slink out into the garden, which is much darker now that most of the lights are out. The only light I have left on is the one inside the massive snowman. The thing Eleanor is the proudest of. The thing she thinks is nicer to look at than my dad's sleigh... Pah!

I rummage around in my handbag to see what's in there – I want something to take the smile off that bloody snowman's face. My hand touches various items before it lands on the one I need. A chunky black kohl eyeliner.

I tap the lid on my lip thoughtfully as I eyeball the snowman. I can feel a massive grin on my face as I look around in the darkness, making sure no one can see me.

I know it's immature, but it makes me feel so much better, to reach up and draw the biggest pair of cartoon boobs I can on its chest. I'm not usually one for immature pranks, but this looks hilarious, and I know that my dad would be proud of me. My mum would be horrified, though. Hey, at least it will just wipe straight off. I wouldn't be surprised if the snow washes it off overnight before anyone gets the chance to see it anyway, but I'm still happy with what I've done. My dad would love this if he was here.

I pop my eyeliner back in my bags and rummage around for my keys as I walk down the dark, slushy driveway. As I pull out my gloves, my keys get caught on them and land in the snow on the pavement below me.

I carefully crouch down to pick them up.

'Freeze,' I hear a man's voice say.

I look up and see DC Dean Gardner looking down at me.

'You *again*,' he says, as soon as he realises it's me.

'Me again,' I say with a smile. 'Hello.'

'We had a report of an individual in a black hooded cloak, creeping around on someone's property.'

'Is this really the calibre of crime they have *detective sergeants* dealing with in Marram Bay?' I ask, changing the subject.

'I live here,' he reminds me. 'I'm the closest person to check out ongoing crimes – which are few and far between usually. Funny, since you've been in town, I've been called out twice.'

'I'm just heading home,' I tell him. 'I dropped my keys.'

I pick them out of the snow and pull myself back to my feet.

'So, you haven't seen any suspicious individuals?' he asks me.

I shake my head.

I watch as Dean's line of sight moves from me to the snow-man. He shines his torch on it.

'What about that snowman?' he asks me.

I look back at it.

'I think it's a snow woman,' I correct him, completely straight-faced. 'And I haven't noticed her doing anything suspicious.'

Dean smiles.

'It wasn't a snow woman two days ago,' he says. 'This is nothing to do with this rivalry I keep hearing about, is it?'

'Huh,' I reply innocently. 'No, it was like that when I got here. And anyway, my dad is on holiday.'

'Okay,' Dean says, nodding thoughtfully, still smiling. 'Well, I'll be off.'

'Do you want to come to my Christmas party?' I call after him.

'What?' he asks.

'I'm having a Christmas party and I think I owe you a drink.'

'Erm... I have a girlfriend, sorry,' he tells me awkwardly.

'Oh, God, no, not like that,' I babble. I feel like all I've done is babble since I arrived here. 'I'm having a proper party, with lots of people. I'm inviting everyone.'

'Are you really?' he asks.

'Yep,' I say. I guess I am now. Well, if people think there is going to be a party, then what other choice do I have? I'll just invite as many people as I can and hope that enough people turn up for it to not be completely tragic. 'Christmas Eve, at my parents' house. Your girlfriend can come too. See you there?'

'Erm, yeah, maybe,' he says. 'My girlfriend is helping out at her parents' B & B in the busy season so she might be working. We'll see. In the meantime, keep out of trouble.'

'Oh, I will, see you later,' I call after him as he heads back to his car.

Wow, I hadn't even noticed his car pull up down the street. Some master criminal I am.

Well, I guess that's it. I am having a party. And I only have one day to organise it all. Fantastic. I can't see this plan backfiring *at all*...

19

Hmm, what beige food to eat for dinner tonight, I wonder?

It's funny, when you're younger, the idea of having your parents' house to yourself, being able to do whatever you want and eat whatever you want sounds like an absolute dream. In reality, it's not all it's cracked up to be. Aside from the loneliness and the boredom, I'm pretty much sick of eating junk food, and although eating popcorn while I watched a movie in Mum and Dad's bed seemed like a fun act of rebellion last night, I'm still finding sharp bits in it today. I'm going to need to do one hell of a clean-up operation before my parents get home, that's for sure.

I pour a small bag of chicken nuggets into my parents' air fryer – oh, to have room for one of these incredible devices. I've used it a few times now since I arrived, and I swear I love it so much I'm just looking for things to cook in it. They've even got one of those super-fancy ones, with two compartments, so I can cook some French fries at the same time, to create myself a sort of homemade McDonald's. I sure know how to live it up – and I'm making the most of it, before it's back to business as usual when I finally go home.

With dinner basically cooking itself, I pour myself a glass of wine and take a seat at the kitchen island. I used to love sitting at the breakfast bar, at Tom's place, while dinner was cooking, or to eat my breakfast on a morning. There was this contrasting combination of feeling like I was such a grown-up, sophisticated lady, but at the same time there was always something about it that brought me back to here, to my childhood, sitting on these exact same stools while Mum cooked dinner and Dad hovered behind her, pinching bits of food. I'll never forget the time Mum was making stew, and my dad mistakenly picked up the lid of the cooking oil, thinking it was a piece of sliced carrot, and popped it in his mouth. My mum whacked him on the back – not because he was choking, but because the second he realised his mistake he spat it out, sending the lid flying across the kitchen, landing on the island right in front of me. Dad and I thought it was hilarious. So did Mum, eventually. Looking back, remembering the good times, makes me feel even worse about life going back to normal after Christmas. I've been looking at my situation as a sort of temporary state but, if I'm being honest, it's only temporary in the same way that anything is until you change it, but unless I actually make the moves to make a difference, it very much is my normal life. I know I sound like a broken record, but I *need* this Leeds job.

My phone vibrates on the countertop in front of me. It's a message from Rex.

Quick Zoom?

It's funny how we've managed to maintain the level of closeness we formed in London, even over Zoom. It almost feels as though we're in a long-distance relationship – or at least it would, if things between us weren't so one-sided. The biggest distance between us of all has to be that I'm into him, whereas he just sees me as a friend. It's a step up from being an invisible colleague, at least.

I punch a quick reply to Rex, telling him that I'm free to talk, before I fire up the app. As I wait for his link to come through, I dash to the downstairs loo and check myself over in the mirror quickly. I was eating cheese puffs about half an hour ago and I still feel like I'm covered in orange stuff. I know, I know, it's unfathomable how sexy I am. How is Rex resisting me?

Certain that I'm clean, I head back to the kitchen and join the call. I can see myself, smiling like a maniac when he answers, because I always am so pleased to see him. It's funny, until we got to know each other, his presence alone used to anger me. I'd feel better on the days when he wasn't working, or was working out of the office and, honestly, I think it's just because it used to mess with my self-confidence, feeling like he didn't see me when I was there. I suppose, deep down, I've never quite been able to deny having the most basic kind of attraction towards him, so I begrudged the way he made me feel – and I somehow let him make me feel that way by him doing nothing, which, looking back, doesn't make a ton of sense. It sounds kind of crazy, when I think about it like that.

Of course, now that I have his attention, it almost feels worse. I hated having a sexual attraction towards a man who I thought was nothing more than a dirtbag. Now I've got to know him, seeing all sides of him, I've enjoyed spending time with him and felt just how caring and comforting he can be, and somehow this feels even worse. Now I want all of him. Of course, I am over-looking certain things, but don't we always when we develop such strong feelings for someone? Aside from the fact that Rex clearly has no interest in me as anything more than a friend, I must be out of my mind to even be fantasising about a relationship with him, because I've seen him date a lot of girls, but I don't think I've ever seen him with the same girl twice. What is it about us that makes us think we can change men, trying to shape them into what we want them to be, just because we wish we could?

My smile drops when I notice the look on his face. It's subtle, but there's something muted about his smile. Something lurking behind his eyes. Ah, shit. It's the job. He's going to tell me that there's a problem or, worse, that I can't have it full stop. I need to get ahead of this, make it seem like I'm fine and calm and professional and, well, all of the other things I absolutely am not right now.

'Look, I knew this was going to happen,' I tell him as sincerely as I can, really hoping that I'm wrong in reacting to the worst-case scenario. 'It's fine.'

'Really?' he replies in disbelief. 'I guess I thought you would be more upset about it – obviously, I'm pleased that you aren't.'

I bat my hand. It's getting harder to hide it with each second that goes by.

'I know you're over him, but still,' Rex continues.

My eyes widen. What on earth does that even mean?

'Wait, what?' I blurt. 'What are you talking about?'

'What are *you* talking about?' he replies, confused.

I furrow my brow as I search his expression for an explanation, anything to tip me off to what the hell is going on because I feel so stupid.

Now Rex looks as confused as I feel.

'I thought this was about the job,' I say, without a hint of confidence. 'The Leeds job.'

I throw in unnecessary information, for clarity, even though there are no other jobs I could possibly be talking about.

I watch Rex's face fall. He looks sick.

'Oh, my God, Dani, I'm so sorry,' he says quickly. He looks as though he truly means it, but what is he sorry for?

'Okay, you need to tell me what's going on,' I insist. 'What am I missing here?'

'I assumed you would have found out by now,' he replies. 'It's Tom. He's engaged.'

My heart sinks. I feel like I've just been slapped across the face. Tom is engaged? Already? After so little time? Even with the overlap, it's been little more than six months.

'How do you know?' I ask. I don't know why I ask. It hardly matters, does it?

'They sent out a company notification, announcing the *good news*,' he says, going extra sarcastic on the last couple of words. 'It's also all over Tom's socials.'

'One minute,' I tell him, swiping Zoom away, opening up Instagram instead. I click in the search box and start typing Tom's name, but nothing comes up. Well, my Tom (for lack of a better way of describing him) doesn't come up – *the* Tom Jones comes up, but I doubt Sir Tom can shed much light on the situation. I type his username, to make sure, but no user is found. I go back to Rex.

'Oh, my God, he's blocked me,' I blurt. '*He's* blocked *me*. And I didn't get the email, so I've been left out of that too.'

'I'm so sorry you had to find out this way,' Rex insists. 'I would have found a much better way to tell you if I'd thought for a second that you might not know yet.'

'I don't think there's any positive way to find out your ex has got engaged to the person he dumped you for pretty much right away,' I reply. 'Even if I am over the cheating bastard. It just feels shit, to know that he *does* want to get married, but that he just never wanted to marry me. And the fact he cheated on me makes it so much worse. I was a placeholder. Someone to amuse him, share his bed, cook him meals – but only until the real deal came along. The younger, prettier, more intelligent real deal.'

'Let me start by saying that, just because Mia is studying to be a doctor, it doesn't mean she's more intelligent than you,' Rex insists. 'I had a chat with her about holidays and she thinks the Bahamas are part of the US. And one time, I saw her eat the paper case around a mini cheese soufflé at a party. Anyone can be studying to be anything – it doesn't make them smarter than anyone else. Also, you're way hotter than her. You're no one's placeholder, Dani. Don't ever think that.'

'She ate a paper case?' I ask through a slight smile, playfully implying that's my only takeaway from everything Rex just said. To be honest, I'm floored by his compliments. It's taking every bit of control I have over my body to not let myself blush and giggle and go all googly-eyed.

'She did,' he replies, clearly relieved to see me smiling again. 'And do you know what else? I let her. I didn't stop her. She had two before she decided they were "too dry".'

'Thanks,' I reply, keeping the smile on my face, even if it's taking every facial muscle I have right now.

'Listen, Dani, don't let it get to you, okay?' Rex continues. 'Tom is an asshole. And Mia, well, she's marrying someone who she stole from someone else. She might feel good about that now, but eventually she's going to realise she needs to live her whole life looking over her shoulder. She'll always wonder, now she isn't the other woman any more, whether Tom will be in the market for a new one. And he will. Cheaters rarely call it a day – especially if they feel like they come out on top.'

'That's an excellent point,' I reply.

'You're too good for him, Dani,' Rex says simply. 'He had a great thing with you, and he blew it. He's the one who should be upset, not you. And who knows? Maybe that's why he's done it, to make himself feel like it was all for something.'

'You're right,' I reply confidently. 'I don't care. I don't need him – I definitely don't want him. He can't upset me ever again. I'm above this, I'm a grown woman.'

The air fryer beeps.

'Sorry, that's just my dinner,' I explain, jumping up to silence it.

'That's okay,' Rex says. 'What are you having?'

'Chicken nuggets,' I admit – so perhaps not that much of a grown woman after all.

'Go, enjoy your dinner,' he insists. 'And don't waste another second thinking about that guy. I'll check in on you later, yeah?'

'That would be great, thank you,' I say with a smile – one that feels so easy again.

God, he really is something, isn't he? If I had found out about Tom any other way, I probably would have been upset and angry and I absolutely would have taken it out on myself, mentally, using it as an opportunity to wonder what was wrong with me, rather than considering what could be wrong with Tom and Mia.

Rex knew just what to say and exactly how to make me listen. He's really outdone himself and, yet again, somehow seems even more attractive to me.

I'm starting to wonder what I'll do when he isn't around any more. Well, we can't keep up the Zoom-pals thing forever, can we? This is just because of the snow. Even if I do get the job in Leeds, Rex will be going back to London, and if I don't, well, I'm being pushed out of the London office anyway. It's only a matter of time.

I can't believe he's been right here, under my nose, this whole time. I never would have guessed just how much I would miss him, but I can definitely feel it now.

Is it strange that I care about my fake break-up with Rex far more than I do about my real one with Tom now? It is, isn't it? Well, I need to snap out of that, ASAP, because once Christmas is over, that will be it. Suddenly it's hard to imagine a happy life without him in it, though.

20

It's the evenings on my own that are the longest, loneliest part of my day.

And you know what time alone means, right? Oh, yeah! Time to overthink.

Tonight, I'm taking a break from wondering about whether or not I'm going to get the Leeds job, and whether or not Rex is really alone in his hotel. Tonight, I'm overanalysing Ben's choice of words.

Making a dinner date – what the hell does that mean?

I know what dinner is. I know what a date is. I know that making a date is different again. Asking someone if they fancy making a dinner date is a confusing mix of all of the above.

What's more confusing than what this dinner date is, is thinking about what I want it to be. Do I want it to be a date-date? Do I want it to be old mates catching up? Obviously, I'm taking all the company I can get at the moment, but that doesn't have to be romantic, does it?

It's funny, considering this now, because I had a crush on Ben for years. For Dani at so many different ages, this is her dream come true.

For present-day Dani, annoyingly, I can't stop thinking about Rex. I flit between missing him, wondering about him, being intrigued by him and wishing we were together, and just being absolutely furious at myself for feeling like I've succumbed to something I shouldn't have, like I've fallen victim to some kind of scam.

It is strange how much we have in common – especially considering I'd always considered him my exact opposite – and we do have so much fun together. It's like we know how to just be around each other. Sometimes I feel like he can read my mind.

Zoom?

This message from Rex not only makes me jump as my phone vibrates on the coffee table, but it freaks me out, just a little, wondering if perhaps he can actually read my mind.

'Hello,' I say when the call connects.

'Hey,' he replies. 'Where are Mom and Dad tonight?'

'They're asleep,' I tell him – he's going to think all they do is sleep.

'Fancy some company?' he asks. 'I am lone-ly.'

I smile. Perhaps he really can read my mind. And it's so like Rex to say something that makes him seem so vulnerable, in such a silly way, to try to deflect from what he's actually saying.

'Not found anyone to keep you company in your hotel room yet?' I tease. 'That doesn't seem like you.'

'A gentleman never tells,' he replies. 'But no.'

'Well, you're no gentleman,' I point out, persisting in lightly ribbing him. 'So who knows what to believe?'

'You wound me, Dani, you really do,' he replies. You can tell he loves it when I tease him, though.

'Any news?' I ask, changing he subject.

'Not yet,' he replies. 'But I was thinking, I'm alone, you're alone – you know what we can do together, right?'

When he says things like this, honestly, I feel like my heart is going to stop. I hold my breath, willing him to say exactly what I want him to say.

Rex holds up a booklet.

'We can play the lame Zoom games head office sent around to everyone,' he says with exaggerated enthusiasm.

Yeah, okay, that's definitely not what I wanted him to say.

'All certified safe for everyone to play,' he continues. 'They get all the new hires to play them. Honestly, they're terrible. I thought we could give them a go. Quick fire, though, just one round on each, so we can get through them all.'

'Yay,' I say sarcastically but, truthfully, it does sound like a lot of fun.

'Do you have a pen and paper there?' he asks me.

I rummage around in the drawer, underneath the coffee table, and pull out a wad of Post-it notes and a biro.

'Got them,' I reply.

'Okay, draw something,' he instructs. 'And it's my job to guess what it is.'

'Oh, I can't draw,' I insist. 'And I don't mean that in a cute way, or a modest way, or to imply that I'm just not great. I am honestly, sincerely, I promise you, awful at drawing.'

'Challenge accepted,' he replies. 'You have to choose something in the room you are sitting in, something in front of you, so that you can show if I'm right, or if I'm wrong. And... go.'

'Erm...'

With no other choice, I set my phone down on the table while

I draw one of the china swans that sits on the fireplace. Mum has two, one that looks up and another that's looking down, burying its beak into its feathers.

I pick my phone up again and hold up the Post-it.

'Dani, this is supposed to be a family-friendly game,' Rex ticks me off.

'Har-har,' I reply. 'Come on.'

'I'm not screwing around,' he insists. 'Is that not a dick, or a willy, or whatever it is you like to call them here?'

'We call them a Rex,' I joke. 'I know it's bad but it's not that bad, is it? I did warn you.'

'You did, I thought you were just being cute or modest,' he teases. 'I don't even think I want to know what it really is, I like the mystery so, okay, game two, twenty questions. We all know how it goes, ask away.'

'Am I a man?' I ask.

'Yes,' he replies.

'Famous?'

'Yes,' he says again.

'Am I a musician?'

'Yes! Wow, you're pretty good at this,' Rex says.

'Am I under sixty?'

'No,' he confirms.

'Am I from England?' I ask.

'*No,*' Rex replies, but he does so in a tone that suggests I'm close.

'Scottish?'

'Nope,' he replies.

I think for a moment. Suddenly it's obvious.

'Oh, my God, am I Tom Jones?' I ask through a smile.

'Ding, ding, ding, we have a winner,' he announces. 'The Tom Jones everyone likes, not the one we hate.'

'Very funny,' I insist.

'Want to play a few more?' he asks.

'Absolutely,' I reply. 'These are actually quite fun.'

'I know how to show a girl a good time,' he jokes. 'Right then, up next...'

Honestly, I think I could do this with Rex all night, which just makes my crush on him even more infuriating, because it's only getting stronger as each day goes by. Let's just hope I get the Leeds job, then at least it will have been worth pretending all I want to be is friends. I'm just really hoping that one day, in the future, when the job is mine, maybe something could happen between us, but I'm sure he will have moved on by then – I'll bet he has already, let's be real.

So, for now at least, there's only one thing we can do, and that's keep playing games. That's the way it's been from the start, so I suppose it should be easy. Here's hoping.

21

I've never planned a party before, not as an adult, at least – the ones I threw as a teenager definitely didn't have any planning involved, people just sort of turned up with cheap booze and hung out while loud music played. But a proper, grown-up party is new to me, and that's just regular parties I'm talking, not one being thrown where I don't really have any friends any more, in a venue where I absolutely do not have permission to throw one, that needs to be planned in a day – and one that will be taking place on Christmas Eve, no less, the day before I'll be spending Christmas all alone. I could go on.

I mean, I suppose it will be nice for me to have a Christmas Eve party, if I'm going to be alone the day after, but that is heavily reliant on people actually showing up to the damn thing, and so far, I have invited my old crush, Ben, his sister/my frenemy, Eleanor, and Dean, the local policeman who I am clearly driving to distraction at the moment – I highly doubt he'll turn up, unless he has cause to arrest me at some point. We can't really rule it out, can we?

But even though I've only invited three people to the party, there's nothing I can do but to throw it, my hands are tied, I'm in too deep now. I *have* to go through with it.

You can guarantee Eleanor will turn up, if only to see if it's something she can make fun of, which it probably will be, so at least she'll be getting what she wants for Christmas. If she and her brother are the only guests, she will no doubt find it absolutely hilarious. She'll laugh for a while, make some jokes, and then she'll leave, and it will just be me and Ben and then I really will feel like a sad cow. I need to do everything I can to stop that from happening, even if it means I have to endure a little short-term embarrassment in the meantime. The long-term gain will be that I can continue to show my face on the island.

It's lucky that I bought some party food at the farm shop the other day, but I'm going to need more. It's easy enough to buy snack foods, and I can just tell people to bring their own booze, that's simple but effective. Boom. That's a party. It's basically the party I threw when I was a teenager, I suppose, but it's the best I can do. Now all I need to do is sort some guests.

I do have an angle I'm going to try, so I'm going to go out and collect the food I need and try to drum up some guests in the process. I just need to figure out how to execute my plan.

My phone rings. It's Rex.

'Hello?' I answer brightly. 'Any news?'

'Not yet,' he replies. 'I swear, I'm just waiting on one piece of information, and then we can try to figure things out. What are you up to?'

I decide that a little truth might be a good thing for once – any more lies and I'm going to need to start writing them down.

'I'm a bit stressed out, to be honest,' I confess.

'How so?' Rex replies.

'Well, my parents' house is on a street that goes over the top with the Christmas lights each year, but it's become sort of a thing, and people love to come and see it, so one year they started putting out a charity box, to collect for good causes.'

This is the angle I was telling you about, and it's hopefully a great way to turn something stupid into something that can do some good.

'I've sort of wound up saying I'll throw a party at my parents' house – just a fun Christmas Eve thing,' I explain. 'The only thing is, I haven't exactly invited many people yet, and the party is tomorrow night. My problem is that I don't really know anyone around here any more, and I don't know how to ask strangers. It's embarrassing.'

'Well, I'm great at talking to strangers,' Rex insists. 'And do you know who needs to be good at talking to anyone? Showbiz journalists.'

'Meh, I know,' I reply. 'It's mostly just because I feel so cheeky, and really awkward. I need you to teach me how to talk to strangers.'

'Okay, so take me with you,' he suggests.

'Oh, what, like in my pocket?' I reply sarcastically.

'Yes,' he says simply. 'Pop an AirPod in, I'll listen in on your interactions, I'll tell you what to say, what to reply – it will be fun, and it will not only help you get people to come to your party, but it will be good for you professionally too. We need to build your confidence up.'

He does have a point.

'Erm, okay,' I say with a nervous laugh.

'Okay, great,' he replies. 'Just give me a call, when you're out. I once again have zero plans.'

'Okay,' I say again, trying to sound less nervous this time, but possibly sounding even more so.

Perhaps having Rex in my ear really will help me. More than that, though, I'm excited to be spending more time with him, even if he is only going to be a voice inside my head. Ah, well, his voice may as well be in there. He's already taking up too much room in my head anyway.

22

Walking down the street, with Rex in my ear, does bizarrely make it feel like he is here with me; although, in a way, it feels a little like having an imaginary friend. I never had one when I was younger – although I suppose one is more use to me now, being the 'Dani no mates' that I am.

Rex isn't imaginary, which has its pros and cons. Obviously, I'm glad that he's real, but if he was a figment of my imagination, then my unrequited crush might not seem so sad. I can't believe I have a crush on my ex-fake boyfriend – it's a tale as old as time.

I have one AirPod in my right ear, hidden perfectly under my long hair. I feel a little bit like a secret agent on a mission. Operation: invite strangers to the party. Whether I need Rex's help or not (I probably do, let's be real), it's a lot of fun having him whispering in my ear.

'Where are we now?' he asks curiously. 'Describe it to me. I want to feel like I'm there with you.'

'Well, it's bloody freezing, so imagine that you're cold,' I reply. 'I'm just taking a shortcut through the park.'

'It can't be a very big park, if it's a shortcut,' he replies.

'It used to be the garden for a massive house, dating back to Victorian times, I believe,' I explain, not remembering the exact details. 'The house is gone but the garden remains. He was a rich local businessman who had all these grottoes and caves built that twine around a massive lake – not that you can tell they're man-made, though. I spent so much time here as a kid. If you were brave, you could walk up the spiral stone steps inside one of the caves, and walk across a skinny stone bridge. It only has a wall on one side. The other side is completely open. I used to run across it when I was a kid, like it was nothing.'

'Are you doing that today?' he asks. I swear, I can hear him smiling.

'Erm, no,' I admit with a laugh. 'I am currently walking over the stone bridge instead. And it's kind of icy, so I'm holding on to the sides.'

'Baby,' he teases.

'I'm not a baby,' I insist, sounding a bit like a baby. 'It takes guts to have you in my ear, being willing to take your advice. I've seen you flirt, remember.'

'The one rule is, anything I tell you to say, you have to say it,' Rex replies.

'Oh, I don't know about that one, buddy,' I say. 'Have you heard some of the things you say?'

He laughs.

'Trust me, I know how to charm people,' he insists. 'So, where is our first stop?'

'To the deli,' I say, lowering my voice as I approach the door.

The deli is a gorgeous little old stone building. It looks so warm and inviting. As I open the doors and step inside, the heating envelops me, pulling me in. I close the door behind me, cutting off the cold air, leaving it outside.

'Hello again,' Channy says brightly. 'Back for *more*?'

'Oh, no, Dani, how hard are you hitting this deli?' Rex teases in my ear. 'If they have sausage rolls, I totally get it.'

I laugh, styling it out as a warm greeting, but secretly acknowledging Rex's running commentary.

'I'm just here to get some party supplies,' I tell her.

Gosh, it really is warm in here, after being out in the cold. I unfasten my coat to let some cool air in.

'Oh, well, we're great for that,' she replies. 'Can I just say, that is one sexy top. Sometimes I feel like I'm the only person around here who dares to be different.'

Channy has a sort of gothic look going on, but in a way that seems to be entirely fashionable, rather than because she's a big Marilyn Manson fan. Her hair is jet black and her foundation is pale. She has large black flicks of liquid eyeliner and a red wine-coloured lipstick on. She's more permanently committed to the look, though, with a septum piercing and large tattoo covering most of her chest, peeking out from above her square neckline.

'I want to see what you're wearing,' Rex tells me. 'It sounds exciting.'

I'm wearing a black mesh top with the red slip under it that I found in my old room. I suppose it is a little different, but it's not exactly daring.

'Oh, this old... oh, my God.' Looking down stops me in my tracks. Now I remember why I stopped wearing this top. It's because the adjustable straps on the slip had lost their grip. They've extended so much the slip is now resting comfortably below my black bra, which you can very, very clearly see.

'You've got 'em, flaunt 'em, sis, that's what I say,' Channy tells me.

I quickly fasten my coat again.

'Erm, it's a bit of a wardrobe malfunction,' I confess. 'They're not supposed to be so... out.'

'No!' Rex says. 'Now you have to show me. I need to see this.'

'Well, I think it looks great,' Channy insists. 'I just assumed you were ready for your party later.'

I pick out the bits I want. Channy starts packaging them up for me.

'No, it's a Christmas Eve party,' I tell her. 'Over on Sycamore Crescent, you know the one, with all the Christmas lights.'

'I know it well,' she replies. 'When me and my brother were little, we used to have our mum drive us there almost every night in December.'

'Now's your chance,' Rex says. 'Invite her.'

'Oh, well, erm, it's like a party for anyone who wants to come,' I explain, rather terribly.

'That makes it sound non-exclusive,' Rex tells me. 'Tell her about the charity.'

'You know how there's a charity box on the street, some people who come to see the lights can donate? Well, what better way to increase donations than by throwing a big party for all the locals?'

'Ooh, did I hear someone say "big party"?' a woman asks as she emerges from the back room.

'This is Lily, she's the manager here,' Channy says.

'She sounds cute,' Rex points out.

'And the little angel on her hip is baby Sally.' Channy continues with the introductions.

'Never mind,' Rex quickly adds.

'Yes, I'm throwing a Christmas Eve party on Sycamore Crescent,' I tell her. 'I'm inviting all the local businesses. It's a bring-your-own-booze, casual kind of thing, but I'm putting on some food, and the idea is that hopefully guests will donate to the charity box while they're there.'

It wouldn't be true to say that my intention was always to raise money for the street's chosen charity this year, but as soon as I realised I was going to have to throw this damn party, it made perfect sense to me, to at least use it as a platform to raise more funds for good causes. If that's the only thing that comes out of all of this, then it will have been more than worth it.

'You don't know how much I miss parties,' Lily says with a sigh. 'I've got a one-year-old and a thirteen-year-old, AKA, a toddler and a teenager. It really is the worst-case scenario – not that I don't love them to pieces.'

'Tell her she can bring her kids,' Rex instructs.

'Ah, got you,' I reply. 'Well, kids are more than welcome. Boyfriends and husbands too.'

'Thank you,' Lily replies. 'I'll have a word with Alfie, my fella.'

'Yeah, if my parents don't have anything planned, I'll be there,' Channy adds.

'Okay, well, maybe see you then,' I reply as I take my bag of goodies.

'Have a nice day,' Channy calls after me.

'You too,' I reply.

Once I'm outside, I turn my attention back to Rex.

'What do you reckon?' I ask him. 'Pretty non-committal, right?'

'I have high hopes for them,' Rex says. 'The one with the kids sounded desperate to let her hair down.'

'I'll bet,' I reply. 'It sounds like she's got her hands full.'

'A toddler and a teenager – can you even imagine?' Rex says.

'I sort of can,' I reply. 'You're always either acting like a toddler or a teenager.'

'Ouch,' he says with a laugh. 'What a burn. Okay, where are we going next?'

'Fruitopia,' I reply.

'What's Fruitopia?' he asks curiously.

'It's a jam shop,' I reply with a giggle.

'No!' Rex replies. I can hear his smile.

'There's just one man working in there, behind the counter,' I tell Rex.

'Then I would advise you to make sure that, whatever that intriguing top is that you're wearing, you have it on show,' he suggests.

'Erm, I don't think so,' I reply.

Sitting behind the counter at Fruitopia is a man who, without a doubt, looks exactly as you would expect a real Yorkshire man to. He's a broad-shouldered man in his late fifties or early sixties. His hair and his bushy beard are almost entirely grey – he's got one hell of a set of sideburns on him.

'Now then,' he says, just as I expected him to. 'What can I do you for, love?'

'I'm Dani, my parents live over on Sycamore Crescent,' I start.

'What do you want, a medal?' he replies rather curtly. 'Whatever you're selling, I'm not buying. If you're here to buy some jam, buy it. I'm sick of your lot just coming in just to take pictures with the funny sign.'

'Your lot?' Rex says in my ear.

'My lot?' I ask.

'Your generation,' he replies, sounding like he's got a bad taste in his mouth. 'Gen Z.'

Geez, *I wish* I was young enough to be considered Gen Z.

'You're not going to get anywhere with this one,' Rex advises in my ear. 'I can tell.'

'I'm not selling anything, it's actually a charity event,' I persist. I'm not ready to give up on him just yet.

'Your lot don't do anything for charity,' he continues. Again with the 'your lot'! 'It's all put on for the socials, so you can say you're "winning" or that you "did a thing"—'

Okay, maybe now I am ready to give up. Rex was right. I'm really not going to get anywhere with this one. How can someone with such a fun shop name be so joyless?

'Never mind,' I interrupt him. 'Sorry to bother you.'

'Well, he was delightful,' Rex says sarcastically.

'Wasn't he just?' I say with a sigh. 'I'd be ready to give up, but I may as well try my luck in the boutique, I need to buy a top that isn't obscene, so that I can take my coat off. I'm roasting everywhere I go. Everyone has their heating on full whack.'

'Full whack,' he repeats back to me through a snigger. 'An English whack?'

I shake my head as I laugh.

'Right, I'm heading into the boutique,' I say, lowering my voice again as I step inside.

Pandora's Boutique is unbelievably cool. Potentially too cool to be in a seaside town. Everything is so stylish and so unique. I can't see more than one of anything, and of the things I can see, no two pieces are remotely alike.

It doesn't take me long to find that special something, a top that stands out from all the others. It's a black cold-shoulder top with a hanky hem. It's sort of plain and understated, but still kind of unusual. It will look great with a pair of jeans and some black boots.

'Am I okay to try this on?' I ask the lady behind the counter.

'Sure,' she replies, hopping to her feet.

She's a petite forty-something who is wearing too many bangles – her accessories probably weigh as much as she does. She's very stylish, in her own way, layering lots of colours and textures. She looks great. If I were to try and do that, I would just look like Joey, from *Friends*, when he's wearing all of Chandler's clothes in 'The One Where No One's Ready'.

'I'm Erin,' she says as she shows me into the fitting room. 'If you need anything, just give me a shout.'

'Thanks very much,' I reply. I wait for her to get back to her post before I speak to Rex, keeping my voice low so that Erin doesn't think I'm talking to myself. 'If you lose me for a second, it's probably because I've knocked my AirPod out. To be honest, you can get going, if you want? It'd probably weird that you're here for this part.'

'Are you taking your top off?' he asks curiously.

Something about him asking, the way he asks perhaps, does things to me. Good things, but I can't let him know that.

'Only you could leer over a topless girl from miles away, over the phone,' I point out.

'So you *are* topless,' he jokes. 'You know I'm only screwing around. Are you going to invite her to the party while you're here?'

'Yeah,' I reply. 'She seems nice.'

I wrestle my way into the new top, careful to keep my AirPod in my ear as I do it. Eventually it's on. I smooth out the creases and look at myself in the mirror.

'Okay, I love this top,' I say, still keeping my voice low. 'Do you think she'll let me keep it on? I'm heading to the Christmas shop next, where I have actual friends, ones who will definitely insist I take off my coat. I can't turn up in a see-through one.'

'So that's why it was sexy,' Rex muses through a chuckle. 'I don't have skin in the game with this one so... why not? I'm sure she'll let you keep it on.'

I stuff my own top into my bag and head back out into the shop, making a point to carry my coat, so it doesn't look like I'm trying to steal the top underneath it. DC Dean would have a field day if he were called out to that scenario.

'Excuse me, this is going to sound weird, but if I buy this top, can I wear it?' I ask.

Erin looks at me blankly for a moment.

'You need to be more specific,' Rex points out. It's actually quite useful, having him in my ear.

'I mean, can I keep it on right now?' I correct myself. 'I had a bit of a wardrobe malfunction, with what I had on when I came in. I could do with leaving in something that isn't going to get me arrested.'

'Nice,' Rex says.

'Of course, sweetheart,' Erin says. 'We've all been there.'

'Thank you so much,' I reply. 'I'm prepping for a big Christmas Eve party, so I don't really have time to go home and get changed.'

'Oh, nice, working into the conversation,' Rex says.

'So, is that what the new top is for? For this big party?' Erin asks.

'She's angling for an invite, quick, shoot your shot and invite her,' Rex says.

Unfortunately, at the same time, I reply, 'I have a date.'

'With who?' Rex asks. 'With Ben?'

'It's just to the pub, on the seafront,' I explain. 'I haven't been in years, I'm mostly curious to see what it's like now.'

'Erm, okay,' Erin replies through a smile, obviously not knowing I was talking to Rex.

'Dani, I'm getting a call, I need to go,' Rex tells me. 'Talk later.'

He hangs up before I can say goodbye.

I try to seem less weird, inviting Erin to the party, before getting on my way. Her reaction is like everyone else's – enthusiastic, but non-committal.

It's oddly lonely, heading to the Christmas shop without Rex in my ear. I'd been enjoying his company.

I hope I'm being smart with the whole party thing. I'm not inviting people I hardly know to my sad-sack party which, until a day ago, was a party for one, which is not only kind of pathetic, but it doesn't exactly sound like a social engagement people will want to attend. Pitching it as a party on the street where everyone goes to see all the Christmas lights, saying that anyone is welcome to come for a drink – I don't want to seem like I'm desperate for company, even though I am, but the way I see it is, if I make it more about the street than it is about me, then people can come, have a good time, have a drink, spread some festive cheer and hopefully put a little something in the street's donation box. At least that way it will all have been for something good.

After inviting a few more people I don't/hardly know to a party I haven't planned, I'm finally at the Christmas shop, to invite some people that I not only know, but who I really like, and hopefully like me too.

I was in two minds whether or not to still come here in person, given the weather, but with the snow not being nearly as heavy as threatened today, I figured I might as well get out of the house while the causeway was open, do everything I needed to do, then get back home in time to get ready for my dinner with Ben. It would be just my luck to miss the causeway crossing, throw off all my plans and ruin everything.

'Hello again,' Santa/Gaz greets me the second I walk through the door.

'Hello,' I say brightly. I know what I'm up against now.

Gaz follows me as I walk through the shop.

'How are you?' he asks me.

'I'm fine, thanks. You?'

'I can't complain,' he says. 'Are you seeing anyone at the moment?'

I stop in my tracks and turn to face him.

'You've got to be the worst Santa Claus I've ever met in my life,' I point out with an amused laugh.

'It's been said before,' he replies thoughtfully. 'But I'm actually the best, just ask Ivy.'

'I'll do that,' I reply with a smile.

We approach the busy counter. It's weird to see it with staff behind it, I keep expecting to see Ivy working behind it on her own, just like her mum used to.

Ivy is behind a laptop, tapping away. Next to her is a very tall, very handsome man. He's wearing a suit, looking very Fifty Shades of Something. I notice that he has a hand on her shoulder. This must be her husband, the one I've heard so much about. Wow, he really is good-looking.

'Dani, hello again!' she beams when she notices me, snapping her laptop shut immediately, just to talk to me. She's such a sweetheart. Her mum was exactly the same. She always had time for anyone who wanted it.

As she walks around the counter to hug me, I can't help but stare at how much taller her husband is than her – there must be a foot between them! Still, they make such a gorgeous couple.

'Hello,' I say as I squeeze her. 'I won't keep you long...'

'Oh, don't be daft,' she says. 'Come into the back with us, let me make you a hot chocolate.'

'I don't want to put you out...'

'Of course you're not putting me out,' she says, ushering me into the back room.

'Can I come?' Gaz asks.

'Sure, why not?' she replies. 'Even Santa Claus needs a break.'

'Pretty sure Santa gets a break three hundred and sixty-four days of the year,' Ivy's husband muses.

'Well, I'm talking about Gaz,' she tells him with a smile and a roll of her eyes.

'So am I,' he says with a chuckle.

Ivy laughs.

'By the way, this is Seb. Seb, this is Dani.'

'Nice to meet you,' he says.

'Yeah, you too,' I reply.

At the back of the shop is a large kitchen area with a big wooden table and chairs in the centre. It's so homely, yet so professional. I would love to see what kind of mess I could make in here.

'This is where we make things for the café, and to sell in the shop,' she says. 'I'm still hiring, if you fancy a change of scenery. They might have made our food tech teacher cry, but I think your fake mince pies would be a huge hit here.'

'Fake mince pies?' Seb enquires curiously as he removes his jacket and undoes his top button. Gosh, he's a babe. I feel like I just watched all that in slow motion.

'Yeah, I really didn't like mince pies – I still don't,' I explain. 'They feel like such a huge part of Christmas, though, so I always felt like I was missing out on something when everyone else was making them and eating them.'

'She baked brownies into pastry,' Ivy says giddily, cutting to the chase.

'Marry me?' Gaz blurts, totally straight-faced. 'They sound so good.'

I give Gaz a half-smile. It seems weird to me that, even though we're in the back room, he is still dressed as Santa Claus. I still don't really know what he looks like. I definitely couldn't pick him out of a police line-up.

'I might make some, if I get the chance,' I say. 'But I'm a little scared to mess up my mum's kitchen, especially the day before the party, which reminds me... I was wondering if you guys wanted to come to my party?'

'Even me?' Gaz asks.

'Of course,' I reply. 'Holly too, if she's free.'

'Oh, wow, that would be so good,' Ivy replies. 'We did make plans with Holly and her husband and the kids, but I'm sure they'd love to come, I could ask them?'

'Oh, don't worry about it too much,' I insist. 'Don't change your plans, it's not a big deal.'

'I'll have a word with her,' Ivy says enthusiastically. 'In the meantime, though, the least I can do is offer you my kitchen, and my lesser baking skills, to help you whip up some party bites – unless you've got plenty of food?'

'Oh, no, wow, that would be great,' I reply. 'Are you sure?'

'Of course,' she says. 'We can even call it an informal job interview, just in case you decide to make the move. All I ask in return is that you make me some of your fake mince pies, to give Gaz for Christmas.'

'You've got yourself a deal,' I reply excitedly.

I'm sure she's joking about the job, but it's weirdly comforting to feel like I have a backup plan, even if it would be a huge departure from what I'm doing now.

'I'll leave you ladies to it,' Seb says, kissing Ivy on the cheek. 'Lovely to meet you, Dani. Gaz, let's leave them to their baking.'

'Okay,' he replies. 'I'm definitely invited to the party, though, right?'

'Definitely,' I say. I'm pretty sure Ivy is just trying to let me down gently, but if Gaz comes, he'll be maybe my third or fourth guest. I'll take that.

'Do you want me to wear the suit?' he says, gesturing downwards.

'Oh, no, you don't have to do that…'

'It's okay, I'll wear the suit,' he says. 'I think you kinda like it.'

Seb laughs to himself as he leads Gaz back out into the shop.

'I don't suppose I'd recognise him if he didn't wear the suit,' I muse.

'He's actually kind of hot under all that,' Ivy whispers. 'But don't ever tell him I said that.'

I laugh.

'I won't, I promise.'

'So, how are you finding it back on Hope Island?' Ivy asks as she starts removing everything we could possibly need from the cupboards.

'Not too bad,' I tell her. 'It's weird without my parents, though.'

'I bet,' she replies. 'I'm surprised you came, with them going away for Christmas.'

I wonder whether now could be the time to confess to someone that I didn't know my parents weren't going to be here when I turned up, but I'm so deep in this mess now. She's being so generous, letting me use her kitchen to make party food, I'd feel awful telling her it was all for nothing. I really want to make something of this party now, and it feels like I'm in with a chance, if I can just pull some guests out of the bag. Instead, I deflect, and confess something else.

'It's given me more time to see my old friends, and I've spent a little time with Ben,' I tell her. 'In fact, he's taking me out for dinner tonight.'

'Oooh,' Ivy coos. 'Remember what a massive crush you had on him when we were at school?'

I feel my cheeks flush.

'Dani Newman, after all these years, do you still have a crush on him?' she asks, immediately stopping what she's doing.

'I don't know,' I reply sheepishly. 'Maybe? It's hard to forget old feelings, isn't it? Trying to work out if you're still feeling them, or just remembering what they felt like back in the day. "Maybe" is as close as I am to figuring it out.'

It's impossible to know how I would be feeling about Ben right now if Rex hadn't turned my head.

Ivy gasps.

'You do! Oh, my God, this is amazing. He's single, you know. There's nothing wrong with him, not that I know of, I think he just works too much. Spends all his time with bits of wood. Have you seen his work? It's amazing. What's stopping you giving things a go? Give me one good reason why you shouldn't.'

I smile. Ivy is so excited. It's so nice to have someone care about me, I feel like it's been a while. Well, unless you count Rex, which oddly I do. Which reminds me...

'There is someone I'm... sort of... something with,' I admit.

Ivy stops what she's doing, picks up her cup of tea, and turns to give me her undivided attention.

'Okay, tell me everything,' she demands.

'There's this guy at work called Rex,' I begin. I think, when it comes to this story, I can actually be totally honest with Ivy for once. It would be good to get her opinion. 'We've worked together for a while but never so much as exchanged a word with each other. I'm still quiet and like to keep my head down. He's the total opposite – he's so confident, so outgoing, he charms the pants off pretty much every girl who passes through the office.'

'Nice,' Ivy says sarcastically.

'Right?' I reply. 'Anyway, so, he set his sights on the new girl in the office and much to my surprise, and his horror, she rejected him.'

'Good,' Ivy replies. 'I'll bet that brought him down a peg or two.'

'Quite the opposite,' I reply with a laugh. 'He went and told her I was his girlfriend and then kissed me in front of everyone.'

'Shut up,' Ivy says, clearly loving the story and the drama. 'What did you do?'

'I was in shock, I just sort of let him,' I admit. 'But then it turned out that maybe we could help each other out. He needed me to play along as his girlfriend, so that he could get this new girl lusting after him – which worked, by the way, she fancied him so much more when she thought he was taken – but he's also in charge of setting up a new team in our magazine's Leeds office, and I really, really want the job so, we struck up a weird sort of deal that might get us both what we want.'

'Ergh, I hate girls like that,' Ivy replies as she pours a handful of chocolate chips into her hand and throws them back into her mouth. 'So, wait, at what point in this story do you meet your dream man?'

'Ah, well, that's the thing,' I start, only slightly embarrassed about what I'm going to say next. 'It's him. It's Rex.'

'I need another cup of tea,' Ivy says with a playful sigh. 'Go on then, how on earth did you wind up fancying him? It sounds like you thought he was a bit of a tool before.'

'That's the thing, I did,' I insist. 'I would watch him with girls and – other than the fact he's really good-looking and has a sexy American accent – I could never get why they were all falling at his feet. It genuinely baffled me, I knew I could never fancy him. But then I started spending time with him and, I hate to say it, but I totally get it. He's so charming, he's so much fun, he's hilarious, but he's kind and caring, he's thoughtful. And, when all was said and done, when we were at our work Christmas party together, and it was finally time for him to get the girl, he didn't want her, he wanted to hang out with me instead. We hung out all evening, he offered to drive me here the next day – right to my door – and since then, I was supposed to go to Leeds for a meeting with him, but with the snow being so bad we've only been having Zoom meetings, but we're chatting loads, we're getting on really well, and I know I thought he was my opposite to begin with, but it's actually starting to seem like we've got loads in common.'

'Well, I wasn't convinced at first,' Ivy says. 'But you sound like you really like him, and it sounds like he really cares about you.'

'Yeah, I thought so, but...'

'Ahh, there's always a but,' Ivy says with a sigh.

'I tried to kiss him at the party and he pretended not to notice, effectively rejecting me. So on the drive up here I told him I had a date with Ben – a lie, to make him think it was okay that he rejected me, because I really want this job – and he didn't seem to mind. It sounds like he's spending Christmas with a girl.'

'Well, now you really do have a date with Ben,' Ivy reminds me. 'How does that make you feel?'

'Honestly, if I hadn't interacted with Rex, I would have been over the moon,' I reply honestly.

'You should go then, have fun, see how you feel about things after you have a date with someone who is so very clearly interested in you,' she says. 'And if you do get your job from Rex, well, maybe your dynamic will change.'

That's a very good point.

'Perhaps it's not a good idea, to be lusting after the man I'm relying on to save the day,' I point out. 'I hate that I need a man to save me. It doesn't feel like progress.'

Ivy fusses around the kettle as she makes us a cup of tea. I don't know what it is about baking – and gossiping – but it's always much better when you've got a cup of tea in your hand.

'I don't know if you know this, but knowing this village, I'd be surprised if anyone hadn't told you this already. Seb and I didn't meet under the best circumstances,' she explains. 'The landlord who owned the old building the shop was in decided he was selling it, and it was Seb who was planning to buy it, to knock it down and build holiday homes. I was devastated and, believe me, I hated Seb. I did everything I could to try and raise the money to buy the place myself, but it was just too much. But it turned out that, while Seb and I were fighting, we were falling for each other, and when it came down it, we landed on a compromise: he would get to build his holiday homes, but he would also rebuild the shop as a part of it, and I would rent that from him. Doing that meant that I got to keep the business going, and keep my past alive, but it opened a door to a new future with Seb and, honestly, we couldn't be happier. There's no shame in letting a man save the day. Things are never that straightforward. If he cares about you, he'll help you. It's as simple as that.'

'Well, it's not looking good on the job front, I don't think,' I explain. 'So, when I talk to him later, I guess that might tell me everything I need to know.'

'All the more reason to go on this date with Ben after then,' she says with a smile. 'Fifteen-year-old you would be bouncing off the walls with joy, caking herself in black eye make-up, putting on her best denim skirt and leggings combo.'

'Oh, God, don't,' I reply with a laugh. 'Those clothes are probably still at my mum and dad's, I could dig them out.'

'Save them for the party,' she suggests playfully. 'I really will try to make it to the party. It sounds like fun.'

'Don't worry if you can't,' I insist.

'Yeah, you won't mind, if you've got Ben there with you,' she says with a wink.

It's cute how encouraging she is. She's certainly given me a lot to think about. Maybe, if Rex does like me, he'll do everything he can to get me that job. Maybe that's never going to happen. I suppose there's a third option, where he gives me the job, but it's just because he knows how much I want it, and he's a decent person.

I guess we'll just have to wait and see what is said in our meeting later. At least I've got my dinner date to look forward to after. I just kind of wish it was with Rex instead of Ben, no matter what my inner fifteen-year-old is screaming at me.

23

It's been a long time since I got ready for a date (that may not be a date-date, but never mind) – it's been even longer since I got ready for one at my parents' house. I must have been in my teens, probably around the time I was in sixth form. I remember a boy called Mark from A-level English taking me to the cinema on the seafront to see *The Prestige*. He was ever the gent, when he picked me up in his car – you were just naturally cooler, if you were in sixth form, especially if you were one of the first ones to get a car – but he was clearly a little overly inspired by the movie, when he tried to make his tongue disappear down my throat on the back row.

Tonight is different, though. I'm a grown woman… a grown woman going on a date with her school crush. Isn't it funny, how we grow up in some ways but regress in others?

I apply some red lipstick – the finishing touch to my ensemble – and check myself in the mirror. I don't look so bad, you know.

My phone vibrates. It's Rex.

Quick Zoom?

Shit. I wonder if this is it. The news I've been waiting for.

'Wow, you look amazing,' Rex tells me when I join the call. 'Ex-boyfriend Ben is a lucky guy.'

I smile.

'Do you have news?' I ask, cutting to the chase. 'I'm going out of my mind.'

'I do, but I don't know if it's good news,' he admits. 'The problem we've got is that there's only budget for one more hire and that needs to be someone to lead the team.'

'Ah,' I reply.

'Do you have any experience leading a team?' he asks hopefully, although I suspect he already knows the answer.

'No,' I say simply.

'Do you think you could do the job?' he asks.

I think for a second, but who am I kidding?

'Honestly, no,' I reply. 'And it's not a case of me not having faith in myself or anything like that. I don't have the experience. There's no way I could take that position on and do a good job. Not a chance.'

It's hard to say whose fault it is, somehow it feels like everyone's and no one's, but allowing myself to be ushered into the advertorial writing gig means that, as far as real journalistic experience goes, I don't really have any to show anyone. What I've been doing is more like copywriting, which doesn't exactly put me at the front of the queue for one of the demanding positions like being on the Showbiz team. There will be thousands of people with more experience than me. And then there's the fact that I have absolutely zero experience managing a team – in recent times, I haven't even been working in one.

Rex sighs.

'I want to give it to you, I really do,' he insists – and I believe him. 'But I need you to tell me something, anything, that means I can sell you as the right person to the higher-ups.'

'I appreciate you trying, and I really appreciate everything you've done for me,' I tell him sincerely – but then the bullshit kicks in. 'I really need to go, though, or I'm going to be late for my date.'

'Yeah, of course,' he replies. 'Have an awesome time, we'll talk later.'

'Yeah, have a good evening,' I tell him as I end the call.

Obviously, I wasn't rushing him off the phone because I'm running late (I'm not, for once), it's because I'm devastated. I really, really wanted that job. I understand why I can't have it, of course I do, I'm a big girl. And now I'm even more annoyed because what I also want is Rex, and I tanked that too, in favour of the job I'm not going to get.

'Do not cry,' I command myself in the mirror, sternly waggling a finger at my reflection.

My game face firmly in place, I head downstairs. I just need to forget about it all, go and meet Ben, and see what happens. I can figure out what I'm going to do with the rest of my life in the morning, at least.

24

Just across the causeway, on the edge of the water, sits a pub called the Hopeful Ghost. That's where Ben is taking me for dinner tonight.

I suppose it's kind of a creepy name for a pub, when you think about it. Even more if you know the history of Hope Island, which I do, because growing up here, it was one of the horror stories we used to tell each other as kids.

The pub was named after Hope Island's resident ghost – yes, we've even got our own ghost – if you believe in that sort of thing.

There are some old abbey ruins over on Hope Island which have somehow become the island's top romantic spot, despite being where the ghost is said to live (well, not *live*, but you know what I mean), and the completely unromantic rumours about what went on there a long time ago.

It's an urban legend, so the chances are it didn't actually happen, as is always the case with such things. I can't remember when this is supposed to have happened but, even if I did, I can't imagine it's a fact that will enrich such an unbelievable story.

Legend has it a bride and groom were tying the knot in the

abbey. Shortly after the ceremony, which went down without a hitch, the groom was nowhere to be found. The bride, in a mad panic, searched high and low for him. Eventually, she found him, tucked away in the corner of one of the old rooms, talking with the bride's younger sister. The sister was upset, telling the groom that he should have married her instead, and then they kissed – and it made the bride go mad. She decided that she wanted to teach her no-good husband a lesson, to show him what it feels like when your partner disappears, so she found a hiding place and, to give him a scare, she went into hiding there.

According to the rumours, there is a secret tunnel underneath the island that the monks would use to escape the abbey back in the day. The bride is said to have gone down there to hide, but then couldn't find her way back out again, so she died down there. Supposedly, she haunts the abbey, looking for her husband, and terrorising any loved-up couples she sees while she's searching. Yes, somehow that story has made the Hope Island abbey ruins the most romantic place to be in these parts. I'm not exactly sure I believe in ghosts but, whether you do or you don't, the whole thing is just beyond creepy – I'd rather not take my chances. People still get married in the ruins, talk about tempting fate. I'm much happier over here, at the pub, with Ben, eating burgers and fries and catching up on everything that has happened since school.

It's such a warm and cosy place. It's so rustic, and I really appreciate that it is a dog-friendly pub, I've spotted some really cute dogs while I've been sitting here. You just don't get places like this, with this particular brand of warmth and charm, in the city. It's nice, being somewhere that is quiet without being dead, and with a friendly cast of dog characters too. There's a golden retriever at the bar who I can't stop smiling at.

Ben looks good, in a pristine navy-blue jumper and a pair of jeans. He's got some kind of product on his hair, holding it in place, which makes me glad I bought a new top for the occasion. We've both made an effort, but things are still casual.

'Isn't it sad, that neither of us has anything exciting to report?' Ben says with a laugh. 'All these years since we were at school and what do we have to show for it? A few wrinkles, some grey hair...'

'Yeah, and that's just me,' I joke.

'Give over,' Ben insists with a smile. 'You hardly look a day older.'

'I like to think I'm more stylish, at least,' I say. 'I don't think it matters when you grow up, or what the fashion was like at that particular time, I think everyone looks back at photos of themselves when they were at school and can't believe how awful they looked, as far as following the trends goes. To be honest – and this is a good one for you, if you use dating apps – it's impossible to get away with using old pictures because there's one thing that is changing so, so rapidly, from one year to the next, and that's eyebrows. I'm embarrassed of my eyebrows in photos from like three years ago. At the time, they were cool – big blocky things. Forget laughing at your mum's dodgy eighties perm, the kids of our generation are going to be cringing at Mum's brows.'

Ben laughs.

'That's actually an excellent point,' he replies. 'I'll remember that. I haven't tried any dating apps – not yet. Although my love life has been pretty shocking since school. One disaster to the next, really. I was married, for about seven months. It was way too soon for us to be tying the knot, but we were young and we thought we knew what we were doing.'

'Wow,' I blurt. 'Being divorced makes you seem so grown-up.'

Ben laughs.

'I'm glad you think so,' he replies. 'Being divorced doesn't usually give off a great impression. Thanks for saying something that doesn't make me feel like a failure.'

'Ah, there's no shame in failed relationships,' I reassure him. 'We've all got those in our back catalogue. Some more spectacular than others.'

'That sounds like more of a story than you let on before,' Ben says, clearly detecting my tone. 'I told you mine. Want to tell me yours?'

'Ah, mine's not that interesting, and luckily I didn't marry him, obviously,' I reply. 'Not that he asked. He's actually my boss now, though – and he cheated on me, so I don't love seeing him almost every day.'

'My ex cheated on me,' he says with a knowing nod. 'I let all the air out of her tyres and threw her clothes out onto the lawn and then I felt a bit better. Did you do anything to your ex? Any petty acts of revenge?'

'I was embarrassingly weak, to be honest,' I admit. 'I just shut down, shut up and tried to move on with my life. That said, just before I left for Christmas, I did get a little satisfaction from something.'

'That sounds interesting, what did you do?' he asks.

I feel a massive smile cross my face.

'He got jealous, seeing me with someone at work, thinking we were a couple,' I reply. 'It looked like it was driving him mad.'

'Nice,' Ben replies. 'Were you a couple?'

My face falls.

'Oh, erm, no,' I reply. 'My ex just thought we were.'

'I'll bet he regrets cheating on you now,' Ben says with a smile. 'Good work.'

'Yeah,' I reply. 'Maybe.'

God, why can't I stop thinking about Rex? This is tragic. He's the one person in the office I always judged people for falling for and, look at me now, I'm falling hook, line and sinker.

I must wander off in my thoughts because Ben pulls me back with a subject change.

'I still can't believe your parents agreed to let you have a party, not after the ones we had as teens,' he says. 'That one at your house...'

Oh, he doesn't know the half of it.

'I know I mentioned it the other day, but Eleanor was there, so I didn't think you'd appreciate me bringing up how we almost kissed.'

I feel my cheeks flush, and it isn't from the roaring fire in the heart of the pub.

'I remember,' I say coyly.

'You know, I'm pretty sure she spilled that drink on purpose, to stop us by any means necessary,' he says thoughtfully. 'I think she could tell I had a bit of a crush on you. She must not have liked the idea of her friend and her brother.'

'*You* had a crush on *me*?' I blurt.

'Erm, yeah,' he says awkwardly.

'But... I used to try and talk to you all the time, when I felt brave enough, and you were always so quiet.'

'Yeah...'

'Oh.'

'People are quiet when they have a crush on people,' he says.

'Or they try and talk to them at every opportunity,' I say. 'Like I did.'

Ben just smiles.

It's quite funny now, looking back, knowing we both had a crush on one another but were both too scared to do anything about it.

'Maybe I'll feel braver at this party,' he says casually.

'Ha, maybe,' I reply, assuming he's just being cute and funny.

It's also funny in a way that only I would get – well, he wouldn't need much courage to kiss me in front of almost zero people, would he? I wonder what it would be like, to kiss him now. I wonder if I want him to try.

I'm sure Ben is just being flirty. He's so much more confident these days.

'I'm surprised your parents didn't want to be there,' he says, pushing the subject.

'They fancied a holiday,' I tell him with a casual shrug, hopefully putting the issue to bed – I should change the subject slightly. 'I need to go to Christmas Every Day tomorrow morning, to pick up everything that Ivy and I baked together today. I had to leave it all there to cool. So as long as the snow doesn't get any heavier, it shouldn't be a problem. It was so much fun, baking together, like old times.'

'I'll give you a lift in my four-by-four, if you like?' he suggests. 'And I can help you get set up for the party.'

'Thanks, that would be great. I wouldn't want to not have enough food for everyone.'

Hilarious.

'Are lots of people coming?' he asks.

He's asking a lot of questions. It's making me nervous that I'm going to mess up and expose my lie. Honestly, when it feels like the heat is on, like it is now, I feel like it would have been easier to tell the truth. Of course, it's far too late to do that now.

'Erm, a fair few,' I say vaguely. 'I'd love to see some of your work.'

Yes, I'm unsubtly changing the subject now, but it is also true.

'I have some pictures on my phone,' he says, popping a chip into his mouth before reaching into his pocket for his phone.

Ben taps on the screen a few times before holding up his phone for me to see.

'This is my latest commission,' he says. 'It's nearly finished, I just have a little more work to do.'

'Oh, my gosh, Ben, it's incredible.'

It's a large four-poster bed with peppermill-shaped posts. It's so beautiful, a real work of art.

'I'm also working on a chair and a wardrobe,' he says as he flicks through his camera roll.

'Ooh, what's that?' I ask.

I just about catch a glimpse of a table with wheels at the bottom before Ben quickly swipes it away.

'Ah, that's nothing,' he says. 'Just something I had left over that I'm trying to turn into something else. Fancy some dessert?'

Now I feel like he's changing the subject. Perhaps he's a little shy, showing people his creative work.

'You know what? I can't believe I'm saying this, but I think I'm full. That was one of the biggest – but nicest – burgers I've ever had in my life.'

It wasn't your typical burger, it was a Yorkshire Christmas burger. Turkey, a sausage patty, honey mustard parsnips, stuffing, cranberry sauce, all served – not in a bun – in between two Yorkshire puddings, held together with a wooden skewer, with a pig in a blanket stabbed at the top. It came with roast potatoes and gravy, and I'm so full I can hardly move.

'Yeah, I'm pretty stuffed too,' Ben agrees. 'Do you want to go for a short walk?'

'Now?' I ask.

It must be after 9 p.m.

'Yeah, walk the food off, plus I want to show you something. It's not far and I'll take you home after, promise.'

'Erm, okay,' I say with a smile.

I wonder what he's going to show me...

I wrap up warm in my floor-length coat, my cosy hooded scarf and my mittens before we head outside into the cold.

It's snowing, but it's that rare, absolutely perfect kind of snow where lots of tiny flakes drift down from the sky ever so gently before lightly settling on the floor. No icy winds, no getting soaked through, just a delicate dust dancing around in the air. The sky looks thick with it, like there's more to come, but it doesn't seem all that dark out because all of the pretty little lights are bouncing off the snow that has already settled. It's a picture-perfect moment, like something off the cover of a Christmas card, or a scene from a romance movie.

Ben, ever the gent, takes me by the arm and leads me down towards the seafront. With Marram Bay being such a tourist hotspot, especially around Christmas, there are little clusters of people everywhere, some making their way back from the annual Winter Wonderland festival with armfuls of sweets and prizes, others just appreciating the landscape – well, when you think of the coast you have images of sea, sand, sunshine, ice cream, deckchairs... not snow! It really is a beautiful sight.

We make small talk while we stroll, eventually taking cover under a cute little bandstand.

'So, what are you showing me?' I ask impatiently once we're still.

'This,' he says, looking around.

'This?'

'This bandstand.'

I raise my eyebrows while I wait for an explanation.

'I made it,' he says nervously.

'What?' I squeak. 'Ben, it's stunning. It's so detailed and so beautiful and...'

I twirl around underneath it, taking it all in. The fancy little carvings in the wood, combined with the fairy lights, make pretty shadows on the floor inside. Otherwise, we're completely surrounded by snow, it's almost like being on a boat, or floating in the sky.

'It was my first commission,' he says. 'Sort of. It was an unsolicited commission. You know those crazy storms we had a while back? The old bandstand was destroyed, so I decided to rebuild one for the town. It was mostly just to see what I could do, to try out new things, but it was a big hit.'

'Don't try and make out like you did this for yourself,' I tell him. 'This was you doing a nice thing. You're a nice man.'

Ben blushes a little. That's what I like about him, what I've always liked about him, he's always there, ready to do what he can to help people. It's been good seeing him again, having some real-life company while I'm home alone – and he may well be the only guest at my party. I'm glad we bumped into one another again.

As far as romantic feelings go, yes, Ben is gorgeous, and he's lovely, and kind, and maybe I could see myself falling for him again, given time, if it weren't for Rex, hanging around in my thoughts, but nothing is going to happen between us, so I just need to try and forget about him. I need to get on with my life. I can't quite put my finger on whether or not there's a spark between us. Perhaps the idea of an instant spark, or some kind of sign, is something fresh out of a romance movie too, maybe real life isn't so clear-cut. Strong feelings build and develop, they're not handed to you on a plate, are they?

I think a combination of being unexpectedly alone for the holidays, being stuck in a big house, on a small island that is routinely cut off from the rest of the world – it's all making it so hard to figure out what I'm actually thinking and feeling. Plus the fact that every time my mum asks if she can call, I tell her I'm busy with work, or with Tom (who she still doesn't know I'm no longer with), and I text her instead. I just cannot bring myself to speak to her, partly because I don't want to lie to her, but also because I'm terrified that, if I hear her voice, that will be it. I'll want my mum – and I cannot believe I'm saying that when I'm in my thirties.

'Are you okay?' Ben asks me, placing his hands on my shoulders. 'I feel like I've lost you to something.'

'Sorry, just deep in thought,' I tell him.

'You looked kind of sad.'

'I'm fine,' I say with a smile. 'Really, I'm fine.'

It's hard to say who initiates, but we transition from Ben having his hands on my shoulders into more of an embrace. There's a hint of *something* between us. As Ben's face gravitates towards mine, I move slightly closer to him, I wonder whether I should meet him in the middle, but I don't get the chance.

One minute, it seems like my old crush is going to kiss me, the next minute, I'm on the floor.

'Dani, are you okay?' he asks, helping me to sit up.

'Yeah, I just... ow.'

My arse is killing me. It turns out falling on a solid wooden bandstand is not a soft landing at all – who knew?

'Crap, there's a patch of ice on the floor, just a small one, right where you stepped,' he says. 'You must've slipped on it.'

'Hmm, if only I knew who to sue,' I wonder out loud with a cheeky smile to let him know that I'm joking. Making a joke is the best way to defuse an embarrassing moment because it changes the narrative of what everyone is laughing at – at least, that's what I hope it does.

'I think you'll find that's more of an act of God,' he says with a laugh. 'And not my fault in the slightest.'

I laugh, but it gets me thinking. What are the chances I

should slip on some ice, a split second before Ben and I could have locked lips? Something stopped us back in the day and something is stopping us now.

Ben must see the look on my face.

'Shall we get you home?' he suggests. 'I'm pretty sure the causeway is closing soon anyway.'

'Oh, yes, okay,' I reply, slightly awkwardly. 'We'd better get a move on.'

Ben helps me to my feet and sits me down on a bench for a moment. I can feel it, freezing through my clothes, but it helps to soothe where I'm aching from my fall.

'I'll go get the car,' he says.

'Thanks,' I call after him.

For whatever reason, now just isn't the time for us to kiss, and it could be down to an act of God, but I think I know what's more likely. It's the man who thinks he's God's gift, Rex, who I infuriatingly can't stop thinking about, but who I must stop thinking about at all costs, or my next fall might be my worst one yet.

25

Since Ben dropped me off, there's been only one thing on my mind: Rex.

You've really got to hand it to me, I know how to make a mess, and my timing is so shockingly bad that it probably swings back around into being impressive again.

Take Ben, for starters. I spent years swooning over that boy, imagining growing up and marrying him, naming our future babies, and writing his surname after mine in the back of my notebooks, just to see how it looked. The thing with teenage crushes is that, as much as you want to be with that person, and you feel so sure that they're the right person for you, and even though you spend hours upon hours imagining the two of you being together... well, ultimately, you never actually think it's going to happen. In fact, your crush almost flourishes in the safety of that knowledge. It's oddly fine, living with the unre-quited love, even seeing them get on with their lives, have girl-friends and so on, because you just know that it's never going to happen. Now, years later, when he actually tries to kiss me, and it finally feels as though something could happen between us, that's when I decide I'm no longer interested.

Then we've got Rex. I have actively disliked him since the day he started at *Livin' It London*. He's infuriated me, repulsed me, and when he kissed me – using me to get a girl – it didn't exactly endear me towards him. But then I spend a couple of days with him and suddenly I'm trying to kiss him again and he doesn't want me. It's like I just can't get in sync with what I want, and what I can actually have.

I don't blame him for not being able to give me the Leeds job, it's not his fault I don't have enough experience to lead a team, and if that's the only role left within the budget, well, there's nothing any of us can do about that.

I suppose there's a different life on offer for me now, if I want it. I could move back home – see if my parents will take me in for a bit, set up more permanently in my old room, it would definitely help with saving for a deposit. I could take up Ivy's job offer, helping out in the kitchen there, I could try to strike something up with Ben, see where that takes us.

None of it feels like progress, though. It feels like walking backwards. I want to be a writer, I want to live in a city centre, I want to be with Rex.

Oh, God. I want to be with Rex. I really do, I can't ignore it any more. He got me on the hook with the time we spent together back in London but it's all his cute little Zoom calls, long chats, playing games together, somehow having such fun even though we're miles apart. If you can feel a spark with someone through a screen then that spark must be something special, right?

I'm curled up next to the fire in my parents' living room, working my way through a cheap bottle of white wine, feeling spectacularly sorry for myself, wondering what I'm supposed to do about absolutely everything, when my phone vibrating catches my attention. It's Rex.

You still awake?

I am still up, obviously, but Rex is the last person I want to talk to right now. Confusingly, he's also the person I want to talk to the most.

Yes. Is everything OK?

I wait for a reply. It doesn't take long to come through.

Are you alone?

Big time. More than he knows.

Yeah. What's up?

I wait again. Eventually his reply comes through. It's a Zoom link.

I jump to my feet and check myself out in the living room mirror. Thankfully, I'm too lazy to have taken my make-up off yet, but I am wearing a particularly uncool set of baby-pink plaid pyjamas that I found in my room. I'd really rather Rex didn't see me in them, so I whip off the top. I've got a plain black vest top on underneath it. I'd go get dressed up, but I'm sensing something between the lines of Rex's messages. Well, between the words, at least. His messages are short, that's why I'm concerned.

I plonk myself back down in the armchair next to the fire, grab my wine in one hand, and hold up my phone in the other, ready to join his call.

'Oh, snap,' I say cheerily, noticing that Rex has a glass of wine too. He also has a bottle next to him, also verging on being empty. I also can't help but notice that he's shirtless, although I'm trying not to stare, even though his muscular body is pretty impressive.

'Hey,' he says, with a little less warmth than usual. He takes the bottle and pours the last of it into the glass. 'Where are you?'

'I'm at home – at my parents' house.'

I turn my phone, to show him the fireplace, before pointing the camera back at myself.

'Are you in your underwear?' he asks curiously, with his usual playful, flirtatious tone.

Shit, I must've panned down a little too low as I moved my phone.

'It's just a vest,' I reply. 'Not underwear. We haven't all reached a level of sex appeal where we can sit around topless drinking wine.'

Joking about finding Rex attractive is the perfect cover for actually fancying him. Plus, he knows he's attractive, everyone does, so it's not exactly a memorable event when someone points it out to him.

'Where are your folks?' he asks.

'Oh, they're asleep,' I lie – well, they probably are, actually, with France being an hour ahead. That might be the most honest thing I've said all week.

'How was your date with Ben?' he asks, shifting the tone to something a little more serious.

'It was great,' I reply, stretching my mouth into a smile. 'I had a really nice time. The food was amazing. I had a Christmas dinner burger. I know you usually rave about UK cuisine. You've got to try one.'

'Let me guess, it's in a Yorkshire pudding instead of a bun?' he replies with a knowing smile.

'Yes!' I squeak excitedly, my smile genuine this time. 'I really think you would love it.'

Rex gives me a bit of a smile, but he really doesn't look happy at all.

'Rex, is everything okay?' I ask. 'You don't seem yourself tonight.'

'I'm in mourning,' he replies. 'I've lost something important to me, that I didn't realise how much I cared about.'

'Oh?' I prompt. That sounds intriguing.

'My car,' he replies. 'It's still in the shop, but they're not sure they can fix it now. It seems like I might have totalled it in the snow.'

'Wow, you must have really done something to it,' I reply. 'It's a miracle you weren't hurt. At least it was just the car and you're okay.'

'Hmm,' he replies thoughtfully. 'But sometimes you think something doesn't matter all that much to you. But then you realise it's gone. I'm not injured but I wouldn't say I wasn't hurt.'

Okay, this *has* to be about more than a car. No one feels like this about a car, even if it did look like an expensive one. I can tell something is on his mind, but he doesn't seem to want to talk about what is really going on here.

'Well, *I* did injure myself tonight,' I tell him. 'And it was low-key mortifying.'

Perhaps sharing my own embarrassment with him will encourage him to open up a little.

'Oh, yeah?' he replies. 'What happened?'

'I stacked it while I was on my date,' I confess. 'Right down on the cold, hard floor. Just as Ben tried to kiss me, so it was even more embarrassing.'

'Shit, are you okay?' he asks. There's a level of concern in his voice but otherwise his tone still seems pretty flat. I've never seen him like this before.

'Oh, I'm fine,' I insist. 'Ended the date with a bang.'

Rex looks momentarily shocked by what I just said. Then I realise why.

'With an English bang,' I quickly insist. 'Me, hitting the floor. Not an American bang. God, no. We didn't even kiss. I didn't even want to kiss him. If I hadn't fallen like I did, I probably would've thrown myself out of his way anyway.'

'Huh,' Rex says thoughtfully.

He leans back in his chair for a moment with his hands behind his head. I catch myself staring at his muscles again, as he stretches his body, and I feel like a pervert. I quickly avert my gaze for a few seconds. When I look back, it almost looks like Rex is laughing. He *is* laughing.

'I'm glad you find it so funny,' I tease. 'I'm so pleased me injuring myself amuses you.'

'It's not that,' he insists as his laugh dies down into a smile. 'I, er... This isn't like me at all. I was actually feeling a bit, I guess... jealous?'

His voice goes up at the end, as though he's asking a question, almost like he can't quite believe he could feel such a thing.

I feel my eyebrows shoot up. I don't know what to say.

'I know, I know, it's not like me at all,' he says. 'But the thought of you going on a date with someone – someone else – drove me crazy. I don't give a shit about my car. It's all about you. I really haven't been myself this evening. It's so lame.'

I practically chug my wine, while I try to think of the right words to say.

'It's customary for you to say things now,' he points out through an awkward laugh.

'Sorry, I just... this doesn't seem like a very "you" thing,' I dare to suggest. It's not that these aren't the words I've been dreaming of hearing him say, it's more that I need to remind myself that I've been watching Rex for years, and I've never known him date a girl more than once.

'How do you mean?' he asks.

'Well, you date a lot, usually just first dates, whereas I'm into taking things a bit more seriously with people,' I tell him, not wanting to offend him, but keen to make my point.

Rex laughs.

'You think I don't take these things seriously?' he replies. 'Look, Dani, I know I'm a big flirt. I know I go on a lot of first dates but it's not what you think. It's pretty lonely, moving from one country to another, leaving your family and friends behind, trying to start somewhere new, making new connections.'

I sigh. He's not wrong, and I didn't move as far as he did. I know it must have been hard for him.

'I go on a lot of dates because I want to find someone, but please don't think I don't take relationships as seriously as you do, it's the fact that I do that is probably why you see me on so many first dates. If there's no spark, no instant connection, I can tell quite quickly that it's not going to go anywhere, and it isn't fair on anyone to string them along. I could just stick with anyone, date them, see where it goes, even if it doesn't feel like it's going anywhere, just to not feel so lonely, but life is just too short.'

His words hit me like a ton of bricks. Not just because I have so very clearly misjudged him, but because what he just described, well, that's what I did with Tom, isn't it? We just banded together, because I was looking for someone, and he was waiting for something better to come along. We're lucky we didn't waste more of each other's time.

'Dani, I know how I come across, and I know I must seem like I go off basic attraction when it comes to meeting women, but that's why I've been getting it so wrong, I know that now,' he explains. 'I know it's weird, the way we were thrown together, but it's given me a chance to get to know someone I was probably too scared to talk to before.'

'Okay, hang on,' I say, stopping him in his tracks. 'There's no way you were scared to talk to me.'

'You don't think so?' he replies. 'Because I don't usually have a problem talking to girls, they talk to me, but I always kind of felt like you looked at me like you hated me. I guess I prejudged you, and for that I'm sorry. Getting to know you has honestly been... just... amazing.'

'I think I might have prejudged you too,' I tell him, although I know that I have.

'Look, I'm just gonna come out with it,' he says, taking a deep breath. 'I can't stop thinking about you.'

I come out from behind my wine glass.

'While I was on my date, I was thinking about you,' I confess.

'The thought of you being on a date with someone else seriously bugged me,' he adds.

'I wouldn't have even gone on the date if you hadn't dodged me trying to kiss you,' I say bravely. 'Do you think we need to talk about this?'

'I think we do,' he says. 'I also think I need a coffee, so we're not having this conversation while I'm on the verge of being wasted.'

'Good idea,' I reply quickly. If there's a chance he's only saying this because he's drunk, then I would rather he sobered up a little before he said it again. I'm excited, but still so terrified that I'm getting my wires crossed.

'This hotel is driving me nuts,' he says with a sigh. 'Room service didn't replace my coffee today, and this phone is supposed to connect to the lobby, but it doesn't work. Look.'

Rex picks up an old, discoloured phone with a coiled-up wire – the kind I haven't seen in years. He presses the button to reach reception, but nothing happens. He presses it again. Then again.

'See, nothing,' he says. 'Let me dash downstairs and grab some.'

'Okay, no worries,' I say, my heart in my mouth.

Rex throws on a shirt before leaving the room. I dash to my feet and leg it to my bedroom – well, my parents' bedroom. Once I'm there, I quickly sort out my hair and make-up in the mirror, to make it look a little less end-of-the-day. Then I grab my best bra and put it on under my vest, scooping each boob in from the side to make sure my cleavage looks as impressive as possible. If we're going to do this – if there's a chance we might have feelings for each other – then I want to look my best, as sexy as humanly possible. I've never done anything like this over a Zoom before. In person would be so much easier. We could kiss, rip our clothes off, pounce on each other. I know, a few minutes of looking at him without his shirt on, and I'm getting seriously carried away.

I jump on the bed, get myself comfortable in the centre of it, and raise my phone to my face again. I go to look at myself first, to make sure I look okay on-screen, but I spot something else. I quickly hang up and drop my phone down on the bed.

Rex, drunk and looking for coffee, threw on his shirt and left his laptop on with me on the line. But what I just saw is a young, attractive blonde wandering around his room in her nightdress. I should have known he was full of it. He's supposedly all alone, having spent the night in bits over the thought of me going on a date with someone else, and now there's a blonde wandering around his room with practically nothing on? Has she been there this whole time? I can't think of too many explanations for that, can you? I have experience with girls in bedrooms they're not supposed to be in – and even if I hadn't caught Mia and Tom at it, the long brown hair on the white sheet and the baby-blue thong under the bed which I found later would have been a big give-away. I'll always wonder if she left them there on purpose. Either way, when things look bad, it's usually because they are.

Look, I'm over Tom, I know that for sure, but even though you get over the person who cheated on you, you never get over the cheating. It's like a ghost. Even when it isn't popping out at you, making you jump, it's messing with little things that remind you of them. Of what they did. They're not necessarily wounds, more like little paper cuts, ones that don't look all that bad – you can't even see them from certain angles – but my God, do they hurt when you mess with them.

I know that Rex isn't cheating on me, what are we? We're nothing. But this just feels so close to something. Something I don't like.

I snatch up my phone and open my message thread with Rex.

Feeling tired and achy. Going to bed. We can talk another time.

I say that, although it's not a conversation I'll be rushing to have. Honestly, this has all been one big, fat mistake. I was suckered in by the Rex charm, just like all the other girls in the past, and all the girls he'll meet in the future. I'm better off out of it.

Oh, OK. Get some rest and don't forget to ice your butt. Sweet dreams.

A typical Rex response. Sweet, funny, oblivious.

I don't send anything in response. Instead, I snuggle down in bed and squeeze my eyes tightly closed. It really is quite impressive, what an absolute mess I'm making of everything.

26

I remember Christmas Eves from my childhood like they happened yesterday.

Christmas would always feel so far away, all year round, as time passed by so slowly, cycling through the seasons, day-to-day life ticking by as normal. Then, all of a sudden, it would be December, but that immediate countdown to Christmas would drag by even slower. School days would seem longer, the dark evenings cooped up indoors would last a lifetime, and the impatient urge to tear off the entire front of your advent calendar and just eat the whole thing would be overwhelming... but when Christmas Eve arrived, that was it, you knew Christmas was happening – happening tomorrow.

It's an excitement that is unmatchable. Wondering what Santa Claus would bring. Getting to spend time with your family and play games and eat delicious food. Christmas movies playing non-stop, including festive childhood favourites like *The Muppet Christmas Carol*, *Home Alone* and *Jingle All the Way*. But you knew that Christmas Day would fly by so quickly, and that weird week between Christmas Day and New Year's Day when you had no idea what day of the week it was would be over in no time, and then you were pretty much straight back to school. That's why Christmas Eve is so special when you're a kid. You knew all the good bits were immediately ahead of you, and that was something to be excited about.

I suppose, as an adult, all of that goes away. There aren't enough hours in December, to get everything ready, to do all your shopping, all while going to work, keeping the house clean, doing all the dull grown-up stuff that kids just don't have to think about. Today, though… today is different. Today I have that overwhelming excitement I used to enjoy as a kid, only it isn't for Christmas Day, it's for Christmas Eve. It's because tonight is the night of the party.

That's what I'm focusing on. Not the fact that I slept in my underwired bra and now it feels like I've been punched in the ribs. Not falling asleep in a full face of make-up that has transferred on to one of my parents' white pillows, like a weird potato print, except I'm the potato. And, boy, do I feel like a potato today. I'm certainly not going to waste a minute thinking about Rex because, for all his grand statements last night, by the end of the night, it was clear that he's all talk.

I'm excited for the party tonight but I'm still nervous. First of all, it's because this party hasn't been very well planned at all. Well, it started out as a fictional party before being forcibly but carelessly morphed into a real one, so there was never a real plan or guest list. The food has just kind of happened, and while I've pretty much invited everyone I have met on my travels, I have no idea if any of them will turn up. I'm allowing myself to be hopeful, though, because today I am in an excellent mood. The second reason I'm nervous is because of Ben. He wanted to kiss me last night but then, the first sniff of interest from Rex, and I was ready to forget about him forever. I feel awful. Ben could be good for me

– a move back to Hope Island could be good for me – but I'm writing the idea off because I don't feel a spark with Ben like I do with Rex, and because the job on offer here isn't exactly what I want to be doing, but life isn't always about getting the best version of everything, is it? I'm always looking for the bigger, fancier thing. I need to stop looking at the stars and start focusing on what's right in front of me.

The problem is that Ben doesn't know how I'm feeling or where I'm at. He thinks the kiss was nipped in the bud because I fell. Does that mean he might try to kiss me again tonight? If he does, I need to work out what I want, fast. He's a nice guy, he's good-looking, he's great – but he isn't Rex. But why do I want Rex anyway? Ergh!

I'm so nervous my tummy is making loud gurgling noises. It's lunchtime, and I know that I should eat something, but I just can't face it right now. Perhaps, when I'm a little further along with the party prep, I'll be able to relax a little. I just want things to be perfect, which is hard to achieve when you're throwing a party that started out as a lie.

I got a call from Ben about an hour ago, saying he was over on the mainland, picking up some stuff for his mum from a few shops on Main Street. With the causeway due to close in just over an hour, he offered to pick up the food that Ivy and I prepared together yesterday, bring it here and then help me to get things ready for the party tonight. That will be a big help and it leaves me with time to make sure everything is clean and tidy here – and that all valuables and smashables are locked away. I've learned from some of my mistakes since I was a teenager.

Luckily, with Simple Simon linked to my Apple Music, I can use it to play some decent music, and he (I'm not quite sure whether to refer to Simple Simon as an 'it' or a 'he' because it might be nothing more than a gadget, but it's a gadget with a name and a lovely, smooth voice – one which has been keeping me company, and probably the only one I'll be spending Christmas Day with) can control the pretty cool party lights too. Huh, it turns out that, when I told Ben I was doing a party 'dry run', testing out the music and the lights, I actually was.

For the first time since I arrived, I hear a knock at the door and don't assume it's two hapless burglars, here to try to steal from my parents while they're on holiday. I'm probably just as – if not more – nervous, though, because I know it is Ben. What if he tries to kiss me while we're alone together? I haven't figured out how I'm supposed to react yet.

I greet Ben at the door. He looks so pleased to see me and I feel bad, for knowing that, despite being pleased to see him too, I don't see him as anything more than a friend.

'Wow, you and Ivy really did some serious baking yesterday,' he says. 'There are a few more boxes in the car.'

I hurry on my Ugg boots and my coat, and follow Ben outside to help him carry the rest of the food in.

'Well, that's the perks of having a friend with a fully stocked commercial kitchen, and I wasn't sure how many people were coming, so we made sure to make plenty – did Ivy say if she was coming tonight?'

'She didn't mention it,' Ben replies.

'Oh,' I say softly. 'She did say she had plans with her husband and her sister. Never mind.'

'Her husband relocated here, you know,' Ben tells me as we carry the boxes up the driveway and into the house. 'He's a southerner who wanted to live somewhere nicer. He'd had enough of city life.'

'Oh, really?' I reply. I feel like this is leading to something.

'Yeah, so, if you ever wanted to move back here,' he says. 'It's not uncommon, to trade in the town for the country.'

He says this like he's given it some serious thought.

'Noted,' I say with a smile.

I don't tell him that moving back home and taking a job here is my plan B – but a plan B I'm not all that jazzed about.

'Ah, I'm disappointed that Ivy won't be here tonight,' I say with a sigh so heavy my shoulders drop. 'It would have been nice to see her and Seb again, and Holly – I hear she has kids.'

'Four,' Ben tells me.

'Four!' I echo. It's still as surprising as when Ivy mentioned it to me.

It's weird to think that someone my age has four kids. I mean, it isn't weird that someone my age has four kids, I just can't imagine it, I can't imagine having that much responsibility. I'm not exactly doing a brilliant job of looking after myself.

'Well, Christmas is a time to be around family,' I reason. 'So, I can't exactly blame them for having plans.'

Ben plonks a box down on the worktop and places an arm around me.

'You must be missing your family,' he says as he gives me a squeeze. 'I'm sure they would have rushed home, if you'd told them you were here, it's not that they don't care about you.'

'I know,' I say with another big sigh. Then his words sink in. 'Wait, what?'

'Your parents love you. I'm sure they would much rather be here with you. If they knew...'

'Sorry, if they knew what?' I ask, pressing him on the matter.

'That you're here on your own,' he says.

'They know that I'm here on my own, they said I could have my party here,' I remind him – it's not true, obviously, but that's the official line.

Ben lets go of me quickly.

'Okay, Dani, come on, you can be straight with me,' he says. 'I know you're here on your own.'

'Yeah, while my mum and dad are away, for the party,' I say slowly.

'Dani, I know that they went on holiday, and that they had no idea you were coming,' he says, frustrated.

'How could you possibly know that?' I ask in disbelief. It isn't a confident disbelief, though, because he is right. I just can't work out how he knows.

'Your dad came to see me the day before they left. He said that, with you spending Christmas with your boyfriend again, he was going to take your mum somewhere nice for a change. Then he gave me a key and asked me to water his plants – I assume you've been watering them?'

'I haven't even noticed plants in the house,' I admit. 'Don't change the subject. You've known all that, all this time, and you've just been lying to me?'

'Erm, hang on a minute,' Ben says with a bemused, kind of angry laugh. '*You've* been lying to *me*. I figured you were just embarrassed, that's why I left you to it, but I made sure to spend lots of time with you, so you weren't alone.'

'Oh, wonderful, so you were just hanging around me because you feel sorry for me,' I say, starting to get a little annoyed myself, although I suspect the main reason for that is because he's rumbled me and I do feel embarrassed. This is exactly what I was trying to avoid.

'I don't feel sorry for you,' he says. 'Well, okay, I do a bit. You're single, you're lonely, your parents aren't here. You care so much about what people think that you're trying to tough it all out. I don't understand why you won't just call your mum and dad, they'll come home. So you're not doing all that well in life, big deal, we all feel like failures now and then.'

'Okay, whoa there,' I say. 'You're the one throwing the F-word around. I never said I was a failure, that seems like perhaps something you think. And saying I care so much about what people think – you really need to mind your own business.'

'You do care what people think,' he points out. 'I've been watching you lie your pants off all week, about this party. It was funny at first...'

'Oh, I'm so glad it's been amusing for you, watching me squirm,' I reply.

I'm sure Ben's heart is in the right place, but he's really rubbing me up the wrong way with this approach. His choice of words isn't ideal.

'And I didn't tell my mum and dad because I didn't want to ruin their holiday, because I knew they would come rushing home – they would feel so guilty,' I explain.

'But they're going to find out at some point – if only because your dad is going to come back to dead plants,' he jokes, but I'm really not in the mood for it.

'They're not going to find out,' I insist.

'Come on, Dani, of course they will. Something will be out of place, someone will mention seeing you – something will tip them off.'

'Can you please just mind your own business?' I say firmly.

'Okay. Okay, sure,' he says. 'I think I'm going to go, I'll leave you to it.'

As much as I want to ask him not to leave, and as much as I don't want to be alone, his words are still echoing around in my head. Ben looks at me and sees someone who 'isn't doing well in life' – however we measure that.

'Yeah, I think that would be best,' I reply.

Perhaps I do want to be on my own after all.

'Okay... yeah...'

Ben heads for the door. I don't stop him.

I don't know if he slams it behind him or if I'm just feeling overly sensitive right now, but the second the door closes, I feel a huge lump in my throat.

I feel awful for upsetting him, and stupid for pushing away a real-life person, but it's Christmas, I'm not having a great time, I'm upset about Rex, and I really don't need someone holding up a mirror that says 'You're a mess' above it.

It also hasn't slipped my attention that I've just upset pretty much the only person who was definitely going to come to this party tonight – the only person who I wanted to be there too – and he's pretty much the reason I wound up having to plan the damn thing in the first place.

Just when it seems like no one is going to show up tonight, I notice someone behind the door. Has he come back to figure things out?

I open the door to find Dennis, everyone's favourite nosy neighbour, standing there.

'Is everything okay, Dani?' he asks.

'Erm, yeah, everything is fine,' I reply. 'Are you okay?'

'Yes, but I heard shouting, and banging, it sounded like someone having a big falling-out,' he says.

Exaggeration of the century.

'Oh, no, everything is fine,' I insist.

'I did call the police,' he says, as I notice a car pull in at the bottom of the drive. Of course he did. And of course it's my new bestie, DC Dean.

'I'll go and tell him everything is okay,' Dennis says.

'Yeah, you do that,' I reply.

I watch as Dennis shuffles down the driveway to tell Dean that it's another false alarm. I'm sure Dean knows what Dennis is like, but I'm proving to be a right pain in his arse at the moment.

I give Dean a friendly wave, by way of an apology for whatever my part is in this. As I do, I notice there's someone in his car with him and, all of a sudden, everything clicks into place.

I hurry inside, to grab my bag and my keys, because there's somewhere I need to go, and I know exactly what I'm going to find when I get there. I can't believe I've been so blind.

27

As I approach a tired wooden door with the number twenty-two on it, I take a deep breath before knocking on it lightly. I may know exactly what I'm going to find on the other side of this door, but what's on the other side of this door has no idea I'm here.

'Hello,' I say with a smile. 'Can I come in?'

'It's not what it looks like,' Rex explains, looking like a deer in the headlights, stepping to one side to let me through the door.

'Really?' I reply. 'Because it looks like you've been in a B & B on the island this whole time. Wow, this room looks much nicer in real life than it does on Zoom. It also looks nothing like – and has never looked anything like – a city-centre hotel. I can't believe I missed that.'

'So, how did you rumble me?' he asks curiously.

'Not so fast,' I insist, sitting down on the bed. 'You're the one up for interrogation first.'

I'm not mad at Rex, for not telling me he's been on the island this whole time. In fact, I'm over the moon, I'm so pleased to see him – and especially delighted, now I know that he didn't have a woman in his room. Well, not in the way I thought he did, at least.

Rex sits down next to me.

'Okay, so I dropped you off, I went for a coffee, I sat down inside to drink it, had a bite to eat and then, when I went to leave, the causeway was closed,' he admits.

'So you, what, booked in here and decided to stay?' I reply. 'Why didn't you just tell me?'

Rex pulls a face.

'Well, first of all, I tried to drive through the water,' he admits. 'Engines don't like water, and Hope Island mechanics don't like people who drive through it. It's going to need some kind of specialist, to see if it can be fixed. The next morning, the snow was down, there was no way I was going anywhere, the Leeds office closed early for Christmas, because no one could get there, so I've just been working from here.'

'And the reason you didn't tell me?' I prompt.

'Because you were so excited for your special family Christmas,' he says. 'And for your date with Ben. I didn't want to mess any of that up. You wouldn't have wanted me at your parents' house, and they would have found me being there so strange.'

I laugh.

'What's so funny?' he asks. 'Besides pretty much this entire situation.'

'Rex, my parents are on holiday,' I blurt. 'I'm home alone. They've gone off for Christmas without telling me. I never told them I was coming, because I wanted to surprise them, so I've been in an empty house this whole time.'

'So, you're not having a party?' he asks, confused.

'Oh, no, I'm totally having a party,' I reply. 'I made up that I was throwing one, so that no one thought I was alone, and it's somehow turned into a real one. Except no one is coming, so I have a house full of food. Tons and tons of buffet stuff, almost all of it beige, if you're interested?'

'Sausage rolls?' he asks with a smile.

'Home-made,' I reply, making my shoulders dance. 'What do you reckon, party for two?'

'That sounds really good to me,' he replies. 'But wait, you still haven't told me how you knew I was here?'

'Last night, while you were off looking for coffee, I saw a woman in your room,' I tell him.

'Oh, my God, that was the girl who works here, I'd pressed some sort of panic button on the phone, trying to get it to work, she rushed out of bed to make sure I was okay, I felt terrible,' he explains. 'It's her parents' place. I swear. I think she has a boyfriend, actually.'

'I know, don't worry,' I insist. 'I know him, actually. He's the local policeman, our paths keep, erm, crossing.'

'Are you being a bad girl?' Rex asks with a smirk.

'Mostly misunderstandings with a little light vandalism in the mix,' I reply. 'I saw her in his car earlier. He'd told me he had a girlfriend who worked in her parents' B & B. I told her I knew you and asked if you were being a difficult guest. She knew who you were, which basically confirmed it. But, thinking about it, there were other things. Most notably, Rex Buckley, were you stalking me last night?'

'What?' he replies, his eyes widening in horror. 'No. Well, not really. Sort of. How did you know? How do you know all this stuff, man?'

He's lightly annoyed and kind of impressed. So am I, to be honest.

'When you messaged me last night, you told me to ice my bum,' I point out. 'I never told you I'd landed on my bum.'

'I've been going to different places to eat,' he tells me. 'Last night, I decided to go to the pub. I knew you said you were going to a pub, and yeah, maybe I had hoped I might get to see you.

When I saw you on your date, saw how romantic and perfect it seemed, man, it didn't feel good. I'm not used to feeling jealous and you've seen how I take not getting the girl. I've been thinking about you a lot, since our fake relationship began. I know you tried to kiss me at the Christmas party, I'm sorry, I panicked. I was having so much fun with you, and I wanted to kiss you too, but then I also knew how badly you wanted the job, and I didn't think you'd want to be involved with someone in the company, after what happened with Tom. I didn't want you to worry about your job. I regretted it instantly. But the next day, you were talking about Ben, I figured I'd missed my chance.'

'I was only saying that because I didn't want you to not give me the job, if you thought I fancied you and you didn't fancy me,' I tell him. 'And then you made it sound like you were spending Christmas with a girl.'

'Because you had mentioned going on a date,' he replies. 'I didn't want you to think the job was dependent on anything.'

'Well, if I'd known then how underqualified I was, this wouldn't have been an issue,' I joke. 'We would probably be where we are now before we were halfway up the A1.'

'Yeah, but you can't do this on the A1,' Rex says as he leans forward, taking my face in his hands. I can feel the tension between us, like pins and needles, like little sparks all over my body. Eventually, he presses his lips against mine. As he starts to kiss me, it's only a few seconds before we're both lying down on the bed, Rex on top of me. My God, he's got moves. I'm letting myself get carried away.

'Wait, wait, stop,' I insist with a giggle. 'Let's not do this here.'

'My car really is busted,' he says, his voice muffled as he kisses my neck. 'I don't know how I'd get us to the A1.'

I laugh.

'Back to mine,' I insist. 'I've got a party to get ready for, remember? Even if it is just the two of us. And later, well, you've got a choice: the bedroom I had when I was a teenager, or my parents' bed. Doesn't that sound like fun?'

'I'm in,' Rex jokes, jumping to his feet. 'Come on then, let's go get these sausage rolls. And, if you're lucky, I might give you your Christmas present early. It's not *that*.'

He adds on the last part after seeing the look on my face. That's a shame, I would have loved *that*.

Rex puts on his shoes and we head out, back to my parents' place, for the most overhyped party of the year. But, even if it is just the two of us, I really don't mind that much. Rex is all I want for Christmas. Who needs anyone or anything else when you've got that?

28

I am most definitely a girl with a healthy appetite. I'm no stranger to shovelling down a tub of ice cream while I watch TV. I ate almost all of the large cheese pizza I bought the other day. Rex is the same. He loves a buffet. He's got a real sausage roll problem. And his metabolism is spectacular because he can really put it away. But, as enthusiastic as our appetites may be, there is no way we can eat all of this party food.

Between the stuff I bought at the farm shop, and all the sweet and savoury bits that Ivy and I made, I have enough food for a lot of guests... but no guests, other than Rex. I should have known that all the random people I invited wouldn't come – I mean, who goes to a party that they're invited to last minute by someone who is basically a stranger? Especially when the invitation comes via a handwritten piece of paper shoved through their letter box out of the blue.

It was always a bad idea, but I had kind of hoped people would turn up, even if it was just a few of them. Most of all, I'm just sad that I've driven Ben away. We may not be on the same page, and there might not be anything between us, but he's been a good friend to me while I've been home. I was a bit annoyed, when I felt like he'd been laughing at me all week, knowing that I was lying all along, but I don't mind so much now. Perhaps I really do worry too much about what people think. I'll have to work on that.

I look at all the food I've laid out across the dining room and the kitchen. We're *never* going to eat all that. At least we'll have loads left for Christmas dinner, though, because we definitely don't have the supplies for turkey and the trimmings lurking in the back of the fridge.

My parents' house is perfect for parties so, even without much notice, I immediately knew how I was going to set it all out. When you walk in the front door, the large staircase stands in front of you. You can go left into the living room or right into the dining room. Both rooms lead into the huge kitchen, which stretches all the way across the back of the house. So, when you're entertaining, people can literally circulate, talking to everyone, picking up drinks and bites to eat while they do a lap of the house.

I plonk myself down on a dining chair and stuff a sausage roll into my mouth. I'm all dressed up, in the black glitzy party dress I packed for New Year's Eve, just in case we were doing something, I've curled my hair, and I even went to the trouble of watching a YouTube make-up tutorial before attempting to recreate the look on my own canvas (the results are questionable, but look good nonetheless). Rex looks amazing too, in one of his trademark crisp shirts that probably cost more than my rent this month, although he's so effortlessly stylish, it could be from anywhere and I would never be able to tell the difference. I would say he scrubs up well, but I don't suppose I've ever seen him not scrubbed up. He takes a real pride in his appearance, which is a quality I appreciate in a man – unless it foreshadows him leaving me for someone else, of course.

'Simon, stop the music,' I say through my mouthful of sausage roll. 'This is stupid. I'm more than happy you're here, don't get me wrong. I'm just disappointed that, of all the people I invited to the party, no one came. Do you want to just watch TV or something?'

'Hey, so what if it's a party for just the two of us?' Rex replies. 'I'm having a great time. In fact, now seems like a perfect time to give you your present.'

'As intriguing as that sounds, I don't like opening presents before the big day,' I reply. 'I'm pretty sure I was the only kid who didn't go hunting for their Christmas presents.'

'Well, this isn't something you unwrap,' he tells me. 'The job at the Leeds office – it's yours, if you want it.'

'What? How?' I reply. 'I thought there was only budget left for someone to run the team?'

'There was,' he replies. 'But I found someone already on the payroll to run the team, so the budget could be used for another writer.'

'Who?' I reply.

'Me,' he says with a smile.

'Rex, you can't do that,' I insist. 'Especially not for me. Don't they need you in London?'

'I fancied a change of scenery, so I've already had it approved, all I need to do is hire someone for London, instead of Leeds,' he says with a casual shrug. 'It will be pretty cool, though, having you there too.'

'You're amazing,' I tell him, looking him in the eye. 'How didn't I see this before?'

Rex just smiles and shrugs.

I stand up and wrap my arms around him. I try to give him a sweet, tender kiss but that tension between us pulls me in with a real force. I literally throw myself at him, onto his lap as we kiss. Rex stands up and leans me back onto the dining table. We knock a bowl of crisps (almost empty, we've been going at them for the last hour) on to the floor. The loud clatter pulls our lips apart for a second.

'Upstairs?' I say breathlessly.

'Sure,' he replies.

We only make it to the hallway before we start kissing again. Rex reaches behind me and slowly undoes my zip as we kiss. We're halfway up the stairs when there's a knock at the door.

I narrow my eyes, trying to make sense of what I can see behind the front door. Is that... is that Santa Claus? Yes, I know that sounds like a stupid question, but I can see a plump figure, dressed all in red, with a big white beard.

'Get rid of him quickly,' Rex suggests. 'You're about to be very naughty.'

I laugh.

'Quick, zip me back up,' I say. 'Flashing Santa won't go down well.'

Rex does as I ask. I head downstairs and approach the door with caution.

'Hello?' I call out.

'Ho, ho, ho,' a voice calls back. 'Can you open this door, little girl, Santa is freezing his baubles off out here.'

Is that Gaz? If it is, then I was wrong when I said that flashing Santa wouldn't go down well. This particular Santa would love to be flashed.

I open the door to see Gaz, Ivy, Seb, Holly, Holly's husband and their four kids all standing there. At the bottom of the drive, I can see a few people getting out of cars, and up the street, I can see people dressed in their best, clutching bottles of booze, trying to keep upright in the snow.

I can hardly control the smile that spreads across my face.

'Hello,' I say brightly.

'Hey,' Gaz replies. He's in his full Santa Claus get-up, as promised, but I can tell it's him. I say that, but I've never actually seen him without the costume, so if he wasn't wearing it, I probably wouldn't recognise him at all.

'Hello,' I say again. God, I feel like I'm going to cry. People are here for *my* party. I can't believe it.

'I think your doorbell must be broken,' he says. 'I've been ringing it for ages.'

'He's exaggerating,' Ivy says as she hugs me. 'Remember Holly?'

'Holly, hi,' I say, hugging her next.

'Lovely to see you again, Dani,' she says. 'This is Lee, my better half, and my kids, Chloe, Harry, Archie and Finn.'

Ivy and Holly still look nothing like each other (they definitely don't look like twins), but you can sense such a lovely closeness between them. I might not have my family here, but I'm happy to be with theirs.

'Come in, come in,' I insist.

I glance down the driveway and see Lily, from the deli, with a man who I imagine is her husband, and their two kids. Walking with her is Malcolm from Fruitopia – he must've heard the details from someone else and had a change of heart, perhaps he's not so bad after all.

People came! They actually came! Oh, my goodness, thank God I wasn't having sex on the stairs.

'Simon, play my Christmas party playlist,' I call out.

As I watch people filter in, I glance up the stairs at Rex. He comes down to join me.

'Talk about playing hard to get,' he jokes. 'But I suppose it can wait until after the party.'

'I suppose it can,' I reply. 'Plus, we do have the whole Christmas break together, with no one to disturb us.'

'I'll drink to that,' he says. 'Come on, let's go entertain our guests.'

How hilarious, to be playing house with Rex – and in my parents' house, no less. Considering I didn't want this party, or even intend for it to happen in the first place, it's mad how happy I am to see guests piling into the house.

I'd been worried about not having my family around me for Christmas, and the idea of spending it alone was really starting to get to me. I'll see my mum and dad when they get home, but in the meantime, family is what you make it, and tonight this house is going to be full of different families, and Rex, of course. What more could I ask for?

29

As far as last-minute parties go – especially parties that were little more than a figment of my imagination a few days ago – this one is amazing. The food is going down a treat, Simon is playing all of the best Christmas music, the lights are flashing, the drinks are flowing. Everyone is having an absolutely wonderful time.

Rex is, naturally, the life and soul of the party. He's on top form: singing, dancing, charming everyone. He and Gaz are getting on like a house on fire, playing the game Rex and I played at our work Christmas party, laughing together like little kids – well, like a kid and Father Christmas, which just makes it all the funnier.

All in all, I'm pretty pleased with myself. To celebrate, I pop a fake mince pie in my mouth and wash it down with another glass of Prosecco. This party really couldn't have turned out any better.

'There's someone at the door,' I hear a voice call out from the living room.

'I'll get it,' I call back.

I dance my way to the front door, the party spirit (and the

glasses of Prosecco) flowing through my veins, as 'Let It Snow! Let It Snow! Let It Snow!' by Dean Martin plays.

'Hello,' I say cheerily as I open the door. 'Oh, hello, officer.'

'No one is ever happy to see the police, are they?' he replies with a sigh.

'That's not true,' I insist. 'If someone were trying to kill me, I'd want *all the police* to turn up.'

Oh, God, I've had a few drinks and I think I'm funny.

'Let me guess, someone has called to complain about the noise and you're here to arrest me?' I say.

'What's that white powder all over your nose?' he asks curiously, his eyes narrowing as he tries to get a better look.

I quickly dash behind the front door, to glance in the mirror by the coat stand. Sure enough, my nose, and all around my mouth, is covered in white powder. I turn back to Dean.

'It's icing sugar, from a fake mince pie,' I explain. 'Like, it's a real pie, but it's not full of fruit, but it's not full of anything worse either.'

I'm babbling again.

Dean just laughs at me.

'Can I have one?' he asks.

'Erm, yes,' I say.

'I am still invited to your party, right? That's why I'm here. My girlfriend, Lola, says she'll drop by after work...'

'Oh, yes, of course you're still invited,' I say. 'Please, come in. The more the merrier.'

Dean steps inside. I'm about to follow him when I notice the snow start to fall again. I hang around outside for a moment, looking up into the blurry sky. If this were a Christmas movie, I'd probably see Santa Claus in the sky – either the real one, or Gaz jumping off the roof because he's had too much cider. He's certainly getting there.

I'm about to head back in when I notice Ben, walking down the street from his parents' house. I hug myself as I wait to see if he's coming here. Of course he is.

'I shouldn't have got involved,' he says apologetically after walking up the driveway. 'And I should have told you that I knew you were here alone. I wasn't laughing at you. I'm sorry.'

'I'm sorry for biting your head off, and for not taking your advice, and for lying and just... well, all of it, really. I'm just sorry.'

Ben smiles.

'Sounds like the party is a hit,' he says. 'Unless it's another dry run.'

'Nope, it's a real party,' I reply. 'Your sister is in there somewhere. Face like thunder. I don't think she wanted it to be a hit.'

'Sounds like Eleanor,' he replies.

For a moment, we just stand in the snow together. I watch as snowflakes land on his hair before quickly fading away to nothing. Eventually, he smiles and it feels like everything is okay.

'Are you coming in?' I ask him.

'Definitely,' he replies.

The first person we bump into inside the house is Ivy.

'Seb is going to put on a ton of weight, eating your mince pies,' she tells me. 'I thought I was his favourite baker, but you've clearly won him over.'

'I am both delighted and very sorry to hear that,' I reply with a smile.

'I promise you this is the last time I'll ask, but have you thought any more about the job?' she asks. 'There's no pressure or anything but, if you want it, I want it to be yours.'

'Thank you so much for the offer,' I tell her sincerely. 'But Rex has come through for me with the Leeds job. I thought about what you said, about how there's no shame in feeling like a man has saved you. He hasn't saved me, but he has made a sacrifice for me. That's what relationships are all about, right? Give and take.'

'Exactly,' she replies. 'Erm...'

Her tone changes as she looks over my shoulder. I turn around and see that Ben is still standing behind me.

'Honestly, I'm made up for you,' he insists. 'But if you're going to be living in Leeds, I hope that means you won't be a stranger. Come back and see us more often, won't you?'

'I will,' I reply. 'I promise. It's been so nice, seeing you all again. I never had friends like this in London.'

I wander back into the kitchen, where I find Rex chatting with someone I don't know. He's about the same height as me, which I suppose is a little on the short side for a man, but he's so muscular it makes him seem massive. He's good-looking, with piercing blue eyes and dirty blonde hair. I can see tattoos peeping out of his partially rolled-up sleeves. I can't tell what they are, though, just that his forearms are basically covered in them.

'Hello,' I say brightly, intrigued to meet Rex's new friend.

'Hi,' he replies.

Realisation hits me like a ton of bricks.

'Oh, my God, hello,' I say again, more excitedly this time, pulling him in for a hug. 'Why am I hugging you like we're meeting for the first time?'

He laughs.

'I suppose we are,' he replies.

One look in those blue eyes and one word from his mouth and it's obvious: it's Gaz, finally out of his Santa Claus costume.

Wow, Ivy was right, he is kind of fit.

'Where's your bog?' he asks me.

Ha! He's still Gaz, though.

'There's a door under the stairs,' I reply. 'If not, top of the stairs, second door on the left.'

Gaz nods before dashing off.

'I like him,' Rex tells me. 'He's a lot of fun.'

'Yeah, he seems like a loveable handful,' I reply.

'Speaking of which...'

Rex pulls me close. He gives my bum a cheeky squeeze before his hands settle on the small of my back.

'Careful,' I warn him playfully.

'Don't get me wrong, I'm happy your party is going well,' he insists. 'But if we get interrupted one more time, I'm going to go crazy.'

'After the party,' I tell him flirtatiously. 'And we're going to be all alone all day tomorrow – you're going to be sick of me.'

'I don't see that happening anytime soon,' he replies with a smile.

'Ah, I can't believe I'm going to be living much closer to home in the new year,' I say with a happy sigh, relaxing into Rex's arms. 'My mum and dad are going to be over the moon.'

'I'm sure they will,' he says. 'Unless you trash their house with this party.'

'At least I'll have a few days to clear it all up,' I say. 'No need to rush to do it tonight or anything.'

'And you know that I'll help you,' he replies.

'I do.'

God, now I *really* can't wipe the smile from my face.

'Okay then, after everything you went through to put this party together, let's go and enjoy it,' he suggests.

'Okay,' I reply, my big, dumb grin firmly cemented on my face now.

This isn't the Christmas Eve I thought I was going to have, but I don't think it could be more perfect. Well, not unless my family were here, but it strangely feels like my Marram Bay family got even bigger tonight. I can't believe I thought I was going to be alone for Christmas. How could I feel alone with all these wonderful people around me?

30

As Christmas Days go, this isn't like any Christmas Day I have ever had before.

The party last night was a roaring success. We partied from the evening into the early hours of Christmas Day. Obviously, the people with kids left – they needed to be home and tucked up in bed, ready for Santa Claus to bring their presents. Santa Claus, incidentally, *was* partying into the small hours. Well, Gaz was, at least. As the night went on, he didn't only remove parts of his costume, he slowly removed most of his clothes, doing a strip-tease to Michael Bublé's version of 'It's Beginning to Look a Lot Like Christmas', which was equal parts bizarre and kind of sexy. He's such a nice bloke, though, and I don't know where he is, or if he ever put his clothes back on, but I've just walked downstairs and found his Santa Claus suit in a pile on the floor. Gaz was one of the last people to leave. I hope someone stopped him from leaving in his boxers.

It was so amazing, having Rex spend the night with me last night. It felt slightly weird (and a little bit naughty) to be sharing my parents' bed with him but mostly it was just so wonderful to have some company.

That said, I did just wake up in bed alone, with no sign of Rex, or any evidence of him ever actually being here. I pause for a moment. Is it possible he's had a change of heart and taken off? The roads are clear again, so it's not impossible – although neither is me reaching a level of delusion where it turns out I imagined yesterday in its entirety, just to feel less bad about my sad little life. None of it would be off-brand for me, especially not this year, but somehow, I just know that Rex would never do that to me. I don't know what it is, perhaps I'm still drunk on the festive spirit (or perhaps that should be the festive spirits) but I've woken up feeling bizarrely optimistic.

My heart skips a beat of relief when I spot Rex in the kitchen. Not because I'm surprised, but because I'm happy. He sets a cup of tea down on the table.

'Good morning,' he says, giving me a peck on the cheek. 'This is for you. You're going to drink it while I dash to the B & B to get a change of clothes. I'll be right back and then we'll figure out how we can make this Christmas Day as Christmas Day-like as possible, okay?'

'I can't argue with any of that,' I say with a smile. 'Thank you.'

'Won't be long,' he says, briefly kissing me on the lips before heading out.

I sit down at the table, cradling the teacup in my hands to try to warm up, when I hear Rex calling my name.

I tighten the belt on my reindeer dressing gown (it's too cold not to wear it, and I wouldn't want to be with anyone who didn't still fancy me in it, to be honest) before rushing to the front door.

'What?' I ask. 'What's wrong?'

'There's something outside you should see,' he tells me as he peers through the little window next to the door.

Oh, God, I'm half expecting to see Gaz, in the nip, asleep in my dad's sleigh.

I hurry next to him, to peer outside too. I gasp and, for a split second, I just stay frozen on the spot. Once my brain is certain that I'm not seeing things, I fling open the front door and run down the driveway to greet my parents at their car.

'Dani,' my mum says softly, grabbing me, pulling me as close as is physically possible.

My dad wraps his arms around both of us.

'Oh, my God, what are you doing here?' I ask them. 'I thought you were on holiday!'

'What are *you* doing here? I thought you were in London, you naughty girl,' my mum replies. 'Why on earth didn't you tell us you were here?'

'I didn't want to ruin your holiday,' I reply. 'I knew you'd come back early, if you knew I was here. Wait, how did you know I was here? Did Ben tell you?'

'I got an angry message from Gerry,' my dad explains. 'He was banging on about the Christmas lights, saying how we promised we'd never get the kids involved, something about a pair of breasts on his snowman that won't wash off and that it was low of me to ask a young lady to do such a disgusting thing.'

'Oh, God...' I blurt.

'Dani, did you draw a pair of tits on Gerry's snowman?' my dad asks, rather seriously, given the words that just left his mouth.

'Maybe,' I reply sheepishly.

'That's my girl,' he says as he pulls me in for another hug.

I don't think I've ever seen my dad so proud.

'Well, the good news about driving back from France is that we passed a lot of shops on the way, so I've got everything we need for Christmas dinner,' my mum explains. 'And your present is in the house, all wrapped up.'

'God, you're amazing,' I tell her. 'I actually have two presents for you. One is all set up in the house.'

That's Simon. Honestly, I think they're going to love him.

'The other...' I pause for dramatic effect. 'Is that I'm moving back up north, to Leeds, so I'll be able to come and see you a lot more often.'

'What?' my mum practically squeals. 'Dani, that's fantastic news!'

'Marvellous,' my dad says. 'Bloody marvellous.'

'Let's go inside, get the kettle on, you can tell me all about it,' my mum says.

We get to the top of the drive. Rex is still lingering in the doorway.

'Erm, Tom?' she asks, confused, pointing at Rex. Obviously, Rex looks nothing like Tom, but my mum is just working with the most recent intel she has.

'This is Rex,' I tell them. 'I'll be working with him in Leeds.'

The second part of my sentence feels so clumsy, but it's suddenly occurred to me that I don't know what else to say. Well, we don't exactly have a label yet and, beyond confessing our feelings for each other, we don't quite know where we stand yet.

'Are you two...' my dad starts awkwardly, but doesn't quite know how to finish his sentence either.

'Yeah, we're together,' Rex says confidently. 'Hi.'

'Oh, fantastic,' my mum says supportively. 'One more for Christmas dinner then. Come on, let's head inside.'

'Rex is staying at the Lighthouse B & B,' I tell them. 'He's just going to get some bits.'

'Get everything you've got while you're there,' my mum tells him. 'Come and stay here with us. No one should be alone at Christmas.'

'Thank you,' he tells her, giving her a hug. 'I'd love that.'

My parents head inside, leaving me on the doorstep with Rex.

'I can't believe they're here,' I say, my heart ready to burst.

'I'm so happy for you,' Rex tells me, giving me a squeeze. 'And it's great to meet your folks. That's that one out of the way.'

I laugh.

'Yeah, you'll have to find a way for me to meet yours, without the big, scary build-up,' I reply. 'Okay, go get your things, and hurry back. Now it really does feel like Christmas.'

'Do you not want me to go later?' he suggests. 'I could help you tidy up the party mess first?'

'Shit,' I reply in a panicked whisper.

'Dani!' I hear my mum bellow from inside the house.

'Oh, my God,' I blurt in a panicked whisper. 'I totally forgot about the party mess. My mum is going to kill me.'

'Hmm, perhaps you're right,' he says. Rex picks me up and throws me over his shoulder. 'You'd better come with me to the B & B, it's only a five-minute walk. We can hide out there until she calms down.'

'But I'm dressed as a reindeer,' I say with a laugh.

'Yes, you are,' he replies. 'And it's adorable.'

I smile to myself as Rex playfully carries me up the street.

As we pass Dennis's front door, I notice him standing there, staring at us in disbelief.

'Don't worry, you don't need to call the police,' I call out to him. 'He's trying to prevent a crime, not committing one.'

31

Considering I was supposed to be spending Christmas Day all on my own, this one has actually worked out quite well. It's a strange combination of a classic Christmas Day with my parents, with the added new and exciting twist of having Rex here with me too.

After grabbing Rex's bags, heading home and deep cleaning the house while my mum prepped things for dinner, everything feels so natural and normal now. Rex is making himself at home, my parents seem to really like him – I must admit, I'm pinching myself. Little more than a week ago, if you had told me this is what my Christmas Day was going to look like, I never would have believed you.

Mum walks into the living room where Dad, Rex and I are watching *It's a Wonderful Life*. She swipes a finger across the top of the coffee table and playfully checks her finger for signs of dirt.

She shoots me a look, narrowing her eyes, just about masking her smile. Then she brushes a hand over the sofa.

'Crumbs!' she exclaims, in a gotcha kind of way, as bits of crisps rain down on to the carpet.

'Oi, I'm not having that,' I say through a laugh. 'Those are from Dad, from maybe five minutes ago.'

'Have you been eating crisps?' Mum asks him accusingly. 'Dinner is in less than an hour!'

'I haven't,' Dad insists, stifling a smile.

'Erm, you definitely have,' I reply. 'This room was spotless before you came in with your crisps – your family-sized bag.'

'Grass,' my dad mutters under his breath before turning to Rex. 'Pal, tell the missus I haven't been eating crisps.'

I look over at Rex, to see what he's going to do. He smiles at me.

'I didn't see anything either way,' he says tactfully.

'Good work, lad, you can stay,' Dad jokes.

'Okay, well, all in all, it's pretty tidy,' Mum eventually says. 'Good work. I suppose you can both have your presents now – even if you did use my house to throw a party.'

'I really am sorry,' I insist.

'It's nice to see you acting like a teenager again, to be honest,' Mum says. 'You were starting to get a bit boring. I always assumed it must be your fella. But now you've got this fine young man!'

Rex gives her a wink.

'And it's not all bad,' Dad joins in. 'The charity collection box is way up on last year already. It seems like the party brought in a tidal wave of donations.'

'Really?' I reply. 'Wow, that's amazing. Perhaps we should make it an annual thing.'

'Do you want your presents or not?' Mum claps back. 'Because if you do, no more parties.'

I laugh.

'Wait, did you say we both get presents?' I ask.

'That's right,' Mum replies.

'But you didn't even know Rex existed until you met him on the doorstep a few hours ago,' I point out.

'You know your mum's batty,' Dad says between swigs of beer. 'She's got that cupboard, the one I'm not allowed to touch.'

'If you're not allowed to touch it, then why are you always in it, stealing boxes of chocolates?' she asks him.

My mum, along with being a very neat and tidy person, boasts many other traits that sit well with her seriously high standards. She's an organised person, ready for anything – whatever we're panic-buying, she's got a place to stash it. I tell you what, one thing I didn't need to worry about, being here alone this past week, was running out of the important stuff like toilet roll or shower gel. There's a cupboard full of tinned food and bottles of water – something my dad has lovingly dubbed her 'zombie supplies' – which is supposed to be for worst-case, unlikely scenarios like extreme weather or wars or God knows what – but you better believe she's ready for them. This isn't the cupboard Dad is referring to, he isn't interested in her stash of tinned tuna, the cupboard he's on about is Mum's supply of gifting materials. Yep, she can never forget birthdays or be unprepared for surprise guests because she not only keeps a steady supply of wrapping paper and cards for every occasion, but she also has a selection of gifts, a little something for everyone, from chocolates to toys to bath bombs. No one will ever leave this house empty-handed, that's for sure.

Dad ignores this comment. All it's probably done is made him hungry for chocolate.

'I do have something from my cupboard for you, Rex, love, but I think you'll like it,' Mum tells him.

'It won't be as good as what you got us,' Dad chimes in again.

My dad loves his Simple Simon and, best of all, he can actually work it which is a huge bonus. So far, I've heard him talk to

Simon more than he's spoken to my mum today. He's asking it to play music, tell him jokes, and it did the lion's share of the work when we did one of the quizzes in the book one of his friends gave him for Christmas.

'I'm glad you like it,' I tell him. 'You're going to find it so useful.'

'Oh, yeah, I love the speaker,' he insists. I can tell he means it. 'But I was on about Gerry's sexy snowman. Honestly, I'm so proud of you. I've never been prouder.'

I'm so glad all those years at school and uni weren't for nothing.

'It was only eyeliner,' I say for the hundredth time. 'I didn't mean for it not to come off. I'll have to find a way to make it up to him, without making it obvious that I was the culprit.'

'I really don't know what's the funniest,' Dad continues, with frankly the biggest grin I've ever seen on his face in my life. 'Earlier, when I saw him trying to rub them off with his hands, and it looked like he was getting off with the bloody thing, or that he's resolved to covering them up with a scarf that keeps slipping down, making it look like it's wearing a bra.'

'Don't, I feel awful,' I insist again.

That does sound very, very funny, though.

'Oh, come on now, enough about boobs,' Mum begs. 'It's a present you can share. Here, open it.'

She smiles like a maniac as she hands me an envelope.

'You have to promise to share it, though,' she reminds me. I smile because I feel like a kid again. Some things never change.

'Okay, I promise to share,' I reply with a roll of my eyes as I tear it open.

'Go on then, what is it?' Dad prompts.

Maybe he knows, maybe he doesn't. You know what it's like with dads. When you're a kid, and you open your presents, they're usually just as surprised as you are by what's inside, if not slightly more because they never knew what you wanted to begin with.

'Oh, my gosh,' I blurt. 'It's vouchers, for plane tickets.'

'We thought you deserved a holiday,' Mum says with a smile. 'You and Rex can go somewhere nice together. You haven't taken a holiday in forever, you need to treat yourself. The break will do you so much good.'

'That's so generous of you,' I say as I pull myself to my feet. I give her a big hug before plonking down on the sofa next to my dad. I kiss him on the cheek.

'Thank you both,' Rex joins in. 'That's amazing. And so generous of you, considering we just met.'

My parents laugh politely.

'Our Dani has always been a great judge of character,' Mum says – and she's entirely wrong, but it's nice that she thinks that way. 'Where's top of your list to go?'

'I hear Malibu is nice this time of year,' Rex suggests with a wink and a knowing smile.

'That's where Rex is from,' I explain to my parents.

'Ooh, meeting the parents, then,' Mum sings. 'It must be serious between the two of you. I look forward to hearing all about how long you've been together and how you met over dinner.'

Uh-oh. She's never going to believe we've only really been together – fake relationships aside – for a day. I'm not saying things are serious between the two of us, but when you know, you know. We've got a good thing going on right now. That's all that matters.

'In the meantime, can the two of you do me a favour, please?' Mum continues. 'Dinner won't be long now. My friend Clara has a spare Christmas pudding…'

'A spare Christmas pudding,' I repeat back to her, highlighting how truly ridiculous that sounds.

'Oh, Dani, love, she always has a spare Christmas pudding, after what happened in 1998,' she replies, like it's a perfectly reasonable thing to say – I decide not to press her on why. 'She's not going to need it this year, so she says we can have it. Be a love, pop over and get it?'

'No worries,' I say with a laugh. 'I can show Rex more of the sights on the way.'

'Okay, but make it the quick version, won't you?' she insists as she hurries back into the kitchen.

Rex and I head into the hallway, to get our shoes and coats on, ready to trek out for my mum's friend Clara's spare Christmas pudding. Let's hope that once we've taken it, there isn't a repeat of 1998.

'You know I'm just joking about Malibu, right?' he insists. 'It wasn't a hint about meeting my parents.'

'You've very much met my parents by accident,' I point out. 'But I'm thinking, from now, perhaps we need to take things slow.'

'Agreed,' Rex says. 'Although, this is all new to me, and I guess I thought I'd feel more freaked out?'

'I definitely feel more comfortable than I expected I would,' I reply. 'Although I'm not sure if that's a good or a bad thing. But taking things slow will help us figure it out.'

'Okay, but let's not take things too slowly,' he says as he steps forward towards me.

Rex places a hand on the small of my back and pulls me close for a kiss. As he lightly pushes me back against the wall, I hook my arms around his neck.

It's strange because this is definitely Rex, no mistaking that, but it's like I've tapped into this whole other side of him. He looks like him, acts like him – he certainly kisses like him. Whatever it was about him that made me dislike him on sight is just not there any more. Perhaps he hasn't changed at all, maybe it's me who is different now.

'Love, get us another beer,' my dad calls out, ruining the moment.

'If we're here next year, we'll book the B & B,' Rex says through a chuckle.

'If we're even still together next year,' I tease.

'Well, we'll see, won't we?' he replies.

'We will,' I say.

And I really, *really* hope it's true.

32

'... and it is funny, because she had such a crush on you when she was younger,' I hear my mum saying.

Oh, God.

'She had your poster on her wall – in fact, you know what, I think she still does. I caught her kissing it once,' my mum continues.

'Waaah, Mum, hi, hello, I think Dad is looking for you,' I insist, physically inserting myself between her and the pop star so she can't say a single other word to him.

It's true, there is still a poster of Brad Nash on my wall – one of him in a tiny pair of white underpants, that was in aid of some kind of charity. And, yeah, my mum did catch me kissing it once, but it was in jest, in front of my friends. I'm pretty sure it was a dare – one that would be lost in the depths of my memory, if my mum walking in hadn't made it so mortifying.

'She's kidding,' I insist to Brad, once we're alone together. 'You know what mums are like.'

Brad is in his late forties now. He's still gorgeous, though, totally cool. He's got that swagger famous male musicians seem to have about them. I feel like a teenager again but I'm putting a professional face on it.

'That's okay,' Brad replies with a laugh as he runs a hand through his wavy brown hair. 'But, if such a poster did exist, you know I'd be more than happy to sign it.'

'Really?' I squeak.

Okay, so perhaps I'm not being all that professional, but it is Christmas.

Being a Showbiz journalist has its perks – perks I never anticipated.

After the success of last year's impromptu Christmas party, and given how much extra money it helped the street raise for charity, I just knew that I needed to throw another one this year, and that it needed to be even bigger, and even better.

This year, my little party has really evolved, from an unsanctioned house party to a full-blown street party. It's taking place earlier in the day this year, but that's just so that it can be more of a family event (although I'm hoping we'll still get to have the crazy party segment later on in the evening for those who want it, because so many people loved letting their hair down last year).

The perks of my job come in the form of celebrity contacts and, even though it's Christmas Eve, I'm seriously impressed with who we've got to put in appearances. Brad Nash may not be the coolest, the most relevant or the most famous, but he's the one I'm the most excited about.

The cul-de-sac is closed off to cars today, so that the street party can stretch out far and wide. All the decorations are up and out and better than ever – special credit has to go to the inflatable snowman that *someone* anonymously gifted to Gerry, although my dad's display is the star of the show, as always, as far as I'm concerned.

My mum and dad are enjoying the party. My mum, who

insisted last year that we wouldn't be having a repeat perfor-
mance, was all for it, when she realised it was going to be more
about the street coming together for charity and less about
people treading crisps into her carpets.

With the way things are going today, there's chatter about
making this an annual thing now, although God knows how we'll
top it next year. I am absolutely loving my new job, though –
although I don't suppose it's all that new any more – so hopefully
I can meet some even more famous people over the next twelve
months, and I'll be able to try to convince them to show their
faces for charity. Next year, I'm aiming for megastars, like movie
star Freddie Bianchi (who I'll be interviewing to talk about his
new movie in a few weeks) or Dylan King (the musician I definitely would've had posters of, and absolutely would've tried to
snog, if twenty-somethings still had posters on their walls).

The only thing we don't have at the party, that we did have
last year, is Rex.

Don't worry, though, he is on his way. This last year with Rex
has been nothing short of amazing. Working together is so much
fun, we're loving living in Leeds and exploring everything the city
has to offer – it's changed so much since I used to visit as a teen,
so all the cool new places we're discovering, we're doing it
together.

Things have been so hectic for us this year, but we finally
managed to take that holiday together, in October, when we
visited Paris – somewhere else we both got to explore together for
the first time, and it really is one of the most romantic places. But
while we did have such a magical, wonderful time, this meant
that I never did take that trip to Malibu to meet Rex's parents.
Well, that's all going to change today.

You see, in a move that is sort of the opposite of what
happened to me last year, Rex's parents have decided to fly over

for Christmas without telling him. He simply received a message from his dad, telling him what time they would be arriving at Leeds Bradford Airport, so that's where he's gone today, to collect them. In a way, it's sort of perfect. I want to meet Rex's parents, of course I do, but meeting the parents is a truly terrifying thing. If I'd had longer to think about it, to try to prepare for it, I probably would have driven myself crazy with worry. This way, there isn't really any time to worry about it, and with what time there is, I've been too distracted with the street party to overthink it too much.

I notice Rex and his parents walking down the street over Brad's shoulder, so I make my excuses and head straight over. Here goes...

'Hey,' Rex says, kissing me on the cheek. 'Dani, these are my parents, Ron and Susie. Mom, Dad, this is Dani.'

'It's so good to finally meet you, hon,' Susie says as she gives me a big hug.

Wow, Susie is an absolute stunner. I don't know how old she is, but she doesn't look old enough to be Rex's mum, that's for sure.

'You're just as beautiful as Rex described you,' Ron says as he hugs me. Ron also gives me a kiss on the cheek.

The amazing thing about Ron is that Rex looks just like him, but younger, obviously. If this is a glimpse into what Rex is going to look like when he's in his sixties, then I'm in luck. And I can clearly see where Rex gets his charm from too.

'It's so lovely to meet you both finally,' I reply.

'And we can't wait to meet your folks,' Susie adds. 'It's so good of them, to have us join them for Christmas dinner, at such short notice too.'

'They're so excited to meet you too,' I reply. 'And my mum is always ready for anything, don't worry. She thrives on last-minute changes.'

'Sounds like someone I know,' Ron says, raising one hand so that his wife can't see him playfully pointing at her with the other.

Wow, Ron and Susie seem so nice, and so normal, it's such a relief. We've only really got one major hurdle left now and that's for our parents to meet each other. Ron and Susie seem so cool. My parents are more like a double act, a regular Punch and Judy – God, I hope they're all going to get on.

'Oh, my goodness, Ron, what are you eating?' Susie asks him.

'Peanuts,' he replies through a mouthful.

'Where the heck did you get peanuts?' she asks.

'On the plane,' he replies. 'What? I'm hungry.'

'We'll be eating soon,' she reminds him, by way of ticking him off.

I smile. I don't think I need to worry about whether or not our parents are going to get on with each other, do you?

Rex wraps an arm around me and gives me a big squeeze.

'Dani, this is just amazing,' he says, looking around. 'Even better than last year.'

'Yeah, it's going great,' I reply. 'Although my mum is hell-bent on embarrassing me in front of the celebrities.'

'Good,' he replies. 'She told me all about you kissing your Brad Nash poster. I can't have you running away with him.'

'Shut up,' I insist through a smile.

It's hard to believe what a difference a year can make. Last December, I was so miserable. I was single, doing a job I hated, living in a rented flat that I really didn't like but also could not really afford. Look at me now, I have a gorgeous boyfriend, I love my job, and I'm rubbing shoulders with the rich and famous at an event I planned. It's taken a bit of doing, getting to where I am in life right now, but it really does seem like it came from nowhere. One day, everything seemed wrong, but the next corner I turned was *the* corner, the one where everything starts to seem good again.

You never really do know what's on the horizon and you can't always see that exactly what you want, what you need, is already right under your nose. I had all the pieces to make myself a happy life, I just wasn't putting them together.

ACKNOWLEDGMENTS

Massive thanks to the brilliant team at Boldwood Books for all of their hard work on yet another book. I'm so lucky to be working with such a brilliant publisher, and to have such a fantastic editor in Nia, who I can't thank enough.

Thank you to everyone who has bought a copy of this book, and all of my other books, because I wouldn't be doing this without you. Extra massive thanks to those of you who take the time to share a review too – I love hearing your thoughts.

Thank you to my amazing mum, Kim (who buys quite possibly the best publication day presents), and to Pino too. To the wonderful Audrey, who has a copy of every single one of my books on her shelf. Thanks as always go to James, my super-patient tech whizz, and Joey, who always knows exactly how to help when I need it most. Thank you to Meera, and to Jess, for the photo shoots, to Rachel for her support, to Darcy for being my muse, and to Sheldon, who really wanted me to thank him for 'all the years of inspiration and encouragement and blah blah blah' – sorry I didn't get to do it while you were still around to see it, buddy.

Finally, thank you to Joe, my husband, for absolutely everything and more. Congratulations on surviving me writing another book – here's to a bunch more!

MORE FROM PORTIA MACINTOSH

We hope you enjoyed reading *Single All the Way*. If you did, please leave a review.

If you'd like to gift a copy, this book is also available as an ebook, digital audio download and audiobook CD.

Sign up to Portia MacIntosh's mailing list for news, competitions and updates on future books.

http://bit.ly/PortiaMacIntoshNewsletter

Discover more laugh-out-loud romantic comedies from Portia Macintosh:

ALSO BY PORTIA MACINTOSH

One Way or Another

If We Ever Meet Again

Bad Bridesmaid

Drive Me Crazy

Truth or Date

It's Not You, It's Them

The Accidental Honeymoon

You Can't Hurry Love

Summer Secrets at the Apple Blossom Deli

Love & Lies at the Village Christmas Shop

The Time of Our Lives

Honeymoon For One

My Great Ex-Scape

Make or Break at the Lighthouse B&B

The Plus One Pact

Stuck On You

Faking It

Life's a Beach

Will They, Won't They?

No Ex Before Marriage

The Meet Cute Method

Single All the Way

Just Date and See

ABOUT THE AUTHOR

Portia MacIntosh is a bestselling romantic comedy author of over 15 novels, including *My Great Ex-Scape* and *Honeymoon For One*. Previously a music journalist, Portia writes hilarious stories, drawing on her real life experiences.

Visit Portia's website: https://portiamacintosh.com/

Follow Portia MacIntosh on social media here:

[f] facebook.com/portia.macintosh.3
[t] twitter.com/PortiaMacIntosh
[ig] instagram.com/portiamacintoshauthor
[BB] bookbub.com/authors/portia-macintosh

Boldw**oo**d

Boldwood Books is an award-winning fiction publishing company seeking out the best stories from around the world.

Find out more at www.boldwoodbooks.com

Join our reader community for brilliant books, competitions and offers!

Follow us
@BoldwoodBooks
@BookandTonic

Sign up to our weekly deals newsletter

https://bit.ly/BoldwoodBNewsletter

Printed in Great Britain
by Amazon